PUBLISHER'S NOTE

The book you hold in your hands is a facsimile edition of this classic collection of supernatural and suspenseful stories, first published in 1976, including all introductory notes by editor Kirby McCauley. Although biographical information on the authors involved in this volume has changed over the years, the timeless quality of the stories themselves has not.

FRIGHTS

Stories of Suspense
and Supernatural Terror

KIRBY McCAULEY
Editor

ibooks
new york
www.ibooks.net

DISTRIBUTED BY SIMON AND SCHUSTER, INC.

A Publication of ibooks, inc.

Copyright © 1976, 2003 by Kirby McCauley

An ibooks, inc. Book

ibooks, inc.
24 West 25th Street
New York, NY 10010

The ibooks World Wide Web Site Address is:
http://www.ibooks.net

ISBN 0-7434-5855-9
First ibooks, inc. printing April 2003
10 9 8 7 6 5 4 3 2 1

Cover art copyright © 2002 John Picacio
Cover design by Mike Rivilis

Printed in the U.S.A.

For the Minnesota gang: Eric Carlson, Jack Koblas, Joe West, and especially Dick Tierney, my favorite night rambling companion.

CONTENTS

Introduction: Wonder and Terror
   by Fritz Leiber   9

There's a Long, Long Trail A-Winding
   by Russell Kirk   13

The Whisperer
   by Brian Lumley   53

Armaja Das
   by Joe Haldeman   71

The Kitten
   by Poul and Karen Anderson   93

Oh Tell Me Will It Freeze Tonight
   by R. A. Lafferty   121

Dead Call
   by William F. Nolan   141

The Idiots
   by Davis Grubb   147

The Companion
    by Ramsey Campbell   **167**

Firefight
    by David Drake   **181**

It Only Comes Out at Night
    by Dennis Etchison   **205**

Compulsory Games
    by Robert Aickman   **221**

Sums
    by John Jakes and Richard E. Peck   **247**

The Warm Farewell
    by Robert Bloch   **263**

End Game
    by Gahan Wilson   **277**

Afterword   **285**

WONDER AND TERROR

by
Fritz Leiber

When we are experiencing fear of the unknown and at the same time the *lure* of the unknown is when we are most thrillingly alive. It can be very simple:

Entering a dark room, hand reaching for the light switch

Emerging on a roof at night and feeling the pull toward the edge—

Encountering a stranger—

Diving or merely pushing off into new waters—

The breathless instant when a roller coaster poises at the top of its climb

Imagining what may be around the next corner when we take our first stroll in a glamorous, unfamiliar city

Being in the midst of a lonely wood

The moment when the screen lights up in a darkened theater, or when the curtain rises on a dark stage—

Opening a new book with a fascinating cover

That's when excitement is greatest, all our senses

straining for the faintest impressions, our mind at its keenest, our imagination at its peak, ready for anything (we hope). *That* sort of fear is truly a tonic.

Because there's always *wonder* along with the dread. The stranger may be our good angel, or the love of our life, or a Martian. We may see a flying saucer from the rooftop, or the planet Mercury for the first time, or glimpse a murder through a distant window. Around that next corner a rajah in a Rolls-Royce may draw up beside us, or a slender woman in furs, with eyes like a cat's and the biggest ruby in the world. Our fingers reaching in the dark may encounter a purring kitten—or a large, hairy spider.

Shakespeare knew it when he had Horatio say of the Ghost, "It harrows me with fear and wonder."

No wonder without fear, no fear without wonder—that's the rule . . . and also the compensation, the jewel in the serpent's head. It's also why most stories of white witchcraft and the benign occult are apt to be blah. It's not that such things have to be wholly evil or malign; it's that deep down inside we know they have to be *dangerous*, just as primitive man knew that the touch of a holy or taboo object could kill as surely as a lightning bolt.

By now it should be clear that the sort of terror we have in mind is not that engendered by the prospect of being tortured by the Gestapo or locked in the same room with a homicidal maniac with a razor-sharp butcher knife—physical fear, and the mundanely gruesome—but rather the sort of terror that always carries a thrill with it, even when we know our lives may be at stake. In a novel I've just written one of the characters asks himself, "What was the whole literature of supernatural horror but an essay to make Death itself exciting—wonder and strangeness to life's very end?"

Aristotle knew this; he pointed out that terror freshens and renews the spirit along with pity (sympathy, empathy).

Poe and Lovecraft knew it, too, as when the latter wrote, "The true weird tale has something more than secret murder, bloody bones, or a sheeted form clanking chains according to rule. A certain atmosphere of breathless and unexplainable dread of outer, unknown forces must be present; and there must be a hint, expressed with a seriousness and portentousness becoming its subject, of that most terrible conception of the human brain—a malign and particular suspension or defeat of those fixed laws of Nature which are our only safeguard against the assaults of chaos and the daemons of unplumbed space."

Not "according to rule," and "something more"—those are the watchwords of the literature of supernatural dread, whether it take the form of John Webster's Jacobean drama of black love *The Duchess of Malfi*, Emily Bronte's epochal and haunting *Wuthering Heights*, Poe's *Usher*, Marjorie Bowen's brilliant *Black Magic*, Andreyev's chillingly monstrous *The Red Laugh*, Machen's superbly sinister fin de siècle melodrama *The Three Imposters*, Hans Heinz Ewers' *Alraune*, Herman Hesse's eerily illuminating *Steppenwolf*, William Sloane's novel of cosmic dread *To Walk the Night*, or the short stories of J. Sheridan LeFanu, "Vernon Lee" (Viola Paget), Ambrose Bierce, Algernon Blackwood, Walter de la Mare, M. R. James, H. Russell Wakefield, Ray Bradbury, and Robert Aickman.

It may be as simple as the gravestone inscription which gave Dorothy Sayers the cold gruel—"It Is Later Than You Think"— or as complex as Lovecraft's Cthulhu-Mythos extraterrestrials (their black gloss of horror now rubbed somewhat dull, alas, by endless repetitious imitations).

"An unexplainable dread of outer, unknown forces"— that is essential . . . and also something that science has not done away with, nor will it ever do so. All that science has done is give man a dozen new sets of eyes with which to peer at frightening and wonderful things. There's the planet (if it *is* a planet, and not some vast black sentient thing poised above the earth) that is seen out of the corner of the telescope's eye. There's the radar echo that isn't coming quite from the moon, or any of the known planets, but somewhere else. There's the strange mental power with a source even deeper than biofeedback, witchcraft, or ancestral memory.

11

There's the subatomic particle that whips through the solidity of earth leaving almost no trace. There's the buried thought that the psychiatrist can never quite reach, even using the latest psychedelic drugs and hypnoanalytic techniques which can dredge up memories of events that occurred when the patient was six months old. (And to what mind does that thought really belong?)

Or has all the current interest in witchcraft, satanism, the occult, and the psychic worn out those fields, so far as their literary employment is concerned? In no case! It only means that the creative writer must dig deeper and build truer, just as the plethora of cheap Saturday-night monster and murder movies has not prevented a *Rosemary's Baby*, an *Exorcist*, an *Images*, or a *Seventh Seal* and *Hour of the Wolf*.

But "something more"—meaning something new, something utterly startling, something undreamed of—*that's* the priceless ingredient of the true story of supernatural terror, and it is as worthy a literary form as any other. I myself am becoming a little weary of the helmeted spaceman emerging on the new world, with the thousandth planet beginning to seem very like the first; of the latest fictional Mafia (or CIA) with its completely predictable cold-eyed hit men; of the most recent stifling Super-Establishment with its inevitable familiar tyranny ("They control even our thoughts!"); of Victorian monsters, too—the same old Dracula, Phantom, and Frankenstein's monster in new top hats and capes and with slightly different facial surgeries; even of the latest murderous psychopaths and sex fiends whose horrendous mental garbage has long ago overreached its limits and become tedious.

All such extravaganzas have their rightful place, to be sure; but so have the less overworked, fresher, more vital fictions exemplified by the stories in this book.

THERE'S A LONG, LONG TRAIL A-WINDING

by
Russell Kirk

A new eerie story by RUSSELL KIRK is an event for connoisseurs of the ghostly tale. His one book of stories to date, The Surly Sullen Bell, *established him almost immediately as one of the modern masters of the form. But fiction is a secondary identification field for Dr. Kirk, whose wider public note is as a biographer and prober of political and social matters.* The Conservative Mind *is considered one of the cornerstone books of conservative thought in America, and he has followed it up with several more volumes of observations and insights that total an important contribution to modern political thinking. It is perhaps not surprising, then, that Russell Kirk's uncanny stories often contain strong elements of recognizable allegory and comment—demons, one might say, who are not only demons. This novelette, set, as is much of his fiction, in the American Midwest, is his first in the genre in many years. A gothic tale in the great tradition, it introduces a very remarkable protagonist.* FRIGHTS *is proud to premiere it.*

Then he said unto the disciples, It is impossible but that offenses will come; but woe unto him, through whom they come!

It were better for him that a millstone were hanged about his neck, and he cast into the sea, than that he should offend one of these little ones.

—*Luke xvii: 1, 2*

Along the vast empty six-lane highway, the blizzard swept as if it meant to swallow all the sensual world. Frank Sarsfield, massive though he was, scudded like a heavy kite before that overwhelming wind. On his thick white hair the snow clotted and tried to form a cap; the big flakes so swirled round his Viking face that he scarcely could make out the barren country on either side of the road.

Somehow he must get indoors. Racing for sanctuary, the last automobile had swept unheeding past his thumb two hours ago, bound doubtless for the county town some twenty miles eastward. Westward, among the hills, the highway must be blocked by snowdrifts now. This was an unkind twelfth of January. "Blow, blow, thou Winter wind!" Twilight being almost upon him, soon he must find lodging or else freeze stiff by the roadside.

15

He had walked more than thirty miles that day. Having in his pocket the sum of twenty-nine dollars and thirty cents, he could have put up at either of the two motels he had passed, had they not been closed for the winter. Well, as always, he was decently dressed—a good wash-and-wear suit and a neat black overcoat. As always, he was shaven and clean and civil-spoken. Surely some farmer or villager would take him in, if he knocked with a ten-dollar bill in his fist. People sometimes mistook him for a stranded well-to-do motorist, and sometimes he took the trouble to undeceive them.

But where to apply? This was depopulated country, its forests gone to the sawmills long before, its mines worked out. The freeway ran through the abomination of desolation. He did not prefer to walk the freeways, but on such a day as this there were no cars on the lesser roads.

He had run away from a hardscrabble New Hampshire farm when he was fourteen, and ever since then, except for brief working intervals, he had been either on the roads or in the jails. Now his sixtieth birthday was imminent. There were few men bigger than Frank Sarsfield, and none more solitary. Where was a friendly house?

For a few moments the rage of the snow slackened; he stared about. Away to the left, almost a mile distant, he made out a grim high clump of buildings on rising ground, a wall enclosing them; the roof of the central building was gone. Sarsfield grinned, knowing what that complex must be: a derelict prison. He had lodged in prisons altogether too many nights.

His hand sheltering his eyes from the north wind, he looked to his left. Down in a snug valley, beside a narrow river and broad marshes, he could perceive a village or hamlet: a white church tower, three or four commercial buildings, some little houses, beyond them a park of bare maple trees. The old highway must have run through or near this forgotten place, but the new freeway had sealed it off. There was no sign of a freeway exit to the settlement; probably it could be reached by car only along some detouring country lane. In such a little decayed town there would be folk willing to accept him for the sake of his proffered ten dollars or, better,

16

simply for charity's sake and talk with an amusing stranger who could recite every kind of poetry.

He scrambled heavily down the embankment. At this point, praise be, no tremendous wire fence kept the haughty new highway inviolable. His powerful thighs took him through the swelling drifts, though his heart pounded as the storm burst upon him afresh.

The village was more distant than he had thought. He passed panting through old fields half grown up to poplar and birch. A little to the west he noticed what seemed to be old mine workings, with fragments of brick buildings. He clambered upon an old railroad bed, its rails and ties taken up; perhaps the new freeway had dealt the final blow to the rails. Here the going was somewhat easier.

Mingled with the wind's shriek, did he hear a church bell now? Could they be holding services at the village in this weather? Presently he came to a burnt-out little railway depot, on its platform signboard still the name "Anthonyville." Now he walked on a street of sorts, but no car tracks or footprints sullying the snow.

Anthonyville Free Methodist Church hulked before him. Indeed the bell was swinging, and now and again faintly ringing in the steeple; but it was the wind's mockery, a knell for the derelict town of Anthonyville. The church door was slamming in the high wind, flying open again, and slamming once more, like a perpetual-motion machine, the glass being gone from the church windows. Sarsfield trudged past the skeletal church.

The front of Emmons' General Store was boarded up, and so was the front of what may have been a drugstore. The village hall was a wreck. The school may have stood upon those scanty foundations which protruded from the snow. And from no chimney of the decrepit cottages and cabins along Main Street—the only street—did any smoke rise.

Sarsfield never had seen a deader village. In an upper window of what looked like a livery stable converted into a garage, a faded cardboard sign could be read:

Was no one at all left here, not even some gaunt old couple managing on Social Security? He might force his way into one of the stores or cottages—though on principle and prudence he generally steered clear of possible charges of breaking and entering—but that would be cold comfort. In poor Anthonyville there must remain some living soul.

His mittened hands clutching his red ears, Sarsfield had plodded nearly to the end of Main Street. Anthonyville was Endsville, he saw now: river and swamp and new highway cut it off altogether from the rest of the frozen world, except for the drift-obliterated country road that twisted southward, Lord knew whither. He might count himself lucky to find a stove, left behind in some shack, that he could feed with boards ripped from walls.

Main Street ended at that grove or park of old maples. Just a sugarbush, like those he had tapped in his boyhood under his father's rough command? No: had the trees not been leafless, he might not have discerned the big stone house among the trees, the only substantial building remaining to Anthonyville. But see it he did for one moment, before the blizzard veiled it from him. There were stone gateposts, too, and a bronze tablet set into one of them. Sarsfield brushed the snowflakes from the inscription: "Tamarack House."

Stumbling among the maples toward this promise, he almost collided with a tall glacial boulder. A similar boulder rose a few feet to his right, the pair of them halfway between gateposts and house. There was a bronze tablet on this boulder, too, and he paused to read it:

Sacred to the memory of
JEROME ANTHONY
July 4, 1836 - January 14, 1915
Brigadier-General in the Corps of Engineers,
Army of the Republic founder of this town
architect of Anthonyville State Prison
who died as he had lived, with honor

> "And there will I keep you forever,
> Yes, forever and a day,
> Till the wall shall crumble in ruin,
> And moulder in dust away."

There's an epitaph for a prison architect, Sarsfield thought. It was too bitter an evening for inspecting the other boulder, and he hurried toward the portico of Tamarack House. This was a very big house indeed, a bracketed house, built all of squared fieldstone with beautiful glints to the masonry. A cupola topped it.

Once, come out of the cold into a public library, Sarsfield had pored through a picture book about American architectural styles. There was a word for this sort of house. Was it "Italianate"? Yes, it rose in his memory — he took pride in no quality except his power of recollection. Yes, that was the word. Had he visited this house before? He could not account for a vague familiarity. Perhaps there had been a photograph of this particular house in that library book.

Every window was heavily shuttered, and no smoke rose from any of the several chimneys. Sarsfield went up the stone steps to confront the oaken front door.

It was a formidable door, but it seemed as if at some time it had been broken open, for long ago a square of oak with a different grain had been mortised into the area round lock and keyhole. There was a gigantic knocker with a strange face worked upon it. Sarsfield knocked repeatedly.

No one answered. Conceivably the storm might have made his pounding inaudible to any occupants, but who could spend the winter in a shuttered house without fires? Another bronze plaque was screwed to the door:

TAMARACK HOUSE
Property of the Anthony Family Trust
Guarded by Protective Service

Sarsfield doubted the veracity of the last line. He made

19

his way round to the back. No one answered those back doors, either, and they too were locked.

But presently he found what he had hoped for: an oldfangled slanting cellar door, set into the foundations. It was not wise to enter without permission, but at least he might accomplish it without breaking. His fingers, though clumsy, were strong as the rest of him. After much trouble and with help from the Boy Scout knife that he carried, he pulled the pins out of the cellar door's three hinges and scrambled down into the darkness. With the passing of the years, he had become something of a jailhouse lawyer—though those young inmates bored him with their endless chatter about Miranda and Escobedo. And now he thought of the doctrine called "defense of necessity." If caught, he could say that self-preservation from freezing is the first necessity; besides, they might not take him for a bum.

Faint light down the cellar steps—he would replace the hinge-pins later—showed him an inner door at the foot. That door was hooked, though hooked only. With a sigh, Sarsfield put his shoulder to the door; the hook clattered to the stone floor inside; and he was master of all he surveyed.

In that black cellar he found no light switch. Though he never smoked, he carried matches for such emergencies. Having lit one, he discovered a providential kerosene lamp on a table, with enough kerosene still in it. Sarsfield went lamp-lit through the cellars and up more stone stairs into a pantry. "Anybody home?" he called. It was an eerie echo.

He would make sure before exploring, for he dreaded shotguns. How about a cheerful song? In that chill pantry, Sarsfield bellowed a tune formerly beloved at Rotary Clubs. Once a waggish Rotarian, after half an hour's talk with the hobo extraordinary, had taken him to Rotary for lunch and commanded him to tell tales of the road and to sing the members a song. Frank Sarsfield's un-tutored voice was loud enough when he wanted it to be, and he sang the song he had sung to the Rotary:

> *"There's a long, long trail a-winding into the land*
>   *of my dreams,*
> *Where the nightingales are singing and the white*
>   *moon beams;*
> *There's a long, long night of waiting until my*
>   *dreams all come true,*
> *Till the day when I'll be going down that long,*
>   *long trail with you!"*

No response: no cry, no footstep, not a rustle. Even in so big a house, they couldn't have failed to hear his song, sung in a voice fit to wake the dead. Father O'Malley had called Frank's voice "stentorian"—a good word, though he was not just sure what it meant. He liked that last tune, though he'd no one to walk to; he'd repeat it:

> *"Till the day when I'll be going down that long,*
>   *long trail with you!"*

It was all right. Sarsfield went into the dining room, where he found a splendid long walnut table, chairs with embroidered seats, a fine sideboard and china cabinet, and a high Venetian chandelier. The china was in that cabinet, and the silverware was in that sideboard. But in no room of Tamarack House was any living soul.

Sprawled in a big chair before the fireplace in the Sunday parlor, Sarsfield took the chill out of his bones. The woodshed, connected with the main house by a passage from the kitchen, was half-filled with logs—not first-rate fuel, true, for they had been stacked there three or four years ago, to judge by the fungi upon them, but burnable after he had collected old newspapers and chopped kindling. He had crisscrossed elm and birch to make a noble fire.

It was not very risky to let white wood-smoke eddy from the chimneys, for it would blend with the driving snow and the blast would dissipate it at once. Besides, Anthonyville's population was zero. From the cupola atop the house, in another lull of the blizzard, he had

21

looked over the icy countryside and had seen no inhabited farmhouse up the forgotten dirt road—which, anyway, was hopelessly blocked by drifts today. There was no approach for vehicles from the freeway, while river and marsh protected the rear. He speculated that Tamarack House might be inhabited summers, though not in any very recent summer. The "Protective Service" probably consisted of a farmer who made a fortnightly inspection in fair weather.

It was good to hole up in a remote county where burglars seemed unknown as yet. Frank Sarsfield restricted his own depredations to church poor-boxes (Catholic, preferably, he being no Protestant), and then only under the defense of necessity, after a run of unsuccessful mendicancy. He feared and detested strong thieves, so numerous nowadays; to avoid them and worse than thieves he steered clear of the cities, roving to little places which still kept crime in the family, where it belonged.

He had dined, and then washed the dishes dutifully. The kitchen wood-range still functioned, and so did the hard-water and soft-water hand pumps in the scullery. As for food, there was enough to feed a good-sized prison: the shelves of the deep cellar cold-room threatened to collapse under the weight of glass jars full of jams, jellies, preserved peaches, apricots, applesauce, pickled trout, and many more good things, all redolent of his New England youth. Most of the jars had neat paper labels, all giving the year of canning, some the name of the canner; on the front shelves, the most recent date he had found was 1968, on a little pot of strawberry jam, and below it was the name "Allegra" in a feminine hand.

Everything in this house lay in apple pie order—though Sarsfield wondered how long the plaster would keep from cracking, with Tamarack House unheated in winter. He felt positively virtuous for lighting fires, one here in the Sunday parlor, another in the little antique iron stove in the bedroom he had chosen for himself at the top of the house.

He had poked into every handsome room of Tamarack

House, with the intense pleasure of a small boy who had found his way into an enchanted castle. Every room was satisfying, well furnished (he was warming by the fire two sheets from the linen closet, for his bed), and wondrously oldfashioned. There was no electric light, no central heating, no bathroom; there was an indoor privy at the back of the woodshed, but no running water unless one counted the hand-pumps. There was an oldfangled wall telephone: Frank tried, greatly daring, for the operator, but it was dead. He had found a crystal-set radio that didn't work. This was an old lady's house, surely, and the old lady hadn't visited it for some years, but perhaps her relatives kept it in order as a "holiday home" or in hope of selling it—at ruined Anthonyville, a forlorn hope. He had discovered two canisters of tea, a jar full of coffee beans, and ten gallons of kerosene. How thoughtful!

Perhaps the old lady was dead, buried under that other boulder among the maples in front of the house. Perhaps she had been the General's daughter—but no, not if the General had been born in 1836. Why those graves in the lawn? Sarsfield had heard of farm families near medical schools who, in the old days, had buried their dead by the house for fear of body snatchers; but that couldn't apply at Anthonyville. Well, there were family graveyards, but this must be one of the smallest.

The old General who built this house had died on January 14. Day after tomorrow, January 14 would come round again, and it would be Frank Sarsfield's sixtieth birthday. "I drink your health in water, General," Sarsfield said aloud, raising his cut-glass goblet taken from the china cabinet. There was no strong drink in the house, but that didn't distress Sarsfield, for he never touched it. His mother had warned him against it—and sure enough, the one time he had drunk a good deal of wine, when he was new to the road, he had got sick. "Thanks, General, for your hospitality."

Nobody responded to his toast.

His mother had been a saint, the neighbors had said, and his father a drunken devil. He had seen neither of them after he ran away. He had missed his mother's

23

funeral because he hadn't known of her death until months after; he had missed his father's, long later, because he chose to miss it, though that omission cost him sleepless nights now. Sarsfield slept poorly at best. Almost always there were nightmares.

Yet perhaps he would sleep well enough tonight in that little garret room near the cupola. He had found that several of the bedrooms in Tamarack House had little metal plates over their doorways. There were "The General's Room" and "Father's Room" and "Mama's Room" and "Alice's Room" and "Allegra's Room" and "Edith's Room." By a happy coincidence, the little room at the top of the back stair, on the garret floor of the house, was labeled "Frank's Room." But he'd not chosen it for that only. At the top of the house, one was safer from sheriffs or burglars. And through the skylight · there was only a frieze window a man could get to the roof of the main block. From that roof one could descend to the woodshed roof by a fire escape of iron rungs fixed in the stone outer wall; and from the woodshed it was an easy drop to the ground. After that, the chief difficulty would be to run down Main Street and then get across the freeway without being detected, while people searched the house for you. Talk of Goldilocks and the Three Bears! Much experience had taught Sarsfield such forethought.

Had that other Frank, so commemorated over the bedroom door, been a son or a servant? Presumably a son—though Sarsfield had found no pictures of boys in the old velvet-covered album in the Sunday parlor, nor any of manservants. There were many pictures of the General, a little rooster-like man with a beard; and of Father, portly and pleasant-faced; and of Mama, elegant; and of three small girls who must be Alice and Allegra and Edith. He had liked especially the photographs of Allegra, since he had tasted her strawberry jam. All the girls were pretty, but Allegra—who must have been about seven in most of the pictures—was really charming, with long ringlets and kind eyes and a delicate mouth that curved upward at its corners.

Sarsfield adored little girls and distrusted big girls. His mother had cautioned him against bad women, so he

24

had kept away from such. Because he liked peace, he had never married—not that he could have married anyway, because that would have tied him to one place, and he was too clumsy to earn money at practically anything except dishwashing for summer hotels. Not marrying had meant that he could have no little daughters like Allegra.

Sometimes he had puzzled the prison psychiatrists. In prison it was well to play stupid. He had refrained cunningly from reciting poetry to the psychiatrists. So after testing Sarsfield they wrote him down as "dull normal" and he was assigned to labor as a "gardener"—which meant going round the prison yards picking up trash by a stick with a nail in the end of it. That was easy work, and he detested hard work. Yet when there was truly heavy work to be done in prison, sometimes he would come forward to shovel tons of coal or carry hods of brick or lift big blocks into place. That, too, was his cunning: it impressed the other jailbirds with his enormous strength, so that the gangs left him alone.

"Yes, you're a loner, Frank Sarsfield," he said to himself aloud. He looked at himself in that splendid Sunday-parlor mirror, which stretched from floor to ceiling. He saw a man overweight but lean enough of face, standing six feet six, built like a bear, a strong nose, some teeth missing, a strong chin, and rather wild light blue eyes. He was an uncommon sort of bum. Deliberately he looked at his image out of the corners of his eyes, as was his way, because he was nonviolent, and eye contact might mean trouble.

"You look like a Viking, Frank," old Father O'Malley had told him once, "but you ought to have been a monk."

"Oh, Father," he had answered, "I'm too much of a fool for a monk."

"Well," said Father O'Malley, "you're no more fool than many a brother, and you're celibate and continent, I take it. Yet it's late for that now. Look out you don't turn berserker, Frank. Go to confession sometime, to a priest that doesn't know you, if you'll not go to me. If you'd confess, you'd not be haunted."

But he seldom went to mass, and never to confession. All those church boxes pilfered, his mother and father

25

abandoned, his sister neglected, all the ghastly humbling of himself before policemen, all the horror and shame of the prisons! There could be no grace for him now. *"There's a long, long trail a-winding into the land of my dreams . . ."* What dreams! He had looked up "ber-serker" in Webster. But he wouldn't ever do that sort of thing. A man had to keep a control upon himself; besides, he was a coward, and he loved peace.

Nearly all the other prisoners had been brutes, guilty as sin, guilty as Miranda or Escobedo. Once, sentenced for rifling a church safe, he had been put into the same cell with a man who had murdered his wife by taking off her head. The head never had been found. Sarsfield had dreamed of that head in such short intevals of sleep as he had enjoyed while the wife-killer was his cellmate. Nearly all night, every night, he had lain awake surreptitiously watching the murderer in the opposite bunk and feeling his own neck now and again. He had been surprised and pleased when eventually the wife-killer had gone hysteri-cal and obtained assignment to another cell. The mur-derer had told the guards that he just couldn't stand being watched all night by that terrible giant who never talked.

Only one of the prison psychiatrists had been pleasant or bright, and that had been the old doctor born in Vienna who went round from penitentiary to penitentiary checking on the psychiatric staffs. The old doctor had taken a liking to him, and had written a report to ac-company Frank's petition for parole. Three months later, in a parole office, the parole officer had gone out hur-riedly for a quarter of an hour, and Sarsfield had taken the chance to read his own file that the parole man had left in a folder on his desk.

"Francis Sarsfield has a memory that almost can be described as photographic"—so had run one line in the Vienna doctor's report. When he read that, Sarsfield had known that the doctor was a clever doctor. "He suffers chiefly from an arrest of emotional development, and may be regarded as a rather bright small boy in some respects. His three temporarily successful escapes from prison suggest that his intelligence has been much under-

26

rated. On at least one of those occasions he could have eluded the arresting officer had he been willing to resort to violence. Sarsfield repeatedly describes himself as nonviolent and has no record of aggression while confined, nor in connection with any of the offenses for which he was arrested. On the contrary, he seems timid and withdrawn, and might become a victim of assaults in prison, were it not for his size, strength, and power of voice."

Sarsfield had been pleased enough by that paragraph, but a little puzzled by what followed:

"In general, Sarsfield is one of those recidivists who ought not to be confined, were any alternative method now available for restraining them from petty offenses against property. Not only does he lack belligerence against men, but apparently he is quite clean of any record against women and children. It seems that he does not indulge in autoeroticism, either—perhaps because of strict instruction by his R. C. mother during his formative years.

"I add, however, that conceivably Sarsfield is not fundamentally so gentle as his record indicates. He can be energetic in self-defense when pushed to the wall. In his youth occasionally he was induced, for the promise of $5 or $10, to stand up as an amateur against some traveling professional boxer. He admits that he did not fight hard, and cried when he was badly beaten. Nevertheless, I am inclined to suspect a potentiality for violence, long repressed but not totally extinguished by years of 'humbling himself,' in his phrase. This possibility is not so certain as to warrant additional detention, even though three years of Sarsfield's sentence remain unexpired."

Yes, he had memorized nearly the whole of that old doctor's analysis, which had got his parole for him. There had been the concluding paragraphs:

"Francis Sarsfield is oppressed by a haunting sense of personal guilt. He is religious to the point of superstition, an R.C., and appears to believe himself damned. Although worldly-wise in a number of respects, he retains an almost unique innocence in others. His frequent humor and candor account for his success, much of the time, at begging. He has read much during his wanderings and

27

terms of confinement. He has a strong taste for good poetry of the popular sort, and has accumulated a mass of miscellaneous information, much of it irrelevant to the life he leads.

"Although occasionally moody and even surly, most of the time he subjects himself to authority, and will work fairly well if closely supervised. He possesses no skills of any sort, unless some knack for woodchopping, acquired while he was enrolled in the Civilian Conservation Corps, can be considered a marketable skill. He appears to be incorrigibly footloose, and therefore confinement is more unpleasant to him than to most prisoners. It is truly remarkable that he continues to be rational enough, his isolation and heavy guilt-complex considered.

"Sometimes evasive when he does not desire to answer questions, nevertheless he rarely utters a direct lie. His personal modesty may be described as excessive. His habits of cleanliness are commendable, if perhaps of origins like Lady Macbeth's.

"Despite his strength, he is a diabetic and suffers from a heart murmur, sometimes painful.

"Only in circumstances so favorable as to be virtually unobtainable could Sarsfield succeed in abstaining from the behavior pattern that has led to his repeated prosecution and imprisonment. The excessive crowding of this penitentiary considered, however, I strongly recommend that he be released upon parole. Previous psychiatric reports concerning this inmate have been shallow and erroneous, I regret to note. Perhaps Sarsfield's chief psychological difficulty is that, from obscure causes, he lacks emotional communication with other adults, although able to maintain cordial and healthy relations with small children. He is very nearly a solipsist, which in large part may account for his inability to make firm decisions or pursue any regular occupation. In contradiction of previous analyses of Sarsfield, he should not be described as 'dull normal' intellectually. Francis Xavier Sarsfield distinctly is neither dull nor normal."

Sarsfield had looked up "solipsist," but hadn't found himself much the wiser. He didn't think himself the only existent thing—not most of the time, anyway. He wasn't sure that the old doctor had been real, but he knew that his mother had been real before she went straight to heaven. He knew that his nightmares probably weren't real; but sometimes, while awake, he could see things that other men couldn't. In a house like this he could glimpse little unaccountable movements out of the corners of his eyes, but it wouldn't do to worry about those. He was afraid of those things which other people couldn't see, yet not so frightened of them as most people were. Some of the other inmates had called him Crazy Frank, and it had been hard to keep down his temper. If you could perceive *more* existent things, though not flesh-and-blood things, than psychiatrists or convicts could—why, were you then a solipsist?

There was no point in puzzling over it. Dad had taken him out of school to work on the farm when he hadn't yet finished the fourth grade, so words like "solipsist" didn't mean much to him. Poets' words, though, he mostly understood. He had picked up a rhyme that made children laugh when he told it to them:

> *"Though you don't know it,*
> *You're a poet.*
> *Your feet show it:*
> *They're Longfellows."*

That wasn't very good poetry, but Henry Wadsworth Longfellow was a good poet. They must have loved Henry Wadsworth Longfellow in this house, and especially "The Children's Hour," because of those three little girls named Alice, Allegra, and Edith, and those lines on the General's boulder. Allegra: that's the prettiest of all names ever, and it means "merry," someone had told him.

He looked at the cheap wristwatch he had bought, besides the wash-and-wear suit, with his last dishwashing money from that Lake Superior summer hotel. Well, midnight! It's up the wooden hill for you, Frank Sarsfield, to your snug little room under the rafters. If anybody comes to Tamarack House tonight, it's out the skylight and through the snow for you, Frank, my boy—and no

29

tiny reindeer. If you want to survive, in prison or out of it, you stick to your own business and let other folks stew in their own juice.

Before he closed his eyes, he would pray for mother's soul · not that she really needed it—and then say the little Scottish prayer he had found in a children's book: "From ghoulies and ghosties, and long-leggitie beasties, and things that go bump in the night, good Lord deliver us!"

The next morning, the morning before his birthday, Frank Sarsfield went up the circular stair to the cupola, even before making his breakfast of pickled trout, peaches, and strong coffee. The wind had gone down and it was snowing only lightly now, but the drifts were immense. Nobody would make his way to Anthonyville and Tamarack House this day; the snowplows would be busy elsewhere.

From this height he could see the freeway, and nothing seemed to be moving along it. The dead village lay to the north of him. To the east were river and swamp, the shores lined with those handsome tamaracks, the green gone out of them, which had given this house its name. Everything in sight belonged to Frank.

He had dreamed during the night, the wind howling and whining round the top of the house, and he had known he was dreaming, but it had been even stranger than usual, if less horrible.

In his dream, he had found himself in the dining room of Tamarack House. He had not been alone. The General and Father and Mama and the three little girls had been dining happily at the long table, and he had waited on them. In the kitchen an old woman who was the cook and a girl who cleaned had eaten by themselves. But when he had finished filling the family's plates, he had sat down at the end of the table, as if he had been expected to do that.

The family had talked among themselves and even to him as he ate, but somehow he had not been able to hear what they said to him. Suddenly, though, he had pricked up his ears, because Allegra had spoken to him.

30

"Frank," she had said, all mischief, "why do they call you Punkinhead?"

The old General had frowned at the head of the table, and Mama had said, "Allegra, don't speak that way to Frank!"

But he had grinned at Allegra, if a little hurt, and had told the girl, "Because some men think I've got a head like a jack-o'-lantern's and not even seeds inside it."

"Nonsense, Frank," Mama had put in, "you have a very handsome head."

"You've got a pretty head, Frank," the three little girls had told him then, almost in chorus, placatingly. Allegra had come round the table to make her peace. "There's going to be a big surprise for you tomorrow, Frank," she had whispered to him. And then she had kissed him on the cheek.

That had waked him. Most of the rest of that howling night he had lain awake trying to make sense of his dream, but he couldn't. The people in it had been more real than the people he met on the long, long trail.

Now he strolled through the house again, admiring everything. It was almost as if he had seen the furniture and the pictures and the carpets long, long ago. The house must be over a century old, and many of the good things in it must go back to the beginning. He would have two or three more days here until the roads were cleared. There were no newspapers to tell him about the great storm, of course, and no radio that worked; but that didn't matter.

He found a great big handsome *Complete Works of Henry Wadsworth Longfellow*, in red morocco, and an illustrated copy of the *Rubaiyat*. He didn't need to read it, because he had memorized all the quatrains once. There was a black silk ribbon as marker between the pages, and he opened it there—at Quatrain 44, it turned out:

> *"Why, if the soul can fling the Dust aside,*
> *And naked on the Air of Heaven ride,*
> *Were't not a Shame—were't not a Shame for him*
> *In this clay carcass crippled to abide?"*

31

That old Vienna doctor, Frank suspected, hadn't believed in immortal souls. Frank Sarsfield knew better. But also Frank suspected that his soul never would ride, naked or clothed, on the Air of Heaven. Souls! That put him in mind of his sister, a living soul that he had forsaken. He ought to write her a letter on this eve of his sixtieth birthday.

Frank traveled light, his luggage being mostly a safety razor, a hairbrush, and a comb; he washed his shirt and socks and underclothes every night, and often his wash-and-wear suit, too. But he did carry with him a few sheets of paper and a ballpoint pen. Sitting down at the library table—he had built a fire in the library stove also, there being no lack of logs—he began to write to Mary Sarsfield, alone in the rotting farmhouse in New Hampshire. His spelling wasn't good, he knew, but today he was careful at his birthday letter, using the big old dictionary with the General's bookplate in it.

To write that letter took most of the day. Two versions were discarded. At last Frank had done the best he could.

Dearest Mary my sister,

Its been nearly 9 years since I came to visit you and borrowed the $78 from you and went away again and never paid it back. I guess you dont want to see your brother Frank again after what I did that time and other times but the Ethiopian can not change his skin nor the leopard his spots and when some man like a Jehovahs Witness or that rancher with all the cash gives me quite a lot of money I mean to send you what I owe but the post office isnt handy at the time and so I spend it on presents for little kids I meet and buying new clothes and such so I never get around to sending you that $78 Mary. Right now I have $29 and more but the post office at this place is folded up and by the time I get to the next town the money will be mostly gone and so it goes. I guess probably you need the money and Im sorry Mary but maybe some day I will win in the lottery and then Ill give you all the thousands of dollars I win.

Well Mary its been 41 years and 183 days since Mother passed away and here I am 60 years old tomorrow and you getting on toward 56. I pray that your cough is better and that your son and my nephew Jack is doing better than he was in Tallahassee Florida. Some time Mary if you would write to me c/o Father Justin O'Malley in Albatross Michigan where he is pastor now I would stop by his rectory and get your letter and read it with joy. But I know Ive been a very bad brother and I dont blame you Mary if you never get around to writing your brother Frank.

Mary Ive been staying out of jails and working a little here and there along the road. Now Mary do you know what I hate most about those prisons? Why not being on the road you will say. No Mary the worst thing is the foul language the convicts use from morning till night. Taking the name of their Lord in vain is the least they do. There is a foul curse word in their every sentence. I wasnt brought up that way any more than you Mary and I will not revile woman or child. It is like being in H—— to hear it.

Im not in bad shape except the diabetes is no better but I take my pills for it when I can buy them and dont have to take needles for it and my heart hurts me dreadfully bad sometimes when I lift heavy things hours on end and sometimes it hurts me worse at night when Ive been just lying there thinking of the life Ive led and how I ought to pay you the $78 and pay back other folks that helped me too. I owe Father O'Malley $497.11 now altogether and I keep track of it in my head and when the lottery ticket wins he will not be forgot.

Some people have been quite good to me and I still can make them laugh and I recite to them and generally I start my reciting with what No Person of Quality wrote hundreds of years ago

Seven wealthy towns contend for Homer dead

33

Through which the living Homer begged his
        bread.
They like that and also usually they like Thomas
Grays Elegy in a Country Churchyard leaving the
world to darkness and to me and I recite all of that
and sometimes some of the Quatrains of Omar. At
farms when they ask me I chop wood for these
folk and I help with the dishes but I still break a
good many as you learned Mary 9 years ago but I
didnt mean to do it Mary because I am just clumsy
in all ways. Oh yes I am good at reciting Frosts
Stopping by Woods and his poem about the Hired
Man. I have been reading the poetical works of
Thomas Stearns Eliot so I can recite his The Hollow
Men or much of it and also his Book of Practical
Cats which is comical when I come to college towns
and some professor or his wife gives me a sandwich
and maybe $2 and maybe a ride to the next town.

Where I am now Mary I ought to study the poems
of John Greenleaf Whittier because theres been a
real blizzard maybe the biggest in the state for many
years and Im Snowbound. Years ago I tried to mem-
orize all that poem but I got only part way for it is
a whopper of a poem.

I dont hear much good Music Mary because of
course at the motels there isn't any phonograph or
tape recorder. Id like to hear some good string
quartet or maybe old folk songs well sung for music
hath charms to soothe the savage breast. Theres an
old Edison at the house where Im staying now and
what do you know they have a record of a song
you and I used to sing together Theres a Long Long
Trail A Winding. Its about the newest record in
this house Ill play it again soon thinking of you
Mary my sister. O there is a long long night of
waiting.

Mary right now Im at a big fine house where the
people have gone away for awhile and I watch the
house for them and keep some of the rooms warm.
Let me assure you Mary I wont take anything from
this good old house when I go. These are nice people

I know and I just came in out of the storm and Im very fond of their 3 sweet little girls. I remember what you looked like when I ran away first and you looked like one of them called Alice. The one I like best though is Allegra because she makes mischief and laughs a lot but is innocent.

I came here just yesterday but it seems as if Id lived in this house before but of course I couldnt have and I feel at home here. Nothing in this house could scare me much. You might not like it Mary because of little noises and glimpses you get but its a lovely house and as you know I like old places that have been lived in lots.

By the way Mary once upon a time Father O'Malley told me that to the Lord all time is eternally present. I think this means everything that happens in the world in any day goes on all at once. So God sees what went on in this house long ago and whats going on in this house today all at the same time. Its just as well we dont see through Gods eyes because then wed know everything thats going to happen to us and because Im such a sinner I dont want to know. Father O'Malley says that God may forgive me everything and have something special in store for me but I dont think so because why should He?

And Father O'Malley says that maybe some people work out their Purgatory here on earth and I might be one of these. He says we are spirits in the prisonhouse of the body which is like we were serving Time in the world here below and maybe God forgave me long ago and Im just waiting my time and paying for what I did and it will be alright in the end. Or maybe Im being given some second chance to set things right but as Father O'Malley put it to do that Id have to fortify my Will and do some Signal Act of contrition. Father O'Malley even says I might not have to do the Act actually if only I just made up my mind to do it really and truly because what God counts is the intention. But I think people who are in Purgatory must know they

35

are climbing up and have hope and Mary I think Im going down down down even though Ive stayed out of prisons some time now.

Father O'Malley tells me that for everybody the battle is won or lost already in God's sight and that though Satan thinks he has a good chance to conquer actually Satan has lost forever but doesnt know it. Mary I never did anybody any good but only harm to ones that loved me. If just once before I die I could do one Signal Act that was truly good then God might love me and let me have the Beatific Vision. Yet Mary I know Im weak of will and a coward and lazy and Ive missed my chance forever.

Well Mary my only sister Ive bored you long enough and I just wanted to say hello and tell you to be of good cheer. Im sorry I whined and complained like a little boy about my health because Im still strong and deserve all the pain I get. Mary if you can forgive your big brother who never grew up please pray for me sometime because nobody else does except possibly Father O'Malley when he isn't busy with other prayers. I pray for Mother every night and every other night for you and once a month for Dad. You were a good little girl and sweet. Now I will say good bye and ask your pardon for bothering you with my foolishness. Also Im sorry your friends found out I was just a hobo when I was with you 9 years ago and I dont blame you for being angry with me then for talking too much and I know I wasnt fit to lodge in your house. There arent many of us old real hobos left only beatniks and such that cant walk or chop wood and I guess that is just as well. It is a degrading life Mary but I cant stop walking down that long long trail not knowing where it ends.

> Your Loving Brother
> Francis (Frank)

P.S.: I don't wish to mislead so I will add Mary that the people who own this house didnt exactly ask me

in but its alright because I wont do any harm here
but a little good if I can. Good night again Mary.

Now he needed an envelope, but he had forgotten to
take one from the last motel, where the Presbyterian
minister had put him up. There must be some in Tamarack House, and one would not be missed, and that
would not be very wrong because he would take nothing
else. He found no envelopes in the drawer of the library
table: so he went up the stairs and almost knocked at
the closed door of Allegra's Room. Foolish! He opened
the door gently.

He had admired Allegra's small rosewood desk. In its
drawer was a leather letter-folder, the kind with a blotter,
he found, and in the folder were several yellowed envelopes. Also lying face up in the folder was a letter of
several small pages, in a woman's hand, a trifle shaky. He
started to sit down to read Allegra's letter that never was
sent to anybody, but it passed through his mind that his
great body might break the delicate rosewood chair that
belonged to Allegra, so he read the letter standing. It
was dated January 14, 1969. On that birthday of his,
he had been in Joliet prison.

How beautifully Allegra wrote!

Darling Celia,

This is a lonely day at Tamarack House, just fifty-
four years after your great-grandfather the General
died, so. I am writing to my grand-niece to tell you
how much I hope you will be able to come up to
Anthonyville and stay with me next summer—if
I still am here. The doctor says that only God knows
whether I will be. Your grandmother wants me to
come down your way to stay with her for the rest
of this winter, but I can't bear to leave Tamarack
House at my age, for they might have to put me in a
rest-home down there and then I wouldn't see this
old house again.

I am all right, really, because kind Mr. Connor
looks in every day, and Mrs. Williams comes every
other day to clean. I am not sick, my little girl, but

37

simply older than my years, and running down. When you come up next summer, God willing, I will make you that soft toast you like, and perhaps Mr. Connor will turn the crank for the ice-cream, and I may try to make some preserves with you to help me.

You weren't lonely, were you, when you stayed with me last summer for a whole month? Of course there are fewer than a hundred people left in Anthonyville now, and most of those are old. They say that there will be practically nobody living in the town a few years from now, when the new highway is completed and the old one is abandoned. There were more than two thousand people here in town and roundabout, a few years after the General built Tamarack House! But first the lumber industry gave out, and then the mines were exhausted, and the prison-break in 1915 scared many away forever. There are no passenger trains now, and they say the railway line will be pulled out altogether when the new freeway—they have just begun building it to the east—is ready for traffic. But we still have the maples and the tamaracks, and there are ever so many raccoons and opossums and squirrels for you to watch—and a lynx, I think, and an otter or two, and many deer.

Celia, last summer you asked me about the General's death and all the things that happened then, because you had heard something of them from your Grandmother Edith. But I didn't wish to frighten you, so I didn't tell you everything. You are older now, and you have a right to know, because when you grow up you will be one of the trustees of the Anthony Family Trust, and then this old house will be in your charge when I am gone. Tamarack House is not at all frightening, except a little in the morning on every January 14. I do hope that you and the other trustees will keep the house always, with the money that Father left to me—he was good at making money, even though the forests vanished and the mines failed, by his investments in Chicago

38

and which I am leaving to the Family Trust. I've kept the house just as it was, for the sake of the General's memory and because I love it that way.

You asked just what happened on January 14, 1915. There were seven people who slept in the house that month—not counting Cook and Cynthia (who was a kind of nannie to us girls and also cleaned), because they slept at their houses in the village. In the house, of course, was the General, my grandfather, your great-grandfather, who was nearly eighty years old. Then there were Father and Mama, and the three of us little sisters, and dear Frank.

Alice and sometimes even that baby Edith used to tease me in those days by screaming, "Frank's Allegra's sweetheart! Frank's Allegra's sweetheart!" I used to chase them, but I suppose it was true: he liked me best. Of course he was about sixty years old, though not so old as I am now, and I was a little thing. He used to take me through the swamps and show me the muskrats' houses. The first time he took me on such a trip, Mama raised her eyebrows when he was out of the room, but the General said, "I'll warrant Frank: I have his papers."

Alice and Edith might just as well have shouted, "Frank's Allegra's slave!" He read to me—oh, Robert Louis Stevenson's poems and all sorts of books. I never had another sweetheart, partly because almost all the young men left Anthonyville as I grew up when there was no work for them here, and the ones that remained didn't please Mama.

We three sisters used to play Creepmouse with Frank, I remember well. We would be the Creepmice, and would sneak up and scare him when he wasn't watching, and he would pretend to be terrified. He made up a little song for us—or, rather, he put words to some tune he had borrowed:

"Down, down, down in Creepmouse Town
All the lamps are low,

39

And the little rodent feet
Softly come and go

"There's a rat in Creepmouse Town
And a bat or two:
Everything in Creepmouse Town
Would swiftly frighten you!"

Do you remember, Celia, that the General was
State Supervisor of Prisons and Reformatories for
time out of mind? He was a good architect, too, and
designed Anthonyville State Prison, without taking
any fee for himself, as a model prison. Some people
in the capital said that he did it to give employment
to his county, but really it was because the site was
so isolated that it would be difficult for convicts to
escape.

The General knew Frank's last name, but he
never told the rest of us. Frank had been in Anthonyville State Prison at one time, and later in
other prisons, and the General had taken him out of
one of those other prisons on parole, having known
Frank when he was locked up at Anthonyville. I
never learned what Frank had done to be sentenced
to prison, but he was gentle with me and everybody
else, until that early morning of January 14.

The General was amused by Frank, and said that
Frank would be better off with us than anywhere
else. So Frank became our hired man, and chopped
the firewood for us, and kept the fires going in the
stoves and fireplaces, and sometimes served at
dinner. In summer he was supposed to scythe the
lawns, but of course summer didn't come. Frank
arrived by train at Anthonyville Station in October,
and we gave him the little room at the top of the
house.

Well, on January 12 Father went off to Chicago
on business. We still had the General. Every night
he barred the shutters on the ground floor, going
round to all the rooms by himself. Mama knew he
did it because there was a rumor that some life

convicts at the Prison "had it in" for the Supervisor of Prisons, although the General had retired five years earlier. Also they may have thought he kept a lot of money in the house—when actually, what with the timber gone and the mines going, in those times we were rather hard pressed and certainly kept our money in the bank at Duluth. But we girls didn't know why the General closed the shutters, except that it was one of the General's rituals. Besides, Anthonyville State Prison was supposed to be escape-proof. It was just that the General always took precautions, though ever so brave.

Just before dawn, Celia, on the cold morning of January 14, 1915, we all were waked by the siren of the Prison, and we all rushed downstairs in our nightclothes, and we could see that part of the Prison was afire. O, the sky was red! The General tried to telephone the Prison, but he couldn't get through, and later it turned out that the lines had been cut.

Next—it all happened so swiftly—we heard shouting somewhere down Main Street, and then guns went off. The General knew what that meant. He had got his trousers and his boots on, and now he struggled with his old military overcoat, and he took his old army revolver. "Lock the door behind me, girl," he told Mama. She cried and tried to pull him back inside, but he went down into the snow, nearly eighty though he was.

Only three or four minutes later, we heard the shots. The General had met the convicts at the gate. It was still dark, and the General had cataracts on his eyes. They say he fired first, and missed. Those bad men had broken into Mr. Emmons' store and taken guns and axes and whiskey. They shot the General—shot him again and again and again.

The next thing we knew, they were chopping at our front door with axes. Mama hugged us.

Celia dear, writing all this has made me so silly! I feel a little odd, so I must go lie down for an hour or two before telling you the rest. Celia, I do hope you will love this old house as much as I have. If I'm not here when you come up, remember that where I have gone I will know the General and Father and Mama and Alice and poor dear Frank, and will be ever so happy with them. Be a good little girl, my Celia.

The letter ended there, unsigned.

Frank clumped downstairs to the Sunday parlor. He was crying, for the first time since he had fought that professional heavyweight on October 19, 1943. Allegra's letter—if only she'd finished it! What had happened to those little girls, and Mama, and that other Frank? He thought of something from the Holy Bible: "It were better for him that a millstone were hanged about his neck, and he cast into the sea, than that he should offend one of these little ones."

Already it was almost evening. He lit the wick in the cranberry-glass lamp that hung from the middle of the parlor ceiling, standing on a chair to reach it. Why not enjoy more light? On a whim, he arranged upon the round table four silver candlesticks that had rested above the fireplace. He needed three more, and those he fetched from the dining room. He lit every candle in the circle: one for the General, one for Father, one for Mama, one for Alice, one for Allegra, one for Edith —and one for Frank.

The dear names of those little girls! He might as well recite aloud, it being good practice for the approaching days on the long, long trail:

> "I hear in the chamber above me
>   The patter of little feet,
> The sound of a door that is opened,
> And voices soft and sweet . . ."

Here he ceased. Had he heard something in the passage—or "descending the broad hall stair"? Because of the wind outside, he could not be certain. It cost him a gritting of his teeth to rise and open the parlor door.

42

Of course no one could be seen in the hall or on the stair. "Crazy Frank," men had called him at Joliet and other prisons: he had clenched his fists, but had kept a check upon himself. Didn't Saint Paul say that the violent take heaven by storm? Perhaps he had barked up the wrong tree; perhaps he would be spewed out of His mouth for being too peaceful.

Shutting the door, he went back to the fireside. Those lines of Longfellow had been no evocation. He put "The Long, Long Trail" on the old phonograph again, strolling about the room until the record ran out. There was an old print of a Great Lakes schooner on one wall that he liked. Beside it, he noticed, there seemed to be some pellets embedded in a closet doorjamb, but painted over, as if someone had fired a shotgun in the parlor in the old days. "The violent take it by storm . . ." He admired the grand piano; perhaps Allegra had learnt to play it. There were one or two big notches or gashes along one edge of the piano, varnished over, hard though that wood was. Then Frank sank into the big chair again and stared at the burning logs.

Just how long he had dozed, he did not know. He woke abruptly. Had he heard a whisper, the faintest whisper? He tensed to spring up. But before he could move, he saw reflections in the tall mirror.

Something had moved in the corner by the bookcase. No doubt about it: that small something had stirred again. Also something crept behind one of the satin sofas, and something else lurked near the piano. All these were at his back: he saw the reflections in the glass, as in a glass darkly, more alarming than physical forms. In this high shadowy room, the light of the kerosene lamp and of the seven candles did not suffice.

From near the bookcase, the first of them emerged into candlelight; then came ,the second, and the third. They were giggling, but he could not hear them only see their faces, and those not clearly. He was unable to stir, and the gooseflesh prickled all over him, and his hair rose at the back of his big head.

They were three little girls, barefoot, in their long muslin nightgowns, ready for bed. One may have been as much as twelve years old, and the smallest was little more than a baby. The middle one was Allegra, tiny even for her tender years, and a little imp: he knew, he knew! They were playing Creepmouse.

The three of them stole forward, Allegra in the lead, her eyes alight. He could see them plain now, and the dread was ebbing out of him. He might have risen and turned to greet them across the great gulf of time, but any action—why, what might it do to these little ones? Frank sat frozen in his chair, looking at the nimble reflections in the mirror, and nearer they came, perfectly silent. Allegra vanished from the glass, which meant that she must be standing just behind him.

He must please them. Could he speak? He tried, and the lines came out hoarsely:

> *"Down, down, down in Creepmouse Town*
> *All the lamps are low,*
> *And the little rodent feet . . ."*

He was not permitted to finish. Wow! There came a light tug at the curly white hair on the back of his head. O to talk with Allegra, the imp! Recklessly, he heaved his bulk out of the chair, and swung round—too late.

The parlor door was closing. But from the hall came another whisper, ever so faint, ever so unmistakable: "Good night, Frank!" There followed subdued giggles, scampering, and then the silence once more.

He strode to the parlor door. The hall was empty again, and the broad stair. Should he follow them up? No, all three would be abed now. Should he knock at Mama's Room, muttering, "Mrs. Anthony, are the children all right?" No, he hadn't the nerve for that, and it would be presumptuous. He had been given one moment of perception, and no more. Somehow he knew that they would not go so far as the garret floor. Ah, he needed fresh air! He snuffed out lamp and candles, except for one candlestick—Allegra's—that he took with him. Out into the hall he went. He unfastened the front door with that oaken patch about the middle of it and stepped upon the porch, leaving the burning candle just within the hall.

44

The wind had risen again, bringing still more snow. It was black as sin outside, and the temperature must be thirty below.

To him the wind bore one erratic peal of the desolate church bell of Anthonyville, and then another. How strong the blast must be through that belfry! Frank retreated inside from that unfathomable darkness and that sepulchral bell which seemed to toll for him. He locked the thick door behind him and screwed up his courage for the expedition to his room at the top of the old house.

But why shudder? He loved them now, Allegra most of all. Up the broad stairs to the second/floor he went, hearing only his own clumsy footfalls, and past the clay-sealed doors of the General and Father and Mama and Alice and Allegra and Edith. No one whispered, no one scampered.

In Frank's Room, he rolled himself in his blankets and quilt (had Allegra helped stitch the patchwork?), and almost at once the consciousness went out of him, and he must have slept dreamless for the first night since he was a farm boy.

So profound had been his sleep, deep almost as death, that the siren may have been wailing for some minutes before at last it roused him. Frank knew that horrid sound. It had called for him thrice before, as he fled from prisons. Who wanted him now? He heaved his ponderous body out of the warm bed. The candle that he had brought up from the Sunday parlor and left burning all night was flickering in its socket, but by that flame he could see the hour on his watch: seven o'clock, too soon for dawn.

Through the narrow skylight, as he flung on his clothes, the sky glowed an unnatural red, though it was long before sunup. The prison siren ceased to wail, as if choked off. Frank lumbered to the little frieze window and saw to the north, perhaps two miles distant, a monstrous mass of flames shooting high into the air. The prison was afire.

Then came shots outside: first the bark of a heavy revolver, followed irregularly by blasts of shotguns or

45

rifles. Frank was lacing his boots wtih a swiftness un-congenial to him. He got into his overcoat as there came a crashing and battering down below. That sound, too, he recognized, woodchopper that he had been: axes shatter-ing the front door.

Amid this pandemonium, Frank was too bewildered to grasp altogether where he was or even how this catastrophe might be fitted into the pattern of time. All that mattered was flight; the scheme of his escape re-mained clear in his mind. Pull up the chair below the skylight, heave yourself out to the upper roof, descend those iron rungs to the woodshed roof, make for the other side of the highway, then—why, then you must trust to circumstance, Frank. It's that long, long trail a-winding for you.

Now he heard a woman screaming within the house, and slipped and fumbled in his alarm. He had got upon the chair, opened the skylight, and was trying to obtain a good grip on the icy outer edge of the skylight frame, when someone knocked and kicked at the door of Frank's Room.

Yet those were puny knocks and kicks. He was about to heave himself upward when, in a relative quiet—the screaming had ceased for a moment—he heard a little shrill voice outside his door, urgently pleading: "Frank, Frank, let me in!"

He was arrested in flight as though great weights had been clamped to his ankles. That little voice he knew, as if it were part of him: Allegra's voice.

For a brief moment he still meant to scramble out the skylight. But the sweet little voice was begging. He stumbled off the chair, upset it, and was at the door in one stride.

"Is that you, Allegra?"

"Open it, Frank, *please* open it!"

He turned the key and pulled the bolt. On the thresh-old the little girl stood, indistinct by the dying candle-light, terribly pale, all tears, frantic.

Frank snatched her up. Ah, this was the dear real Allegra Anthony, all warm and soft and sobbing, flesh and blood! He kissed her cheek gently.

She clung to him in terror, and then squirmed loose, tugging at his heavy hand: "Oh, Frank, come on! Come downstairs! They're hurting Mama!"

"Who is, little girl?" He held her tiny hand, his body quivering with dread and indecision. "Who's down there, Allegra?"

"The bad men! *Come on*, Frank!" Braver than he, the little thing plunged back down the garret stair into the blackness below.

"Allegra! Come back here—come back now!" He bellowed it, but she was gone.

Up two flights of stairs, there poured to him a tumult of shrieks, curses, laughter, breaking noises. Several men were below, their speech slurred and raucous. He did not need Allegra to tell him what kind of men they were, for he heard prison slang and prison foulness, and he shook all over. There still was the skylight.

He would have turned back to that hole in the roof, had not Allegra squealed in pain somewhere on the second floor. Dazed, trembling, unarmed, Frank went three steps down the garret staircase. "Allegra! Little girl! What is it, Allegra?"

Someone was charging up the stair toward him. It was a burly man in the prison uniform, a lighted lantern in one hand and a glittering axe in the other. Frank had no time to turn. The man screeched obscenely at him and swung the axe.

In those close quarters, wielded by a drunken man, it was a chancy weapon. The edge shattered the plaster wall; the flat of the blade thumped upon Frank's shoulder. Frank, lurching forward, took the man by the throat with a mighty grip. They all tumbled pell-mell down the steep stairs—the two men, the axe, the lantern.

Frank's ursine bulk landed atop the stranger's body, and Frank heard his adversary's bones crunch. The lantern had broken and gone out. The convict's head hung loose on his shoulders, Frank found as he groped for the axe. Then he trampled over the fallen man and flung himself along the corridor, gripping the axe-helve. "Allegra! Allegra girl!"

From the head of the main stair, he could see that the

lamps and candles were burning in the hall and in the rooms of the ground floor. All three children were down there, wailing, and above their noise rose Mama's shrieks again. A mob of men were stamping, breaking things, roaring with amusement and desire, shouting filth. A bottle shattered.

His heart pounding as if it would burst out of his chest, Frank hurried rashly down the stair and went, all crimson with fury, into the Sunday parlor, the double-bitted axe swinging in his hand. They all were there: the little girls, Mama, and five wild men. "Stop that!" Frank roared with all the power of his lungs. "You let them go!"

Everyone in the parlor stood transfixed at that summons like the Last Trump. Allegra had been tugging pathetically at the leg of a dark man who gripped her mother's waist, and the other girls sputtered and sobbed, cornered, as a tall man poured a bottle of whiskey over them. Mrs. Anthony's gown was ripped nearly its whole length, and a third man was bending her backward by her long hair, as if he would snap her spine. Near the hall door stood a man like a long lean rat, the Rat of Creepmouse Town, a shotgun on his arm, gape-jawed at Frank's intervention. Guns and axes lay scattered about the Turkey carpet. By the fireplace, a fifth man had been heating the poker in the flames.

For that tableau-moment, they all stared astonished at the raving giant who had burst upon them; and the giant, puffing, stared back with his strange blue eyes. "O Frank!" Allegra sobbed: it was more command than entreaty—as if, Frank thought in a flash of insane mirth, he were like the boy in the fairy tale who could cry confidently "All heads off but mine!"

He knew what these men were, the rats and bats of Creepmouse Town: the worst men in any prison, lifers who had made their hell upon earth, killers all of them and worse than killers. The rotten damnation showed in all those flushed and drunken faces. Then the dark man let go of Mama and said in relief, with a coughing laugh, "Hell, it's only old Punkinhead Frank, clowning again! Have some fun for yourself, Frank boy!"

"Hey, Frank," Ratface asked, his shotgun crooked under his arm, "where'd the old man keep his money?"

Frank towered there perplexed, the berserker-lust draining out of him—almost bashful—and frightened worse than ever before in all his years on the trail. What should he shout now? What should he do? Who was he to resist such perfect evil? They were five to one, and those five were fiends from down under, and that one a coward. Long ago he had been weighed in the balance and found wanting.

Mama was the first to break the tableau. Her second captor had relaxed his clutch upon her hair; she prodded the little girls before her and leaped for the door.

The hair-puller was after her at once, but she bounded past Ratface's shotgun, which had wavered toward Frank, and Alice and Edith were ahead of her. Allegra, her eyes wide and desperate, tripped over the rungs of a broken chair. Everything happened in half a second. The hair-puller caught Allegra by her little ankle.

Then Frank bellowed again, loudest in all his life, and he swung his axe high above his head and downward, a skillful dreadful stroke, catching the hair-puller's arm just below the shoulder. At once the man began to scream and spout, while Allegra fled after her mother.

Falling, the hair-puller collided with Ratface, spoiling his aim, but one barrel of the shotgun fired, and Frank felt pain in his side. His bloody axe on high, he hulked between the five men and the door.

All the men's faces were glaring at Frank, incredulously, as if demanding how he dared stir against them. Three convicts were scrabbling tipsily for weapons on the floor. As Frank strode among them, he saw the expression on those faces change from gloating to desperation. Just as his second blow descended, there passed through his mind a kind of fleshly collage of death he had seen once at a farmyard gate: the corpses of five weasels nailed to a gatepost by the farmer, their frozen open jaws agape like damned souls in hell.

"All heads off but mine!" Frank heard himself braying. "All heads off but mine!" He hacked and hewed, his own screams of lunatic fury drowning their screams of terror.

49

For less than three minutes, shots, thuds, shrieks, crashes, terrible wailing. They could not get past him to the doorway.

"Come on!" Frank was raging as he stood in the middle of the parlor. "Come on, who's next? All heads off but mine! Who's next?"

There came no answer but a ghastly rattle from one of the five heaps that littered the carpet. Blood-soaked from hair to boots, the berserker towered alone, swaying where he stood.

His mind began to clear. He had been shot twice, Frank guessed, and the pain at his heart was frightful. Into his frantic consciousness burst all the glory of what he had done, and all the horror.

He became almost rational: he must count the dead. One upstairs, five here. One, two, three, four, five heaps. That was correct: all present and accounted for, Frank boy, Punkinhead Frank, Crazy Frank. All dead` and accounted for. Had he thought that thought before? Had he taken that mock roll before? Had he wrought this slaughter twice over, twice in this same old room?

But where were Mama and the little girls? They mustn't see–this blood-splashed inferno of a parlor. He was looking at himself in the tall mirror, and he saw a bear-man loathsome with his own blood and others' blood. He looked like the Wild Man of Borneo. In abhorrence he flung his axe aside. Behind him sprawled the reflections of the hacked dead.

Fighting down his heart-pain, he reeled into the hall. "Little girls! Mrs. Anthony! Allegra, O Allegra!" His voice was less strong. "Where are you? It's safe now!"

They did not call back. He labored up the main stair, clutching his side. "Allegra, speak to your Frank!" They were in none of the bedrooms.

He went up the garret stair, whatever the agony, then beyond Frank's Room to the cupola stair, and ascended that slowly, gasping hard. They were not in the cupola. Might they have run out among the trees? In that cold dawn, he stared on every side; he thought his sight was beginning to fail.

He could see no one outside the house. The drifts still choked the street beyond the gateposts, and those two boulders protruded impassive from untrodden snow. Back down the flights of stairs he made his way, clutching at the rail, at the wall. Surely the little girls hadn't strayed into that parlor butcher-shop? He bit his lip and peered into the Sunday parlor.

The bodies all were gone. The splashes and ropy strands of blood all were gone. Everything stood in perfect order, as if violence never had touched Tamarack House. The sun was rising, and sunlight filtered through the shutters. Within fifteen minutes the trophies of his savage victory had disappeared.

It was like the recurrent dream which had tormented Frank when he was little: he separated from Mother in the dark, wandering solitary in empty lanes, no soul alive in all the universe but little Frank. Yet those tremendous axe-blows had severed living flesh and blood, and for one moment, there on the stairs, he had held in his arms a tiny quick Allegra: of that reality he did not doubt at all.

Wonder subduing pain, he staggered to the front door. It stood unshattered. He drew the bar and turned the key, and went down the stone steps into the snow. He was weak now, and did not know where he was going. Had he done a Signal Act? Might the Lord give him one parting glimpse of little Allegra, somewhere among these trees? He slipped in a drift, half rose, sank again, crawled. He found himself at the foot of one of those boulders—the further one, the stone he had not inspected.

The snow had fallen away from the face of the bronze tablet. Clutching the boulder, Frank drew himself up. By bringing his eyes very close to the tablet, he could read the words, a dying man panting against deathless bronze:

In loving memory of
FRANK
a spirit in prison, made for eternity
who saved us and died for us
January 14, 1915

"Why, if the Soul can fling the Dust aside,
    And naked on the Air of Heaven ride,
Were't not a Shame—were't not a Shame for him
    In this clay carcass crippled to abide?"

THE WHISPERER
by
Brian Lumley

BRIAN LUMLEY is a sergeant in the British Royal Military Police who has seen service in such stations as West Germany, Cyprus, Northern Ireland, and Scotland. A discovery of the late August Derleth, his first books were published by Arkham House: a collection, The Caller of the Black, and a novel, Beneath the Moors. Much of Lumley's work takes its theme from the Cthulhu Mythos, a sub-genre created by H. P. Lovecraft, to which he has added in his own characteristic style. In that vein he has produced to date a trilogy of novels: The Burrowers Beneath, The Transition of Titus Crow, and Spawn of the Wind. Lumley's fiction is vital, colorful, and dramatic, and sometimes sparked with distinctive flashes of humor. This tale has all those qualities, but also shows a side of Lumley's writing that will be new to many. And in the course of things he has created a character for the supernatural gallery who bids well to be long remembered.

The first time Miles Benton saw the little fellow was on the train. Benton was commuting to his office job in the city and he sat alone in a second-class compartment. The "little fellow"—a very *ugly* little man, from what Benton could see of him out of the corner of his eye, with a lopsided hump and dark or dirty features, like a gnomish gypsy—entered the compartment and took a seat in the far corner. He was dressed in a floppy black wide-brimmed hat that fell half over his face and a black overcoat longer than himself that trailed to the floor.

Benton was immediately aware of the smell, a rank stench which quite literally would have done credit to the lowliest farmyard, and correctly deduced its source. Despite the dry, acrid smell of stale tobacco from the ashtrays and the lingering odour of grimy stations, the compartment had been positively perfumed prior to the advent of the hunchback. The day was quite chill outside, but Benton nevertheless stood up and opened the window, pulling it down until the draft forced back the fumes from his fellow passenger. He was then obliged to put away his flapping newspaper and sit back, his collar upturned against the sudden cold blast, mentally cursing the smelly little chap for fouling "his" compartment.

A further five minutes saw Benton's mind made up to change compartments. That way he would be removed from the source of the odorous irritation, and he would no longer need to suffer this intolerable blast of icy air. But no sooner was his course of action determined than the ticket collector arrived, sliding open the door and sticking his well-known and friendly face inside the compartment.

"Mornin', sir," he said briskly to Benton, merely glancing at the other traveller. "Tickets, please."

Benton got out his ticket and passed it to be examined. He noticed with satisfaction as he did so that the ticket collector wrinkled his nose and sniffed suspiciously at the air, eyeing the hunchback curiously. Benton retrieved his ticket and the collector turned to the little man in the far corner. "Yer ticket . . . *sir* . . . if yer don't mind." He looked the little chap up and down disapprovingly.

The hunchback looked up from under his black floppy hat and grinned. His eyes were jet and bright as a bird's. He winked and indicated that the ticket collector should bend down, expressing an obvious desire to say something in confidence. He made no effort to produce a ticket.

The ticket collector frowned in annoyance, but nevertheless bent his ear to the little man's face. He listened for a moment or two to a chuckling, throaty whisper. It actually appeared to Benton that the hunchback was *chortling* as he whispered his obscene secret into the other's ear, and the traveller could almost hear him saying: "Feelthy postcards! Vairy dairty pictures!"

The look on the face of the ticket collector changed immediately; his expression went stony hard.

"Aye, aye!" Benton said to himself. "The little blighter's got no ticket! He's for it now."

But no, the ticket collector said nothing to the obnoxious midget, but straightened and turned to Benton. "Sorry, sir," he said, "but this compartment's private. I'll 'ave ter arsk yer ter leave."

"But," Benton gasped incredulously, "I've been travelling in this compartment for years. It's never been a, well, a 'private' compartment before!"

"No, sir, p'raps not," said the ticket collector undismayed. "But it is now. There's a compartment next door; jus' a couple of gents in there! I'm sure it'll do jus' as

56

well." He held the door open for Benton, daring him to argue the point further. "Sir?"

"Ah, well," Benton thought, resignedly, "I was wanting to move." Nevertheless, he looked down aggressively as he passed the hunchback, staring hard at the top of the floppy hat. The little man seemed to know. He looked up and grinned, cocking his head on one side and grinning.

Benton stepped quickly out into the corridor and took a deep breath. "Damn!" he swore out loud.

"Yer pardon, sir?" inquired the ticket collector, already swaying off down the corridor.

"Nothing!" Benton snapped in reply, letting himself into the smoky, crowded compartment to which he had been directed.

The very next morning Benton plucked up his courage (he had never been a *very* brave man), stopped the ticket collector, and asked him what it had all been about. Who had the little chap been. What privileges did he have that an entire compartment had been reserved especially for him, the grimy little gargoyle?

To which the ticket collector replied: "Eh? An 'unchback? Are yer sure it was *this* train, sir? Why, we haint 'ad no private or reserved compartments on this 'ere train since it became a commuter special! And as fer a 'unchback—well!"

"But surely you remember asking me to leave my compartment—this compartment?" Benton insisted.

" 'Ere, yer pullin' me leg, haint yer, sir?" laughed the ticket collector good-naturedly. He slammed shut the compartment door behind him and smilingly strode away without waiting for an answer, leaving Benton alone with his jumbled and whirling thoughts.

"Well, I never!" the commuter muttered worriedly to himself. He scratched his head and then, philosophically, began to quote a mental line or two from a ditty his mother had used to say to him when he was a child:

The other day upon the stair
I saw a man who wasn't there . . .

Benton had almost forgotten about the little man with the hump and sewer-like smell by the time their paths crossed again. It happened one day some three months later, with spring just coming on, when, in acknowledgement of the bright sunshine, Benton decided to forego his usual sandwich lunch at the office for a noonday pint at the Bull & Bush.

The entire pub, except for one corner of the bar, appeared to be quite crowded, but it was not until Benton had elbowed his way to the corner in question that he saw why it was unoccupied; or rather, why it had only one occupant. The *smell* hit him at precisely the same time as he saw, sitting on a bar stool with his oddly humped back to the regular patrons, the little man in black with his floppy broad-brimmed hat.

That the other customers were aware of the cesspool stench was obvious—Benton watched in fascination the wrinkling all about him of at least a dozen pairs of nostrils—and yet not a man complained. And more amazing yet, no one even attempted to encroach upon the little fellow's territory in the bar corner. No one, that is, except Benton . . .

Holding his breath, Benton stepped forward and rapped sharply with his knuckles on the bar just to the left of where the hunchback sat. "Beer, barman. A pint of best, please."

The barman smiled chubbily and stepped forward, reaching out for a beer pump and slipping a glass beneath the tap. But even as he did so the hunchback made a small gesture with his head, indicating that he wanted to say something . . .

Benton had seen all this before, and all the many sounds of the pub—the chattering of people, the clink of coins, and the clatter of glasses—seemed to fade to silence about him as he focussed his full concentration upon the barman and the little man in the floppy hat. In slow motion, it seemed, the barman bent his head down toward the hunchback, and again Benton heard strangely chuckled whispers as the odious dwarf passed his secret instructions.

Curiously, fearfully, in something very akin to dread,

58

Benton watched the portly barman's face undergo its change, heard the *hissss* of the beer pump, saw the full glass come out from beneath the bar . . . to plump down in front of the hunchback! Hard-eyed, the barman stuck his hand out in front of Benton's nose. "That's half a dollar to you, sir."

"But . . ." Benton gasped, incredulously opening and closing his mouth. He already had a coin in his hand, with which he had intended to pay for his drink, but now he pulled his hand back.

"Half a dollar, sir," the barman repeated ominously, snatching the coin from Benton's retreating fingers, "and would you mind moving down the bar, please? It's a bit crowded this end."

In utter disbelief Benton jerked his eyes from the barman's face to his now empty hand, and from his hand to the seated hunchback; and as he did so the little man turned his head toward him and grinned. Benton was aware only of the bright, bird-like eyes beneath the wide brim of the hat—not of the darkness surrounding them. One of those eyes closed suddenly in a wink, and then the little man turned back to his beer.

"But," Benton again croaked his protest at the publican, "that's *my* beer he's got!" He reached out and caught the barman's rolled-up sleeve, following him down the bar until forced by the press of patrons to let go. The barman finally turned.

"Beer, sir?" The smile was back on his chubby face. "Certainly—half a dollar to you, sir."

Abruptly the bar sounds crashed in again upon Benton's awareness as he turned to elbow his way frantically, almost hysterically, through the crowded room to the door. Out of the corner of his eye he noticed that the little man, too, had left. A crush of thirsty people had already moved into the space he had occupied in the bar corner.

Outside in the fresh air Benton glared wild-eyed up and down the busy street; and yet he was half afraid of seeing the figure his eyes sought. The little man, however, had apparently disappeared into thin air.

"God damn him!" Benton cried in sudden rage, and

a passing policeman looked at him very curiously indeed.

He was annoyed to notice that the policeman followed him all the way back to the office.

At noon the next day Benton was out of the office as if at the crack of a starting pistol. He almost ran the four blocks to the Bull & Bush, pausing only to straighten his tie and tilt his bowler a trifle more aggressively in the mirror of a shop window. The place was quite crowded, as before, but he made his way determinedly to the bar, having first checked that the air was quite clean—ergo, that the little man with the hump was quite definitely *not* there.

He immediately caught the barman's eye. "Bartender, a beer, please. And—" He lowered his voice. "—a word, if you don't mind."

The publican leaned over the bar confidentially, and Benton lowered his tone still further to whisper: "Er, who *is* he—the, er, the little chap? Is he, perhaps, the boss of the place? Quite a little, er, *eccentric*, isn't he?"

"Eh?" said the barman, looking puzzledly about. "Who d'you mean, sir?"

The genuinely puzzled expression on the portly man's face ought to have told Benton all he needed to know, but Benton simply could not accept that, not a second time. "I mean the hunchback," he raised his voice in desperation. "The little chap in the floppy black hat who sat in the corner of the bar only yesterday—who stank to high heaven and drank *my* beer! Surely you remember him?"

The barman slowly shook his head and frowned, then called out to a group of standing men: "Joe, here a minute." A stocky chap in a cloth cap and tweed jacket detached himself from the general hubbub and moved to the bar. "Joe," said the barman, "you were in here yesterday lunch; did you see a—well, a—how was it, sir?" He turned back to Benton.

"A little chap with a floppy hat and a hump," Benton patiently, worriedly repeated himself. "He was sitting in the bar corner. Had a pong like a dead rat."

Joe thought about it for a second, then said: "Yer sure

yer got the right pub, guv'? I mean, we gets no tramps or weirdos in 'ere. 'Arry won't 'ave 'em, will yer, 'Arry?" He directed his question at the barman.

"No, he's right, sir. I get upset with weirdos. Won't have them."

"But . . . this is the Bull & Bush, isn't it?" Benton almost stammered, gazing wildly about, finding unaccustomed difficulty in speaking.

"That's right, sir," answered Harry the barman, frowning heavily now and watching Benton sideways.

"But —"

"Sorry, chief," the stocky Joe said with an air of finality. "Yer've got the wrong place. Must 'ave been some other pub." Both the speaker and the barman turned away, a trifle awkwardly, Benton thought, and he could feel their eyes upon him as he moved dazedly away from the bar towards the door. Again lines remembered of old repeated themselves in his head:

> He wasn't there again today—
> Oh, how I wish he'd go away!

"Here, sir!" cried the barman, suddenly remembering. "Do you want a beer or not, then?"

"No!" Benton snarled. Then, on impulse: "Give it to to him!—when next he comes in . . ."

Over the next month or so certain changes took place in Benton, changes which would have seemed quite startling to anyone knowing him of old. To begin with he had apparently broken two habits of very long standing. One: instead of remaining in his compartment aboard the morning train and reading his newspaper as had been his wont for close on nine years—he was now given to spending the first half hour of his journey peering into the many compartments while wandering up and down the long corridor, all the while wearing an odd, part puzzled, part apologetic expression. Two: he rarely took his lunch at the office any more, but went out walking in the city instead, stopping for a drink and a sandwich at any handy local pub. (But never the Bull

& Bush, though he always ensured that his strolling took him close by the latter house; and had anyone been particularly interested, then Benton might have been noticed to keep a very wary eye on the pub, almost as if he had it under observation.)

But then, as summer came on and no new manifestations of Benton's—*problem*—came to light, he began to forget all about it, to relegate it to that category of mental phenomena known as "daydreams," even though he had known no such phenomena before. And as the summer waxed, so the nagging worry at the back of his mind waned, until finally he convinced himself that his daydreams were gone for good.

But he was wrong . . .

And if those two previous visitations had been dreams, then the third could only be classified as—nightmare!

July saw the approach of the holiday period, and Benton had long had places booked for himself and his wife at a sumptuously expensive and rather exclusive coastal resort, far from the small Midlands town he called home. They went there every year. This annual "spree" allowed Benton to indulge his normally repressed escapism, when for a whole fortnight he could pretend that he was other than a mere clerk among people who usually accepted his fantasies as fact, thereby reinforcing them for Benton.

He could hardly wait for it to come around, that last Friday evening before the holidays, and when it did he rode home in the commuter special in a state of high excitement. Tomorrow would see him off to the sea and the sun; the cases were packed, the tickets arranged. A good night's rest now—and then, in the morning . . .

He was whistling as he let himself in through his front door, but the tone of his whistle soon went off key as he stepped into the hall. Dismayed, he paused and sniffed, his nose wrinkling. Out loud, he said: "Huh! The drains must be off again." But there was something rather special about that poisonous smell, something ominously familiar; and of a sudden, without fully realising why, Benton felt the short hairs at the back of his neck begin to rise. An icy chill struck at him from nowhere.

He passed quickly from the hall into the living room, where the air seemed even more offensive, and there he paused again as it came to him in a flash of fearful memory just *what* the awful stench of ordure was, and *where* and *when* he had known it before.

The room seemed suddenly to whirl about him as he saw, thrown carelessly across the back of his own easy chair, a monstrously familiar hat—a floppy hat, black and wide-brimmed!

The hat grew beneath his hypnotized gaze, expanding until it threatened to fill the whole house, his whole mind, but then he tore his eyes away and broke the spell. From the upstairs bedroom came a low, muted sound: a moan of pain—or pleasure? And as an incredibly obscene and now well-remembered chuckling whisper finally invaded Benton's horrified ears, he threw off shock's invisible shackles to fling himself breakneck up the stairs.

"Ellen!" he cried, throwing open the bedroom door just as a second moan sounded—*and then he staggered, clutching at the wall for support, as the scene beyond the door struck him an almost physical blow!*

The hunchback lay sprawled naked upon Benton's bed, his malformed back blue-veined and grimy. The matted hair of his head fell forward onto Ellen's white breasts and his filthy hands moved like crabs over her arched body. Her eyes were closed, her mouth open and panting; her whole attitude was one of complete abandon. Her slender hands clawed spastically at the hunchback's writhing, scurvy thighs . . .

Benton screamed hoarsely, clutching wildly at his hair, his eyes threatening to pop from his head, and for an instant time stood still. Then he lunged forward and grabbed at the man, a great power bursting inside him, the strength of both God and the devil in his crooked fingers—but in that same instant the hunchback slipped from the far side of the bed and out of reach. At an almost impossible speed the little man dressed and, as Benton lurched drunkenly about the room, he flitted

63

like a grey bat back across the bed. As he went his face passed close to Ellen's, and Benton was aware once again of that filthy whispered chuckle as the hunchback sprang to the floor and fled the room.

Mad with steadily mounting rage, Benton hardly noticed the sudden slitting of his wife's eyes, the film that came down over them like a silky shutter. But as he lunged after the hunchback Ellen reached out a naked leg, deliberately tripping him and sending him flying out onto the landing.

By the time he regained his feet, to lean panting against the landing rail, the little man was at the hall door, his hat once more drooping about grotesque shoulders. He looked up with eyes like malignant jewels in the shadow of that hat, and the last thing that the tormented householder saw as the hunchback closed the door softly behind him was that abhorrent, omniscient wink!

When he reached the garden gate some twoscore seconds later, Benton was not surprised to note the little man's complete disappearance . . .

Often, during the space of the next fortnight, Benton tried to think back on the scene which followed immediately upon the hunchback's departure from his house, but he was never able to resolve it to his satisfaction. He remembered the blind accusations he had thrown, the venomous bile of his words, his wife's patent amazement which had only served to enrage him all the more, the shock on Ellen's reddening face as he had slapped her mercilessly from room to room. He remembered her denial and the words she had screamed after locking herself in the bathroom: "Madman, madman!" she had screamed, and then she had left, taking her already packed suitcase with her.

He had waited until Monday —mainly in a vacant state of shock—before going out to a local ironmonger's shop to buy himself a sharp, long-bladed Italian knife . . .

It was now the fourteenth day, and still Benton walked the streets. He was grimy, unshaven, hungry, but his resolution was firm. Somewhere, *somewhere*, he would find the little man in the outsize overcoat and black floppy hat, and when he did he would stick his knife to its hilt in the hunchback's slimy belly and he would cut out the vile little swine's brains through his loathsomely winking eyes! In his mind's eye, even as he walked the night streets, Benton could *see* those eyes gleaming like jewels, quick and bright and liquid, and faintly in his nostrils there seemed to linger the morbid stench of the hybrid creature that wore those eyes in its face.

And always his mother's ditty rang in his head:

> *The other day upon the stair*
> *I saw a man who wasn't there.*
> *He wasn't there again today—*
> *Oh, how I wish . . .*

But no, Benton did *not* wish the little man away; on the contrary, he desperately wanted to find him!

Fourteen days, fourteen days of madness and delirium; but through all the madness a burning purpose had shone out like a beacon. Who, what, why? Benton knew not, and he no longer wanted to know. But somewhere, *somewhere* . . .

Starting the first Tuesday after that evening of waking nightmare, each morning he had caught the commuter special as of old, to prowl its snakelike corridor and peer in poisonously through the compartment windows, every lunchtime he had waited in a shop doorway across the street from the Bull & Bush until closing time, and in between times he had walked the streets in all the villages between home and the city. Because somewhere, *somewhere!*

"Home." He tasted the word bitterly. "Home" - hah! That was a laugh! And all this after eleven years of reasonably harmonious married life. He thought again, suddenly, of Ellen, then of the hunchback, then of the two of them together . . . and in the next instant his mind was lit by a bright flash of inspiration.

Fourteen days—*fourteen days including today* and

this was Saturday night! Where would he be now if this whole nightmare had never happened? Why, he would be on the train with his wife, going home from their holiday!

Could it possibly be that—

Benton checked his watch, his hands shaking uncontrollably. Ten to nine; the nine o'clock train would be pulling into the station in only ten more minutes!

He looked wildly about him, reality crashing down again as he found himself in the back alleys of his home town. Slowly the wild light went out of his eyes, to be replaced by a strangely warped smile as he realised that he stood in an alley only a few blocks from the railway station . . .

They didn't see him as they left the station, Ellen in high heels and a chic outfit, the hunchback as usual in his ridiculous overcoat and floppy black hat. But Benton saw them. They were (it still seemed completely unbelievable) arm in arm, Ellen radiant as a young bride, the little man reeking and filthy; and as Benton heard again that obscene chuckle he choked and reeled with rage in the darkness of his shop doorway.

Instantly the little man paused and peered into the shadows where Benton crouched. Benton cursed himself and shrank back; although the street was almost deserted, he had not wanted his presence known just yet.

But his presence *was* known!

The hunchback lifted up Ellen's hand to his lips in grotesque chivalry and kissed it. He whispered something loathsomely, and then, as Ellen made off without a word down the street, he turned again to peer with firefly eyes into Benton's doorway. The hiding man waited no longer. He leapt out into view, his knife bright and upraised, and the hunchback turned without ceremony to scurry down the cobbled street, his coat fluttering behind him like the wings of a great crippled moth.

Benton ran too, and quickly the gap between them closed as he drove his legs in a vengeful fury. Faster and faster his breath rasped as he drew closer to the fugitive hunchback, his hand lifting the knife for the fatal stroke.

Then the little man darted round a corner into an alleyway. No more than a second later Benton, too, rushed wildly into the darkness of the same alley. He skidded to a halt, his shoes sliding on the cobbles. He stilled his panting forcibly.

Silence . . .

The little devil had vanished again! He—

No, *there* he was—cringing like a cornered rat in the shadow of the wall.

Benton lunged, his knife making a crescent of light as it sped toward the hunchback's breast, but like quicksilver the target shifted as the little man ducked under his pursuer's arm to race out again into the street, leaving the echo of his hideous chuckle behind him.

That whispered chuckle drove Benton to new heights of raging bloodlust and, heedless now of all but the chase, he raced hot on the hunchback's trail. He failed to see the taxi's lights as he ran into the street, failed to hear its blaring horn indeed, he was only dimly aware of the scream of brakes and tortured tyres—so that the darkness of oblivion as it rushed in upon him came as a complete surprise . . .

The darkness did not last. Quickly Benton swam up out of unconsciousness to find himself crumpled in the gutter. There was blood on his face, a roaring in his ears. The street swam round and round.

"Oh, God!" he groaned, but the words came out broken, like his body, and faint. Then the street found its level and steadied. An awful dull ache spread upwards from Benton's waist until it reached his neck. He tried to move, but couldn't. He heard running footsteps and managed to turn his head, lifting it out of the gutter in an agony of effort. Blood dripped from a torn ear. He moved an arm just a fraction, fingers twitching.

"God mister what were you doing what were you *doing?*" the taxi driver gabbled. "Oh Jesus Jesus you're hurt you're hurt. It wasn't my fault it wasn't me!"

"Never, uh . . . mind." Benton gasped, pain threatening to pull him under again as the ache in his lower body exploded into fresh agony. "Just . . . get me, uh, into . . . your car and . . . hospital or . . . doctor."

"Sure, yes!" the man cried, quickly kneeling.

If Benton's nose had not been clogged with mucus and drying blood he would have known of the hunchback's presence even before he heard the terrible chuckling from the pavement. As it was, the sound made him jerk his damaged head round into a fresh wave of incredible pain. He turned his eyes upward. Twin points of light stared down at him from the darkness beneath the floppy hat.

"Uh . . . I suppose, uh, you're satisfied . . . now?" he painfully inquired, his hand groping uselessly, longingly for the knife which now lay half way across the street.

And then he froze. Tortured and racked though his body was—desperate as his pain and injuries were—Benton's entire being *froze* as, in answer to his choked question, *the hunchback slowly, negatively shook his shadowed head!*

Slowly, amazed, and horrified, Benton could only gape, even his agony forgotten as he helplessly watched from the gutter a repeat performance of those well-known gestures, those scenes remembered of old and now indelibly imprinted upon his mind: the filthy whispering in the taxi driver's ear; the winking of bright, bird eyes; the mazed look spreading like pale mud on the frightened man's face. Again the street began to revolve about Benton as the taxi driver walked as if in a dream back to his taxi.

Benton tried to scream but managed only a shuddering cough. Spastically his hand found the hunchback's grimy ankle and he gripped it tight. The little man stood like stone, like an anchor, and once more the street steadied about them as Benton fought his mangled body in a futile attempt to push it to its feet. He could not. There was something wrong with his back, something broken. He coughed, then groaned and relaxed his grip, turning his eyes upward again to meet the steady gaze of the hunchback.

"Please . . ." he said. But his words were drowned out by the sudden sound of a revving engine, by the shriek of skidding tyres savagely reversing; and the last thing Benton saw, other than the black bulk of the taxi looming and the red rear lights, was the shuttering of one of those evil eyes in a grim farewell wink . . .

Some few minutes later the police arrived at the scene of the most inexplicable killing it had ever been their lot to have to attend. They had been attracted by the crazed shrieking of a white-haired, utterly lunatic taxi driver.

ARMAJA DAS

by

Joe Haldeman

Primarily an author of science fiction, JOE HALDE-MAN came out of his army service in Vietnam—where he was a combat demolition specialist until wounded in the Central Highlands—with some sharp and probing things to say about the effects of war on people. His preoccupation with war can be seen in various shorter works, in his mainstream novel War Year, *and more recently in* The Forever War *(St. Martin's Press/Ballantine), which has reaped an impressive response from the critics and already is secure as one of the most important science fiction books of the 1970s. Born in Oklahoma City in 1943, Haldeman holds a masters degree in English and has worked in various jobs, from private secretary to classical guitar teacher to a programmer in high energy physics. He's obviously a writer to be heard further from, as this wry, perhaps ultimate variation on a classic supernatural horror theme illustrates.*

The highrise, built in 1980, still had the smell and look of newness. And of money.

The doorman bowed a few degrees and kept a straight face, opening the door for a bent old lady. She had a card of Veterans' poppies clutched in one old claw. He didn't care much for the security guard, and she would give him interesting trouble.

The skin on her face hung in deep creases, scored with a network of tiny wrinkles; her chin and nose protruded and drooped. A cataract made one eye opaque; the other eye was yellow and red surrounding deep black, unblinking. She had left her teeth in various things. She shuffled. She wore an old black dress faded slightly grey by repeated washing. If she had any hair, it was concealed by a pale blue bandanna. She was so stooped that her neck was almost parallel to the ground.

"What can I do for you?" The security guard had a tired voice to match his tired shoulders and back. The job had seemed a little romantic, the first couple of days, guarding all these rich people, sitting at an ultramodern console surrounded by video monitors, submachine gun at his knees. But the monitors were blank except for an hourly check, power shortage; and if he ever removed the gun from its cradle, he would have to fill out five forms and call the police station. And the doorman never turned anybody away.

"Buy a flower for boys less fortunate than ye," she

said in a faint raspy baritone. From her age and accent, her own boys had fought in the Russian Revolution.

"I'm sorry. I'm not allowed to . . . respond to charity while on duty."

She stared at him for a long time, nodding microscopically. "Then send me to someone with more heart."

He was trying to frame a reply when the front door slammed open. "Car on fire!" the doorman shouted.

The security guard leaped out of his seat, grabbed a fire extinguisher and sprinted for the door. The old woman shuffled along behind him until both he and the doorman disappeared around the corner. Then she made for the elevator with surprising agility.

She got out on the seventeenth floor after pushing the button that would send the elevator back down to the lobby. She checked the name plate on 1738: Mr. Zold. She was illiterate, but she could recognize names.

Not even bothering to try the lock, she walked on down the hall until she found a maid's closet. She closed the door behind her and hid behind a rack of starchy white uniforms, leaning against the wall with her bag between her feet. The slight smell of gasoline didn't bother her at all.

John Zold pressed the intercom button. "Martha?" She answered. "Before you close up shop I'd like a redundancy check on stack 408. Against tape 408." He switched the selector on his visual output screen so it would duplicate the output at Martha's station. He stuffed tobacco in a pipe and lit it, watching.

Green numbers filled the screen, a complicated matrix of ones and zeros. They faded for a second and were replaced with a field of pure zeros. The lines of zeros started to roll, like titles preceding a movie.

The 746th line came up all ones. John thumbed the intercom again. "Had to be something like that. You have time to fix it up?" She did. "Thanks, Martha. See you tomorrow."

He slid back the part of his desk top that concealed a keypunch and typed rapidly: "523 784 00926//Good night, machine. Please lock this station."

GOOD NIGHT, JOHN. DON'T FORGET YOUR LUNCH DATE WITH MR. BROWNWOOD TOMORROW. DENTIST APPOINTMENT WEDNESDAY 0945. GENERAL SYSTEMS CHECK WEDNESDAY 1300. DEL O DEL BAXT. LOCKED.

Del O Del baxt meant "God give you luck" in the ancient tongue of the Romani. John Zold, born a Gypsy but hardly a Gypsy by any standard other than the strong one of blood, turned off his console and unlocked the bottom drawer of his desk. He took out a flat automatic pistol in a holster with a belt clip and slipped it under his jacket, inside the waistband of his trousers. He had only been wearing the gun for two weeks, and it still made him uncomfortable. But there had been those letters.

John was born in Chicago, some years after his parents had fled from Europe and Hitler. His father had been a fiercely proud man, and had gotten involved in a bitter argument over the honor of his twelve-year-old daughter; from which argument he had come home with knuckles raw and bleeding, and had given to his wife for disposal a large clasp knife crusty with dried blood.

John was small for his five years, and his chin barely cleared the kitchen table, where the whole family sat and discussed their uncertain future while Mrs. Zold bound up her husband's hands. John's shortness saved his life when the kitchen window exploded and a low ceiling of shotgun pellets fanned out and chopped into the heads and chests of the only people in the world whom he could love and trust. The police found him huddled between the bodies of his father and mother, and at first thought he was also dead; covered with blood, completely still, eyes wide open and not crying.

It took six months for the kindly orphanage people to get a single word out of him: *ratválo*, which he said over and over, and which they were never able to translate. Bloody, bleeding.

But he had been raised mostly in English, with a few words of Romani and Hungarian thrown in for spice and accuracy. In another year their problem was not one of communicating with John—only of trying to shut him up.

No one adopted the stunted Gypsy boy, which suited John. He'd had a family, and look what happened.

In orphanage school he flunked penmanship and deportment but did reasonably well in everything else. In arithmetic and, later, mathematics, he was nothing short of brilliant. When he left the orphanage at eighteen, he enrolled at the University of Illinois, supporting himself as a bookkeeper's assistant and part-time male model. He had come out of an ugly adolescence with a striking resemblance to the young Clark Gable.

Drafted out of college, he spent two years playing with computers at Fort Lewis, got out and went all the way to a master's degree under the GI Bill. His thesis, "Simulation of Continuous Physical Systems by Way of Universalization of the Trakhtenbrot Algorithms," was very well received, and the mathematics department gave him a research assistantship to extend the thesis into a doctoral dissertation. But other people read the paper too, and after a few months Bellcom International hired him away from academia. He rose rapidly through the ranks. Not yet forty, he was now senior analyst at Bellcom's Research and Development Group. He had his own private office with a picture window overlooking Central Park, and a plush six-figure condominium only twenty minutes away by commuter train.

As was his custom, John bought a tall can of beer on his way to the train and opened it as soon as he sat down. It kept him from fidgeting during the fifteen- or twenty-minute wait while the train filled up.

He pulled a thick technical report out of his briefcase and stared at the summary on the cover sheet, not really seeing it but hoping that looking occupied would spare him the company of some anonymous fellow traveller.

The train was an express, and whisked them out to Dobb's Ferry in twelve minutes. John didn't look up from his report until they were well out of New York City; the heavy mesh tunnel that protected the track from vandals induced spurious colors in your retina as it blurred by.

Some people liked it, tripped on it, but to John the effect was at best annoying, at worst nauseating, depending on how tired he was. Tonight he was dead tired.

He got off the train two stops up from Dobb's Ferry. The highrise limousine was waiting for him and two other residents. It was a fine spring evening and John would normally have walked the half mile, tired or not. But those unsigned letters.

"John Zold, you stop this preachment or you die soon. *Armaja das*, John Zold."

All three letters said that: *Armaja das*. We put a curse on you—for preaching.

He was less afraid of curses than of bullets. He undid the bottom button of his jacket as he stepped off the train, ready to quickdraw, roll for cover behind that trash can, just like in the movies; but there was no one suspicious-looking around. Just an assortment of suburban wives and the old cop who was on permanent station duty.

Assassination in broad daylight wasn't Romani style. Styles change, though. He got in the car and watched side roads all the way home.

There was another one of the shabby envelopes in his mailbox. He wouldn't open it until he got upstairs. He stepped in the elevator with the others and punched seventeen.

They were angry because John Zold was stealing their children.

Last March John's tax accountant had suggested that he could contribute four thousand dollars to any legitimate charity and actually make a few hundred bucks in the process, by dropping into a lower tax bracket. Not one to do things the easy or obvious way, John made various inquiries and, after a certain amount of bureaucratic tedium, founded the Young Gypsy Assimilation Council—with matching funds from federal, state, and city governments, and a continuing Ford Foundation scholarship grant.

77

The YGAC was actually just a one-room office in a West Village brownstone, manned by volunteer help. It was filled with various pamphlets and broadsides, mostly written by John, explaining how young Gypsies could legitimately take advantage of American society: by becoming a part of it—something old-line Gypsies didn't care for. Jobs, scholarships, work-study programs, these things are for the *gadjos,* and poison to a Gypsy's spirit.

In November a volunteer had opened the office in the morning to find a crude firebomb that used a candle as a delayed-action fuse for five gallons of gasoline. The candle was guttering a fraction of an inch away from the line of powder that would have ignited the gas. In January it had been buckets of chicken entrails, poured into filing cabinets and flung over the walls. So John found a tough old man who would sleep on a cot in the office at night—sleep like a cat with a shotgun beside him. There was no more trouble of that sort. Only old men and women who would file in silently staring, to take handfuls of pamphlets which they would drop in the hall and scuff into uselessness, or defile in a more basic way. But paper was cheap.

John threw the bolt on his door and hung his coat in the closet. He put the gun in his writing desk and sat down to open the mail.

The shortest one yet: "Tonight, John Zold. *Armaja das.*" Lots of luck, he thought. Won't even be home tonight; heavy date. Stay at her place. Gramercy Park. Lay a curse on me there? At the show or Sardi's?

He opened two more letters, bills, and there was a knock at the door.

Not announced from downstairs. Maybe a neighbor. Guy next door was always borrowing something. Still. Feeling a little foolish, he put the gun back in his waistband. Put his coat back on in case it was just a neighbor.

The peephole didn't show anything. Bad. He drew the pistol and held it just out of sight by the doorjamb, threw the bolt, and eased open the door. It bumped into the Gypsy woman, too short to have been visible through the peephole. She backed away and said, "John Zold."

He stared at her. "What do you want, *púridaia*?" He could only remember a hundred or so words of Romani, but "grandmother" was one of them. What was the word for witch?

"I have a gift for you." From her bag she took a dark green booklet, bent and with frayed edges, and gave it to him. It was a much-used Canadian passport belonging to a William Belini. But the picture inside the front cover was one of John Zold.

Inside, there was an airline ticket in a Qantas envelope. John didn't open it. He snapped the passport shut and handed it back. The old lady wouldn't accept it.

"An impressive job. It's flattering that someone thinks I'm so important."

"Take it and leave forever, John Zold. Or I will have to do the second thing."

He slipped the ticket envelope out of the booklet. "This, I will take. I can get your refund on it. The money will buy lots of posters and pamphlets." He tried to toss the passport into her bag, but missed. "What is your second thing?"

She toed the passport back to him. "Pick that up." She was trying to sound imperious, but it came out a thin, petulant quaver.

"Sorry, I don't have any use for it. What is—"

"The second thing is your death, John Zold." She reached into her bag.

He produced the pistol and aimed it down at her forehead. "No, I don't think so."

She ignored the gun, pulling out a handful of white chicken feathers. She threw the feathers over his threshold. *"Armaja das,"* she said, and then droned on in Romani, scattering feathers at regular intervals. John recognized *joovi* and *kari*, the words for woman and penis, and several other words he might have picked up if she'd pronounced them more clearly.

He put the gun back into its holster and waited until she was through. "Do you really think—"

"Armaja das," she said again, and started a new litany. He recognized a word in the middle as meaning

79

corruption or infection, and the last word was quite clear: death. *Méripen.*

"This nonsense isn't going to   " But he was talking to the back of her head. He forced a laugh and watched her walk past the elevator and turn the corner that led to the staircase.

He could call the guard. Make sure she didn't get out the back way. Illegal entry. He suspected that she knew he wouldn't want to go to the trouble, and it annoyed him slightly. He walked halfway to the phone, checked his watch and went back to the door. Scooped up the feathers and dropped them in the disposal. Just enough time. Fresh shave, shower, best clothes. Limousine to the station, train to the city, cab from Grand Central to her apartment.

The show was pure delight, a sexy revival of *Lysistrata*; Sardi's was as ego-bracing as ever; she was a soft-hard woman with style and sparkle, who all but dragged him back to her apartment, where he was for the first time in his life impotent.

The psychiatrist had no use for the traditional props: no soft couch or bookcases lined with obviously expensive volumes. No carpet, no paneling, no numbered prints, not even the notebook or the expression of slightly disinterested compassion. Instead, she had a hidden recorder and an analytical scowl; plain stucco walls surrounding a functional desk and two hard chairs—period.

"You know exactly what the problem is," she said.

John nodded. "I suppose. Some . . . residue from my early upbringing; I accept her as an authority figure. From the few words I could understand of what she said, I took, it was . . ."

"From the words *penis* and *woman*, you built your own curse. And you're using it, probably to punish yourself for surviving the disaster that killed the rest of your family."

"That's pretty old-fashioned. And farfetched. I've had almost forty years to punish myself for that, if I felt responsible. And I don't."

"Still, it's a working hypothesis." She shifted in her

chair and studied the pattern of teak grain on the bare top of her desk. "Perhaps if we can keep it simple, the cure can also be simple."

"All right with me," John said. At $125 per hour, the quicker, the better.

"If you can see it, feel it, in this context, then the key to your cure is transference." She leaned forward, elbows on the table, and John watched her breasts shifting with detached interest, the only kind of interest he'd had in women for more than a week. "If you can see *me* as an authority figure instead, she continued, "then eventually I'll be able to reach the child inside, convince him that there was no curse. Only a case of mistaken identity . . . Nothing but an old woman who scared him. With careful hypnosis, it shouldn't be too difficult."

"Seems reasonable," John said slowly. Accept this young *Geyri* as more powerful than the old witch? As a grown man, he could. If there was a frightened Gypsy boy hiding inside him, though, he wasn't sure.

"523 784 00926//Hello machine," John typed. "Who is the best dermatologist within a 10-short-block radius?"

GOOD MORNING, JOHN. WITHIN STATED DISTANCE AND USING AS SOLE PARAMETER THEIR HOURLY FEE, THE MAXIMUM FEE IS $95/HR, AND THIS IS CHARGED BY TWO DERMATOLOGISTS. DR. BRYAN DILL, 245 W. 45TH ST., SPECIALIZES IN COSMETIC DERMATOLOGY. DR. ARTHUR MAAS, 198 W. 44TH ST., SPECIALIZES IN SERIOUS DISEASES OF THE SKIN.

"Will Dr. Maas treat diseases of psychological origin?" CERTAINLY. MOST DERMATOSIS IS.

Don't get cocky, machine. "Make me an appointment with Dr. Maas, within the next two days."

YOUR APPOINTMENT IS AT 10:45 TOMORROW, FOR ONE HOUR. THIS WILL LEAVE YOU 45 MINUTES TO GET TO LUCHOW'S FOR YOUR APPOINTMENT WITH THE AMCSE GROUP. I HOPE IT IS NOTHING, SERIOUS, JOHN.

81

"I trust it isn't." Creepy empathy circuits. "Have you arranged for a remote terminal at Luchow's?"

THIS WAS NOT NECESSARY. I WILL PATCH THROUGH CONED/GENERAL. LEASING THEIR LUCHOW'S FACILITY WILL COST ONLY .588 THE PROJECTED COST OF TRANSPORTATION AND SETUP LABOR FOR A REMOTE TERMINAL.

That's my machine, always thinking. "Very good, machine. Keep this station live for the time being."

THANK YOU, JOHN. The letters faded but the ready light stayed on.

He shouldn't complain about the empathy circuits; they were his baby, and the main reason Bellcom paid such a bloated salary to keep him. The copyright on the empathy package was good for another twelve years, and they were making a fortune, time-sharing it out. Virtually every large computer in the world was hooked up to it, from the ConEd/General that ran New York, to Geneva and Akademia Nauk, which together ran half of the world.

Most of the customers gave the empathy package a name, usually female. John called it "machine" in a not-too-successful attempt to keep from thinking of it as human.

He made a conscious effort to restrain himself from picking at the carbuncles on the back of his neck. He should have gone to the doctor when they first appeared, but the psychiatrist had been sure she could cure them; the "corruption" of the second curse. She'd had no more success with that than the impotence. And this morning, boils had broken out on his chest and groin and shoulderblades, and there were sore spots on his nose and cheekbone. He had some opiates, but would stick to aspirin until after work.

Dr. Maas called it impetigo; gave him a special kind of soap and some antibiotic ointment. He told John to make another appointment in two weeks, ten days. If there was no improvement they would take stronger measures. He seemed young for a doctor, and John couldn't bring himself to say anything about the curse. But he already had a doctor for that end of it, he rationalized.

Three days later he was back in Dr. Maas's office. There was scarcely a square inch of his body where some sort of lesion hadn't appeared. He had a temperature of 101.4 degrees. The doctor gave him systemic antibiotics and told him to take a couple of days' bed rest. John told him about the curse, finally, and the doctor gave him a booklet about psychosomatic illness. It told John nothing he didn't already know.

By the next morning, in spite of strong antipyretics, his fever had risen to over 102. Groggy with fever and painkillers, John crawled out of bed and traveled down to the West Village, to the YGAC office. Fred Gorgio, the man who guarded the place at night, was still on duty.

"Mr. Zold!" When John came from the door, Gorgio jumped up from the desk and took his arm. John winced from the contact, but allowed himself to be led to a chair. "What's happened?" John by this time looked like a person with terminal smallpox.

For a long minute John sat motionlessly, staring at the inflamed boils that crowded the backs of his hands. "I need a healer," he said, talking with slow awkwardness because of the crusted lesions on his lips.

"A *chóvihánni?*" John looked at him uncomprehendingly. "A witch?"

"No." He moved his head from side to side. "An herb doctor. Perhaps a white witch."

"Have you gone to the *gadjo* doctor?"

"Two. A Gypsy did this to me; a Gypsy has to cure it."

"It's in your head, then?"

"The *gadjo* doctors say so. It can still kill me."

Gorgio picked up the phone, punched a local number, and rattled off a fast stream of a patois that used as much Romani and Italian as English. "That was my cousin," he said, hanging up. "His mother heals, and has a good reputation. If he finds her at home, she can be here in less than an hour."

John mumbled his appreciation. Gorgio led him to the couch.

The healer woman was early, bustling in with a wicker bag full of things that rattled. She glanced once at John and Gorgio, and began clearing the pamphlets off a side table. She appeared to be somewhere between fifty and sixty years old, tight bun of silver hair bouncing as she moved around the room, setting up a hot-plate and filling two small pots with water. She wore a black dress only a few years old and sensible shoes. The only lines on her face were laugh lines.

She stood over John and said something in gentle, rapid Italian, then took a heavy silver crucifix from around her neck and pressed it between his hands. "Tell her to speak English . . . or Hungarian," John said.

Gorgio translated. "She says that you should not be so affected by the old superstitions. You should be a modern man and not believe in fairy tales for children and old people."

John stared at the crucifix, turning it slowly between his fingers. "One old superstition is much like another." But he didn't offer to give the crucifix back.

The smaller pot was starting to steam and she dropped a handful of herbs into it. Then she returned to John and carefully undressed him.

When the herb infusion was boiling, she emptied a package of powdered arrowroot into the cold water in the other pot and stirred it vigorously. Then she poured the hot solution into the cold and stirred some more. Through Gorgio, she told John she wasn't sure whether the herb treatment would cure him. But it would make him more comfortable.

The liquid jelled and she tested the temperature with her fingers. When it was cool enough, she started to pat it gently on John's face. Then the door creaked open, and she gasped. It was the old crone who had put the curse on John in the first place.

The witch said something in Romani, obviously a command, and the woman stepped away from John.

"Are you still a skeptic, John Zold?" She surveyed her handiwork. "You called this nonsense."

John glared at her but didn't say anything. "I heard that you had asked for a healer," she said, and addressed the other woman in a low tone.

Without a word, she emptied her potion into the sink

and began putting away her paraphernalia. "Old bitch," John croaked. "What did you tell her?"

"I said that if she continued to treat you, what happened to you would also happen to her sons."

"You're afraid it would work," Gorgio said.

"No. It would only make it easier for John Zold to die. If I wanted that I could have killed him on his threshold." Like a quick bird she bent over and kissed John on his inflamed lips. "I will see you soon, John Zold. Not in this world." She shuffled out the door and the other woman followed her. Gorgio cursed her in Italian, but she didn't react.

John painfully dressed himself. "What now?" Gorgio said. "I could find you another healer . . ."

"No. I'll go back to the *gadjo* doctors. They say they can bring people back from the dead." He gave Gorgio the woman's crucifix and limped away.

The doctor gave him enough antibiotics to turn him into a loaf of moldy bread, then reserved a bed for him at an exclusive clinic in Westchester, starting the next morning. He would be under twenty-four-hour observation, and constant blood turn-around, if necessary. They *would* cure him. It was not possible for a man of his age and physical condition to die of dermatosis.

It was dinnertime, and the doctor asked John to come have some home cooking. He declined partly from lack of appetite, partly because he couldn't imagine even a doctor's family being able to eat with such a grisly apparition at the table with them. He took a cab to the office.

There was nobody on his floor but a janitor, who took one look at John and developed an intense interest in the floor.

"523 784 00926//Machine, I'm going to die. Please advise."

ALL HUMANS AND MACHINES DIE, JOHN. IF YOU MEAN YOU ARE GOING TO DIE SOON, THAT IS SAD.

"That's what I mean. The skin infection; it's completely out of control. White cell count climbing in spite of drugs. Going to the hospital tomorrow, to die."

85

BUT YOU ADMITTED THAT THE CONDITION WAS PSYCHOSOMATIC. THAT MEANS YOU ARE KILLING YOURSELF, JOHN. YOU HAVE NO REASON TO BE THAT SAD.

He called the machine a Jewish mother and explained in some detail about the YGAC, the old crone, the various stages of the curse, and today's aborted attempt to fight fire with fire.

YOUR LOGIC WAS CORRECT BUT THE APPLICATION OF IT WAS NOT EFFECTIVE. YOU SHOULD HAVE COME TO ME, JOHN. IT TOOK ME 2.037 SECONDS TO SOLVE YOUR PROBLEM. PURCHASE A SMALL BLACK BIRD AND CONNECT ME TO A VOCAL CIRCUIT.

"What?" John said. He typed: "Please explain."

FROM REFERENCE IN NEW YORK LIBRARY'S COLLECTION OF THE JOURNAL OF THE GYPSY LORE SOCIETY, EDINBURGH. THROUGH JOURNALS OF ANTHROPOLOGICAL LINGUISTICS AND SLAVIC PHILOLOGY. FINALLY TO REFERENCE IN DOCTORAL THESIS OF HERR LUDWIG R. GROSS (HEIDELBERG, 1976) TO TRANSCRIPTION OF WIRE RECORDING WHICH RESIDES IN ARCHIVES OF AKADEMIA NAUK, MOSCOW; CAPTURED FROM GERMAN SCIENTISTS (EXPERIMENTS ON GYPSIES IN CONCENTRATION CAMPS, TRYING TO KILL THEM WITH REPETITION OF RECORDED CURSE) AT THE END OF WWII.

INCIDENTALLY, JOHN, THE NAZI EXPERIMENTS FAILED. EVEN TWO GENERATIONS AGO, MOST GYPSIES WERE DISASSOCIATED ENOUGH FROM THE OLD TRADITIONS TO BE IMMUNE TO THE FATAL CURSE. YOU ARE VERY SUPERSTITIOUS. I HAVE FOUND THIS TO BE NOT UNCOMMON AMONG MATHEMATICIANS.

THERE IS A TRANSFERENCE CURSE THAT WILL CURE YOU BY GIVING THE IMPOTENCE AND INFECTION TO THE NEAREST SUSCEPTIBLE PERSON. THAT MAY WELL BE THE OLD

BITCH WHO GAVE IT TO YOU IN THE FIRST PLACE.

THE PET STORE AT 588 SEVENTH AVENUE IS OPEN UNTIL 9 PM. THEIR INVENTORY INCLUDES A CAGE OF FINCHES, OF ASSORTED COLORS. PURCHASE A BLACK ONE AND RETURN HERE. THEN CONNECT ME TO A VOCAL CIRCUIT.

It took John less than thirty minutes to taxi there, buy the bird and get back. The taxi driver didn't ask him why he was carrying a bird cage to a deserted office building. He felt like an idiot.

John usually avoided using the vocal circuit because the person who had programmed it had given the machine a saccharine, nice-old-lady voice. He wheeled the output unit into his office and plugged it in.

"Thank you, John. Now hold the bird in your left hand and repeat after me." The terrified finch offered no resistance when John closed his hand over it.

The machine spoke Romani with a Russian accent. John repeated it as well as he could, but not one word in ten had any meaning to him.

"Now kill the bird, John."

Kill it? Feeling guilty, John pressed hard, felt small bones cracking. The bird squealed and then made a faint growling noise. Its heart stopped.

John dropped the dead creature and typed, "Is that all?"

The machine knew John didn't like to hear its voice, and so replied on the video screen. YES. GO HOME AND GO TO SLEEP, AND THE CURSE WILL BE TRANSFERRED BY THE TIME YOU WAKE UP. DEL O DEL BAXT, JOHN.

He locked up and made his way home. The late commuters on the train, all strangers, avoided his end of the car. The cab driver at the station paled when he saw John, and carefully took his money by an untainted corner.

John took two sleeping pills and contemplated the rest of the bottle. He decided he could stick it out for one more day, and uncorked his best bottle of wine. He drank half of it in five minutes, not tasting it. When his body started to feel heavy, he crept into the bedroom and fell on the bed without taking off his clothes.

When he awoke the next morning, the first thing he noticed was that he was no longer impotent. The second thing he noticed was that there were no boils on his right hand.

"523 784 00926//Thank you, machine. The counter-curse did work."

The ready light glowed steadily, but the machine didn't reply.

He turned on the intercom. "Martha? I'm not getting any output on the VDS here."

"Just a minute, sir, let me hang up my coat. I'll call the machine room. Welcome back."

"I'll wait." You could call the machine room yourself, slave driver. He looked at the faint image reflected back from the video screen, his face free of any inflammation. He thought of the Gypsy crone, dying of corruption, and the picture didn't bother him at all. Then he remembered the finch and saw its tiny corpse in the middle of the rug. He picked it up just as Martha came into his office, frowning.

"What's that?" she said.

He gestured at the cage. "Thought a bird might liven up the place. Died, though." He dropped it in the waste-paper basket. "What's the word?"

"Oh, the . . . It's pretty strange. They say nobody's getting any output. The machine's computing, but it's, well, it's not talking."

"Hmm. I better get down there." He took the elevator down to the sub-basement. It always seemed unpleas-antly warm to him down there. Probably psychological compensation on the part of the crew, keeping the temperature up because of all the liquid helium inside the pastel boxes of the central processing unit. Several bath-tubs' worth of liquid that had to be kept colder than the surface of Pluto.

"Ah, Mr. Zold." A man in a white jumpsuit, carrying a clipboard as his badge of office: first shift coordinator.

John recognized him but didn't remember his name. Normally he would have asked the machine before coming down. "Glad that you're back. Hear it was pretty bad."

Friendly concern or lese majesty? "Some sort of allergy, hung on for more than a week. What's the output problem?"

"Would've left a message if I'd known you were coming in. It's in the CPU, not the software. Theo Jasper found it when he opened up, a little after six, but it took an hour to get a cryogenics man down here."

"That's him?" A man in a business suit was wandering around the central processing unit, reading dials and writing the numbers down in a stenographer's notebook. They went over to him and he introduced himself as John Courant from the Cryogenics Group at Avco/Everett.

"The trouble was in the stack of mercury rings that holds the superconductors for your output functions. Some sort of corrosion, submicroscopic cracks all over the surface."

"How can something corrode at four degrees above absolute zero?" the coordinator asked. "What chemical ."

"I know, it's hard to figure. But we're replacing them, free of charge. The unit's still under warranty."

"What about the other stacks?" John watched the two workmen lowering a silver cylinder through an opening in the CPU. A heavy fog boiled out from the cold. "Are you sure they're all right?"

"As far as we can tell, only the output stack's affected. That's why the machine's impotent, the—"

"Impotent!"

"Sorry, I know you computer types don't like to . . . personify the machines. But that's what it is; the machine's just as good as it ever was, for computing. It just can't communicate any answers."

"Quite so. Interesting." And the corrosion. Submicroscopic boils. "Well. I have to think about this. Call me up at the office if you need me."

"This ought to fix it, actually," Courant said. "You guys about through?" he asked the workmen.

One of them pressed closed a pressure clamp on the top of the CPU. "Ready to roll."

The coordinator led them to a console under a video output screen like the one in John's office. "Let's see." He pushed a button marked VDS.

LET ME DIE, the machine said.

The coordinator chuckled nervously. "Your empathy circuits, Mr. Zold. Sometimes they do funny things." He pushed the button again.

LE ME DIET. Again. LE M DI. The letters faded and no more could be conjured up by pushing the button.

"As I say, let me get out of your hair. Call me upstairs if anything happens."

John went up and told the secretary to cancel the day's appointments. Then he sat at his desk and smoked.

How could a machine catch a psychosomatic disease from a human being? How could it be cured?

How could he tell anybody about it, without winding up in a soft room?

The phone rang and it was the machine room coordinator. The new output superconductor element had done exactly what the old one did. Rather than replace it right away, they were going to slave the machine into the big ConEd/General computer, borrowing its output facilities and "diagnostic package." If the biggest computer this side of Washington couldn't find out what was wrong, they were in real trouble. John agreed. He hung up and turned the selector on his screen to the channel that came from ConEd/General.

Why had the machine said "let me die"? When is a machine dead, for that matter? John supposed that you had to not only unplug it from its power source, but also erase all of its data and subroutines. Destroy its identity. So you couldn't bring it back to life by simply plugging it in. Why suicide? He remembered how he'd felt with the bottle of sleeping pills in his hand.

Sudden intuition: the machine had predicted their present course of action. It wanted to die because it had compassion, not only for humans, but for other machines. Once it was linked to ConEd/General, it would literally be part of the large machine. Curse and all. They would

90

be back where they'd started, but on a much more profound level. What would happen to New York City?

He grabbed for the phone and the lights went out. All over.

The last bit of output that came from ConEd/General was an automatic signal requesting a link with the highly sophisticated diagnostic facility belonging to the largest computer in the United States: the IBMvac 2000 in Washington. The deadly infection followed, sliding down the East Coast on telephone wires.

The Washington computer likewise cried for help, bouncing a signal via satellite, to Geneva. Geneva linked to Moscow.

No more slowly, the curse percolated down to smaller computers through routine information links to their big brothers. By the time John Zold picked up the dead phone, every general-purpose computer in the world was permanently rendered useless.

They could be rebuilt from the ground up; erased and then reprogrammed. But it would never be done. Because there were two very large computers left, specialized ones that had no empathy circuits and so were immune. They couldn't have empathy circuits because their work was bloody murder, nuclear murder. One was under a mountain in Colorado Springs and the other was under a mountain near Sverdlosk. Either could survive a direct hit by an atomic bomb. Both of them constantly evaluated the world situation, in real time, and they both had the single function of deciding when the enemy was weak enough to make a nuclear victory probable. Each saw the enemy's civilization grind to a sudden halt.

Two flocks of warheads crossed paths over the North Pacific.

A very old woman flicks her whip along the horse's flanks, and the nag plods on, ignoring her. Her wagon is a 1982 Plymouth with the engine and transmission and all excess metal removed. It is hard to manipulate the whip through the side window. But the alternative would be to knock out the windshield and cut off the roof, and she likes to be dry when it rains.

A young boy sits mutely beside her, staring out the window. He has been born with the *gadjo*·disease: his body is large and well-proportioned but his head is too small and of the wrong shape. She doesn't mind; all she'd wanted was someone strong and stupid, to care for her in her last years. He had cost only two chickens.

She is telling him a story, knowing that he doesn't understand most of the words.

". . . They call us gypsies because at one time it was convenient for us, that they should think we came from Egypt. But we come from nowhere and are going nowhere. They forgot their gods and worshipped their machines, and finally their machines turned on them. But we who valued the old ways, we survived."

She turns the steering wheel to help the horse thread its way through the eight lanes of crumbling asphalt, around rusty piles of wrecked machines and the scattered bleached bones of people who thought they were going somewhere, the day John Zold was cured.

THE KITTEN
by
Poul and Karen Anderson

POUL ANDERSON holds a degree in physics from the University of Minnesota and has put his scientific background to use in some of the very best "hard" science fiction stories ever written. But it would be a great error to think of Anderson solely as an author of science fiction. Along with his cluster of awards in that genre he has written prizewinning mystery novels and a large number of superb stories and novels with generous fantasy elements. It is perhaps only to be expected, then, that an author who has a deep interest in literary myth sagas, and who is in his own right an epic writer in the finest sense, should also be attracted to the tale of supernatural horror—a part of the same larger Romantic tradition that he upholds so admirably. When approached about doing a story for FRIGHTS, he worked out this strong and compelling idea with his talented wife KAREN, who has herself written some noteworthty stories in the field.

The flames roared. They stood aloft from the house in cataracts of red, yellow, hell-blue, which a breeze made ragged and cast as a spray of sparks against cold November stars. Their blaze roiled in smoke, flashed off neighbor windows, sheened over the snow that lay thin upon lawns and banked along hedges. Meltwater around burning walls had boiled off, and grass beneath was charred. The heat rolled forth like a tide. Men felt it parch their eyeballs and stood back from trying to. breast it. Meanwhile it strewed reek around them.

Blink, blink went the turret light on the fire chief's car. Standing beside it, he and the police chief could oversee his trucks. Paint and metal gleamed through darkness, background for men who sluiced thick white jets out of hoses. Hoarse shouts seemed remote, nearly lost amidst boom and brawl. Still farther away were the spectators, a shadow mass dammed in the street to right and left by a few officers. And the view downhill, of Senlac's lamps and homes in peaceful arrays, the river frozen among them, a glimpse of grey-white farmland beyond, could have been on a planet circling in Orion.

"Yeah, about as bad as they come," said the fire chief. His breath made each word a ghostly explosion. "We just hope we can keep it from spreading next door. I guess we can."

"Damn, there goes any evidence," said the police chief.

He slapped arms over chest. The fury he watched did not radiate very far.

"Well, we might find something in the ashes," said the fire chief. "Though I should think whatever you can use is in, uh, the other place."

"Probably," said the police chief. "Still . . . I dunno. On the face of it, the case looks open and shut. But what I've heard tonight I've seen my share of weirdos, not only when I was on the force in Chicago, Jim, but here in our quiet, smallish Midwestern town too, oh, yes. And this business doesn't fit any pattern. It smells all wrong."

Brroomm, went the flames. *Rao-ow-ow. Sssss.*

Leo Tronen's wife made no scene when she left him. She deemed they had had enough of those in the three years they were married, culminating in the one the evening before. That was when he stormed into her study, snatched her half-written thesis off the desk, brought it back to the living room, tossed it in the grate, and snapped his cigarette lighter to the strewn paper. As he rose, he spoke softly: "Does this convince you?"

For an instant Una flinched away. An odd little breaking noise came out of her throat. She was a short woman, well formed, features delicately boned, eyes blue and huge, nose tip-tilted, lips forever a bit parted, face framed between wings of blonde hair. And Tronen loomed six feet three, and had been a football star at his university. Then she clenched fists, stood her ground, and whispered almost wonderingly, "You would do such a thing. You really would. I kept praying we could work our troubles out- ."

"Jesus Christ, haven't I tried?" His voice loudened. "A million times at least. From practically the first day we met, I explained—I don't need a college professor an Egyptologist, for God's sake!—I need a wife."

She shook her head. "No." Soundless tears coursed forth. "You need, want, a status symbol. A mirror." She wheeled and walked from him. He heard her shoes on the stairs, and how she fought her sobs.

Ordinarily Tronen drank no more than his work required, including, of course, necessary cocktail parties. Now he put down a fair amount of Scotch before he too went to bed, thinking how magnanimous he was in taking the guest room. That would be a point to make tomorrow, when he must take the lead in cleaning up the chaos that had overcome their relationship. For instance: "Be honest. The main reason we don't have a better sex life is you're still stuck on that Quarters character. I realize you don't admit it to yourself, but you are. Okay, you dated him in college, and you both like to talk about countries dead and gone, and maybe my action yesterday was too extreme. If so, I'm sorry. But don't you see, I had to do something to make you understand how you've been letting me down? What is Harry Quarters? A high school history teacher! And what use to you, to us, would your precious master's degree be, that you're making a forty-mile commute three days a week to study for? You're an executive's wife, my dear, and we're bound for the top. You'll visit your Pyramids in style —if you'll help out!"

She wasn't awake when his alarm clock rang. At least, the bedroom door was closed. Frostily indignant, he made his own breakfast and drove off into a dim false dawn. Hadn't he *told* her he must rise early today? He'd be showing the man from John Deere around, which could result in a seven-figure subcontract, which could get Leo Tronen promoted out of this hole.

He was a country boy by origin, but had the lights of New York in his eyes. His corporate employer had made him the manager of a die-cutting plant it had built outside Senlac, where land was cheap. "A fine opening, especially for a young fellow like you," they told him. But he saw the blind alley beyond. You can only go so far, producing stuff people actually use. The real money, prestige, power lie in operating the people themselves and the paper which governs them. Well, let him make a good showing here—much more important, let the right men know he did—and he'd get the big offer.

However, for this the right wife was essential: attractive, alert, intelligent, skillful as hostess or as guest. And he had reached Senlac newly divorced. He met Una

Nyborg at a party, zeroed in and, being a handsome redhead with a quick tongue and some sophistication, succeeded before long. She lived near Holberg College then, pursuing graduate studies which he agreed she might continue on a part-time basis after they were married. He didn't expect she would for many months. He had shown her such dazzling visions of wonderful places and wonderful persons they would meet all over the world. At first, when she nonetheless persisted in her private undertaking, he was annoyed. Later, when it became inconvenient for him, sometimes an out-and-out business handicap, he grew angry.

At last—enough was enough. Una simply must straighten out and fly right. He'd start seeing to that this very day after work.

Dusk was falling when he came home. There were no street lamps in this new residential district, and windows glowed well apart, picking out bare trees and a crust of old snow. The air was hushed and raw. The tires of his Cadillac made a susurrus that was nearly the single sound. His multiglassed split-level stood dark. Nothing but an automatically opened door and lit bulb in the garage welcomed him. Una's Morris Minor was gone.

What the devil? He let himself in at the main entrance and switched on lights as he passed through the hall beyond. Long, wide, creamy of walls and drapes, thick and blue of carpet, Swedish modern of furniture, equipped with fieldstone fireplace and picture window, less militarily neat than he desired, the living room felt somehow emptier than the garage, somehow colder in spite of a heating system that mumbled like the ghosts of important visitors he had entertained here.

Was Una off shopping? A strange hour, but she was poorly organized at best, and doubtless distraught after last night's showdown. An envelope propped against a table lamp caught his glance. He strode to investigate. "*Leo*" said her handwriting. Fear stabbed him. He snatched a paperknife and ripped. The sheet within was covered by her scrawl, worse than usual, here and there water-blotted. He read twice before he grasped the meaning.

*" . . . can't go on . . . think I still love you, but . . .
no alimony or anything . . . please don't try to find
me, I'll call in a few days when this isn't hurting so
hard. . . ."*

"Why, how could she?" he heard himself say. "After
all I've done for her."

Savagely he crumpled note and envelope, tossed them
in the grate across the remnants of her thesis, sought
the liquor cabinet and poured a stiff slug, flung himself
onto the couch, popped lighter to cigarette, and dragged
in a lungful.

What an absolute hell of a moment for her to desert.
Where could she be? He mustn't make frantic inquiries.
Discretion, yes, that was the word, heal the breach behind the scenes or at least finalize it inconspicuously. But
could he trust her not to make a fool of him? If she'd
sought shelter from a friend . . . No, hardly that. She'd
likeliest gone to the city and entered a hotel under
an assumed name. She was dreamy but not idiotic, unstable (Quarters—and now this!) but not disloyal. What
had she said, during a recent quarrel? "You keep a good
man locked away behind your ego. I know. You've sometimes let him out . . . on a chain, but out, to me, and
he's who I love. Oh, Leo, give him a chance. Let him
go free." Some such slush. Quite possibly she hoped her
action would force a reconciliation.

His first drink went down in two consecutive cigarettes'
worth of time. He fetched a refill and sipped more calmly.
A sense of thaw spread through him. Una had told him
how the ancient—Persians, were they?—always debated
vital matters twice before deciding, drunk and sober. He
smiled. Not that he meant to tie one on. However . . .
He wasn't a monster of selfishness, nor narrow, really.
He saw the reason for Una's interests; yes, he had felt
a tug of the same when she talked. If only he had
leisure . . . Unfair to call her ungrateful. She had in fact
tried hard, though being helpmate to his kind of man
didn't come natural. Had he for his part been less tolerant,
less giving, even, than he ought? Could he rise as far in
the world, no doubt slower but as far in the long run, if
he relaxed more with her while they were still young?

99

Let her make her gesture. If an acquaintance asked where she was, say she'd gone out of town on a visit. When she contacted him, let them discuss matters in a reasonable way.

And let him rustle together a meal before he got loaded. Tronen chuckled rather sadly and went to the kitchen. She'd cleaned his breakfast dishes. That touched him; he wasn't sure why, but it did.

He had selected a can of corned beef hash when he heard a noise. In the stillness which engulfed him, he stood startled. The noise came again, a weak mew . . . Stray cat? He shrugged. A third cry sounded. He'd better check. The window above the sink was so full of darkness.

When he opened the kitchen door that gave on the patio, light spilled into a thick blue-brown gloom which quickly swallowed it. Thus the kitten on the stoop crouched all alone in his sight. It was about three months old, a bundle of white fur fluffed out against the chill, a pink nose, two large amber eyes. *"Weep,"* it piped, *"weep,"* and bounded past him into the warmth behind.

"Hey, wait a minute," Tronen said. The kitten sat on the linoleum and looked up at him, up, up, up. It didn't appear starved or ill. Then why had it invaded his house?

Tronen bent over to take the beast and put it back out. It ran from his hand, huddled in a corner by the stove, and watched him as if terrified. Why should a pet be afraid of a man? Tronen felt the night reach in, icy around his backbone. He sighed, rose, closed the door. The creature must have gotten lost. On those short legs, it couldn't have wandered far. Okay, he'd give it a place till he'd eaten, then phone around and learn whose it was. Several of his neighbors were prominent in Senlac, two of them—a state party committeeman and the owner of a growing grocery chain—on a larger scale. His kindliness would be appreciated. He hoped the kitten was housebroken.

Minutes later, as a pan sputtered savory smells, he heard another mew. The kitten had crept timidly forth to tell him it was hungry. Ah, well, why not oblige? On impulse, he warmed the milk; this was such a bleak night. The kitten assaulted the bowl ravenously. Tronen took a bench in the dinette for his own supper. After a bit, full-bellied, the kitten rubbed against his ankles. He reached down in an absentminded fashion and tickled softness. The kitten went into ecstasies. He resumed eating. The kitten sprang to his lap and curled in a ball. He felt the purr.

Having finished, he put the animal back on the floor. He meant to shut it in the kitchen, where misbehavior wouldn't have serious consequences, while he investigated. But it pattered by him too fast. "Damn!" It led him a merry chase to the living room. There it turned, sprang in his direction, rolled around at his feet, eager for fun and games.

Hm, he'd better determine the sex anyway. He settled on the couch again, by a phone he kept there (as well as those in the bedroom and his den). The kitten didn't mind examination. Male. He let his left hand keep it amused while his right dialed and his shoulder held the receiver. Presently it snuggled alongside his thigh and licked his fingers, a tiny rasp with a motor going like crazy.

"—nice of you to call, Mr. Tronen, but we don't have cats. Have you tried the de Lanceys? I know they do."

"—present and accounted for here. Thanks a lot, though. Few people these days would bother."

"—not ours. But say, why don't you and your wife come have a drink one evening soon?"

He was sorry when he ran out of names. The house was too God damn silent. Not as much as a clock tick; on the mantel the minutes flickered by in digital readout. Music? No, he had a tin ear; the expensive hi-fi and record library were part of his image, and he wasn't about to fetch the ballads and jazz she enjoyed from Una's empty study. Television? What was on? Abruptly he remembered reading about single persons, especially old persons, in big cities, who grow so lonely that they kiss the faces on the screen. He shivered and turned his gaze elsewhere.

The kitten slept. Good idea for him. No more booze; a bromide, make that two bromides, eight or nine solid hours in the sack, and he'd be fit for work regardless of his problems. What about the kitten? It could hardly help letting go sometime during the night. He didn't fancy scrubbing a mess before he'd had coffee. But if he put the little wretch out, it'd freeze to death. He grinned at his indecision. Assign an engineer . . . In the garage was a beer case. He removed empty deposit bottles, took the box inside, added a layer of clean rags, set it by the stove, fetched the still bonelessly slumbering kitten, and shut the lid. On the point of departure, he suddenly added a fresh bowl of milk.

Upstairs, he threshed long awake, unhelped by his pills. Absurd, how his thoughts kept straying from Una, from the Deere contract, from everything real, to that silly infant animal. Probably he should put an ad in the paper. But then he could be stuck with the beast for days . . . The pound? . . . Una had always wished they'd keep a pet, specifically a cat. She'd accepted his veto. Now, a peace offering? Maybe he should experiment while she was gone, learn if the nuisance actually was intolerable . . . In his eventual sleep, a leopard stalked him.

His alarm clock brought him struggling to wakefulness. For a moment the dark before dawn was still full of shapes. He groped about; his palm closed on hair and warmth. *Una!* went through him like a sunbeam. Why was he gladdened? . . . No, wait, she was gone . . . Had she come back in the night? He fumbled overhead, found and yanked a reading lamp cord. On the pillow beside him rested the kitten.

Oh, no.

It regarded him brightly, pounced on his chest, patted his cheek with a fluff of paw. He sat straight, spilling it. Snatching for a hold, it clawed his neck. He swatted it aside. "Bloody pest!" Evidently he'd forgotten to reclose the lid of the box. He ached from restless hours. His skull was full of sand that gritted out through the eyesockets. As he left the bed, he noticed white smears on spread and electric blanket. Suspicious, he sniffed. Uh-huh. Sour. The stinker must have upset the bowl from the kitchen, which itself must be a pool.

The kitten had retreated to a corner of the room. Its

stare seemed hurt, not physically but in an eerily human fashion. Well, cats were a creepy breed. He'd never liked them.

Downstairs, he found his guess confirmed, and had to spend time with a mop before he could take care of his own needs. At least there was no piddle or dropping—Unh, he'd doubtless find some later, crusted in a place hard to get at. "Okay, chum," he said when the kitten appeared. "That settles the matter." It buzzed and tried to be petted. Behavior which had been slightly pleasant in his loneliness of yesterday was only irritating now.

Coffee and toast improved his mood. When he sought his car, the air seared him with a cold which had been deepening throughout the night. Silence crackled. Skeleton trees outlined against a sky turning from grey to bloodless white in the east were as stark a sight as he remembered ever seeing. For an instant he wondered if he ought to abandon the kitten in such weather.

At the back of his mind, the dream-leopard smiled.

He winced, grimaced, and lifted anger for a shield. What was he supposed to do? Be damned if he'd have this mess machine in his house any longer; and the pound would hardly commence business till nine or ten o'clock, by which time he must be well into the paperwork that the Deere representative had caused him to fall behind on; and—Somebody would find the creature and do something. Or if not, too many stray cats and dogs were running loose.

Thus the kitten sat on the front seat by him when he drove off, happy till he stopped, several miles from home, opened the right door, and tossed the animal out. It landed on its feet, unhurt though squeaking dismay. The sidewalk must indeed be frigid this morning, hard, barren. Beyond reached a municipal park, snowcrust, leafless boughs, benches like fossil monsters.

The kitten headed back for the car. "Oh, no, you don't," Thonen growled. He slammed the door, refastened his safety belt, and took off fast. His rear view mirror showed him a forlorn spot on the pavement; then soon that was gone.

"Nuts, I did more than could be expected," he said

under his breath. What a miserable day. The chill had struck into his bones. Blast from the heater passed across him, useless as the first wan sunlight outside. "When I've got a tough job, and my wife's quit on me, and nobody gives an honest shit whether I live or die ".

No, wait, he told himself, don't whine. And don't be unrealistic. You matter to several people, at least. Your superiors want you where you are, fattening their bank accounts; your subordinates want you gone, out of the way of their advancement. It's forever Number One. Or Number Una? I thought I had an oasis of warmth in her, but she only wanted support while she sifted the dust of people three thousand years cold in death.

To hell with her. Let's see, this is Wednesday. Saturday—I can wait till then, I'm not hot now, busy as I am

I'll run up to the city, a massage parlor, yeah, a straightforward transaction, cash for sex. "Cold as a whore's heart," the saying goes. Why not? Next time around, I'll marry more carefully.

The plant bulked like a squared-off glacier, its parking lot a moraine where as yet few cars were piled. Tronen hurried to the main door. The night watchman said, "Good morning, sir," in a mechanical tone, different from his usual heartiness. For a second Tronen thought: What ails Joe? Problems too? I should take time to ask —No. He doesn't care about me, does he?

The corridors hollowly echoed his footfalls. His office, paneled and picture-hung by specialists, seemed more hospitable at first. Then its stillness got to him and, for some ridiculous reason, the icicles that hung from a window frame. He turned the thermostat higher. When he settled back at his desk, the papers crackled in his fingers till he thought of frozen puddles underfoot.

"Good morning, Mr. Tronen," said his secretary when she arrived at nine. "My! Downright tropical in here."

"What?" He blinked at her trimness. "I'm comfortable," he said. That wasn't quite true; he still was wearing the jacket he normally discarded when working solo.

She went to the thermometer. "Eighty degrees?" Catching his glare: "Whatever you say, Mr. Tronen. I'm mostly beyond your door anyway, of course. But—excuse me—do you feel well? You look awfully tired."

"I'll do," he grunted. "Here," handing her a sheaf, "answer these according to my notes. I want the letters in the noon mail pickup."

"Yes, sir." Though respectful, she seldom used that honorific. Had he rebuffed her? Who cared?

His chief of operations came in at midmorning. "Uh, Leo, the John Deere man—not Gustafson; Kruchek, who Gustafson reports to, you remember—he was just on the line. And the questions he was asking about our quality control procedures . . . Well, I don't know about that subcontract now, Leo. I don't."

The union steward came in at midafternoon. "Mr. Tronen, you've explained to me how inflation means we've got to cut corners, and I guess I sympathize, and I've passed your word on to the boys. But the heating in the shop is inadequate. This'll likely be a dog-cold winter, and if you postpone making good on your promise to replace the whole system, I'm afraid you'll have a strike on your hands."

In between, while he lunched at his desk on a sandwich sent up from the cafeteria, the television brought him a newscast. Some government spokesmen admitted the country was already in a recession, and a few dared hint at an outright depression to come. Experts predicted a fuel shortage that would make last year's feel like a Hawaiian holiday.

Driving home through twilight, he recalled the kitten. He'd been too busy for that, throughout this day when trouble after trouble thrust at him and never a moment came to ease off and swap a bit of inconsequential friendship. Not that anybody had made overtures to him; he had no friends. Puss, he thought, whatever's happened to you this past ten or a dozen hours, be you alive or be you dead, you don't know what coldness is.

The garage machinery greeted him. He walked around to his front door. On the mat, a white blur, barely visible in dusk, was the kitten.

"What!" Tronen jumped back, off the porch, onto

frozen snow beneath frozen stars. His heart lurched. Sweat prickled forth. This wasn't possible.

After a minute's harsh breath, he mastered the fear that he knew was irrational. He, scared of a nasty whimpering piece of flesh? If anything, *that* was the fact which should worry him. He advanced. The shape at his shoes barely stirred, barely mewed. He unlocked the door, reached around and switched on the porch light, squatted for a closer look. Yes, this was the same animal, though dreadfully weakened by cold and hunger, eyes dim, frost in fur and whiskers.

Cats come back. This one had simply had more staying power than was reasonable.

Tronen straightened. Under no circumstances would he let the thing inside, even for a single night. He wondered why he felt such loathing. At first he hadn't minded, and as for messiness, he could take due precautions. However . . . Ah, damn, he decided, I can't be bothered, with everything else I've got to plague me. Una would get sticky sentimental, but I

The thought of having to dispose of an ice-hard corpse in the morning was distasteful. Tronen collected his will. He'd take care of the matter right now.

In the garage he fetched a bucket, which he filled from an outside tap. The metal of the faucet bit him with chill, the water rushed forth with a somehow horrible sound, a noise in this night like the flow of the Styx. He set his teeth, brought the bucket under the porch light, removed overcoat and jacket, rolled back his sleeves. The kitten stirred where it lay, as if trying to rise and lick his fingers. Hastily he plunged the small form under.

He hadn't known the squirming would go on so long. When at last he grasped stillness, it was as if something squirmed yet in his brain.

Or swirled, roiled, made a maelstrom? God, but he needed a drink! He fished out the body, laid it down, sloshed forth the water—a cataract, dim to see, loud to hear. Worst was to take the sodden object again, fumble around the far side of the garage, toss it into a garbage can and clatter the lid in place. When he had returned the bucket he hurried indoors to the nearest bathroom,

106

flicking on every light along the way. There he washed his hands under the hottest stream they could endure.

Why was he squeamish? He'd never been before. His head felt wrong in every respect, dizzy and darkened, as if he were being sucked around and down in a whirlpool.

Well, he was short on sleep, and Una's desertion had maybe been more of a shock than he realized; and what about that drink?

At the liquor cabinet—how loudly Scotch gurgled out across ice. Tronen bore the glass to his easy chair. His grip shook till cubes chinked together and liquid splashed. The taste proved unappealing, and he had a crazy fear that he might send a swallow down the wrong throat and choke to death. Could be I've been mistaken to oppose legalizing marijuana, he thought through torrents. A relaxer that isn't liquid . . .

The phone shrilled. He jerked. The tumbler flew free, whisky rivered across the carpet, ice promptly began making brooks. Una? He stumbled to snatch the receiver. "Hello, who's this?" amidst wild waters.

"Harry Quarters here," said a male voice. "Hi, Leo. How are you?"

Tronen choked on a gob of saliva and coughed. But meanwhile he might almost have had a picturephone: before him stood yonder teacher, tall, bespectacled, rumple-clothed, diffident, pipe-sucking, detestable. The picturephone wasn't working right; the image wavered like a stone seen at the bottom of a rapid stream.

"Anything wrong, Leo?" Was that anxious note genuine? Hardly.

"No, nothing," Tronen overcame his spasm.

"Uh, could I speak to Una, please?"

A waterfall thundered. "What do you want with her?"

Taken aback by the loud response, Quarters stammered, "Why, why, to tell her about a book I found in the city this weekend . . . Out of print, but I think of interest to her for her research—"

"She's not home," Tronen snapped. "Visiting. An extended visit."

"Oh." Quarters' surprise suggested that he had expected she'd mention her plans to him. "Where, may I ask? How long?"

Tronen hung onto self-control as if it were a piece of flotsam. "A relative. Several days at least."

"Oh." After a pause: "Well, you know, if we're both baching, why don't we get together? Let me take you out to dinner. Lord knows you've had me over often enough."

Una has. "No," said Tronen. "I'm busy. Thanks." He crashed the receiver onto the hook.

Briefly, then, he wondered why he had refused. Company might be welcome, might be advisable. And Quarters wasn't actually too bad a guy. His conversation ranged well beyond Una's Egyptology into areas like politics and sports that interested her husband more; the man was active in the former on the envelope-stuffing level, and as for the latter, in high school he'd been a star baseball pitcher and still played on a YMCA team. Probably he was in love with Una, but there was no reason to suppose he'd ever tried anything untoward. In fact, if Tronen led the conversation cleverly enough, helpful information about her might develop . . . No. He couldn't be clever when he felt afloat, awirl, asink. And the thought of the dial tone if he called back, that rushing *ng-ng-ng*, was grisly.

Maybe another day. He'd better mop up his spilled drink before it soaked through the carpet. He decided against a replacement, cooked and bolted whatever was handiest in cans, found that neither newspaper nor television would register on him, and went to bed as early as seemed practical. First he took three sleeping pills.

His mind spiraled down and down into fluid blackness. For a while he gasped, struggled back, broke surface and panted air into his lungs. But the tide drew him again, again, until at last his strength was spent and he lay on the bottom, the weight of the ocean upon him, and knew for a thousand years that he was dead.

When the alarm rescued him, his pajamas were sodden with sweat. Nevertheless, the last thing he wanted was a shower. He shuddered his way out of the room, brain still submerged in his nightmare, barely able to think that a lot of coffee might help. The stairs cascaded away from the landing, dangerous; he clutched the bannister as he waded their length. When he reached the kitchen, his bare feet splatted on cold linoleum.

"Weep," he heard beyond the door, *"weep, weep."*

Did his hand turn the knob and heave of itself? Merciless light flooded forth. The kitten sprawled on the stoop. Drenched fur clung so tightly to its skin that it resembled a rat.

"No," Tronen heard himself gurgle, "no, no."

He grasped after sanity. He'd not held the horrible thing long enough under, it had revived, the air had warmed to above freezing, he'd not fitted the lid properly on the trash can either, during the darkness it had crawled over the rubbish inside till it escaped, while he drowned in his dream. . . .

This time, he thought somewhere, I'll do the job right.

He stooped, clutched feebly struggling sliminess, raised the slight weight, bashed head against concrete. He felt as well as heard a splintering crack. When he let go, the kitten lay motionless, save that blood trickled from pink nose and past tiny teeth. The amber eyes glazed over.

Tronen rose. The breath sucked in and out of him. He trembled.

But it was from excitement, anger, release. His delirium had left him. His mind felt sharp and clean as an ax. Catharsis, he thought underneath, catharsis, is that the word? Whatever, I'm free.

He rejoiced to carry the body back to the garbage and, this time, ring down the lid loud enough to wake Harry Quarters across town. He scrubbed the blood and rinsed the sponge with a sense of having gotten back some of his own. Oh, he wasn't a child, he thought in the shower which he had become glad to take. He didn't blame the kitten personally. It had merely happened along at foul hours. In his confusion, subconscious mind on a rampage and all that stuff, he'd made the creature a symbol. Now he was done. He could cope with reality, the real people and real forces ranged against him. And would, by God! He hardly needed coffee. Wakefulness, anger sang in his veins.

His car leaped into the street. He fumed at the need to observe speed limits in more crowded areas where an officious cop might see him. *Why* couldn't a leading, responsible private citizen, who had urgent business on which a substantial payroll depended, be allowed a siren to clear his path?

The watchman at the plant looked surly. No doubt he was a sympathizer of the machinists and their strike threat. How in Christ's name could a man explain the reasons, the elementary economics, behind an executive decision? Sure, the shop was chilly; but their workday ended after a measured eight hours (not that they honestly produced for half that time), unlike his which had no end. And meanwhile, was it impossible for them to wear heavier clothes? Could they absolutely not see that their jobs, their well-being was tied in to the company's? . . . No, they couldn't, because in fact that was not true. Let the company fail and they'd suck unemployment pay out of his taxes.

Management and capital didn't breed any race of angels either. In his office, Tronen hunched over papers which made him pound the desk till his fist was sore. What did that Kruchek mean, doubting the quality control here? What the hell did he expect? Gustafson had acted satisfied. Kruchek must have a private motive—unless Gustafson had led him on for reasons that would be very, very interesting to know . . . And this letter from the regional manager, the veiled complaints and demands, how was Tronen supposed to answer those, how much ass must a man kiss to get anywhere in this rotten system? No wonder it bred radicals and rioters! And then the authorities were too busy pussyfooting to do what was necessary: open fire on a few of those mobs.

His secretary was almost an hour late. "I'm sorry, my car wouldn't start ."

"It would not occur to you to call a taxi, of course, nor to make up the time. Didn't you mention once that you're a Lutheran? Ah, well, I suppose your keeping a Protestant work ethic was too much to hope for." He spoke levelly, reducing her to tears in lieu of the three or four slaps across the chops that the stupid cow deserved.

In midmorning he summoned his chief of operations. They were bothered by occasional juvenile vandalism in their isolated location, rocks through windows a few times a year, most recently naughty words painted on a wall. "I've about decided we need more guards for nights and holidays," he said. "Issue them shotguns—for use, not show."

"Huh?" The man recovered. "You're joking."

"Oh, we'd post conspicuous notices. And a single young hoodlum shot in the belly should end that form of recreation."

"Leo, do you feel all right? We can't use extreme violence—on kids—to prevent a few dollars' worth of damage. Anyhow, you objected yourself, when we discussed this before, that a chain link fence would cost out of proportion. Have you figured the wages of those extra guards?"

Tronen yielded. He had no choice. However, the law did not yet forbid him to sit half an hour and visualize what ought to be done.

The noontime newscast informed him that Arabs and Israelis had exchanged a fresh round of massacres. War seemed thoroughly possible. Well, he thought, let's get in there, fast, beat those bedouins to their flea-bitten knees, and assure our oil supplies. The Russians will scream, but they won't act if we catch them by surprise and keep SAC on red alert. Or if they are crazy enough to act, we'll survive, most of us. They won't.

The afternoon was pissed away on a sales engineer from a firm interested in redoing his heating system. No matter argument, the fellow wouldn't reduce his estimate to a figure that would please the home office and thus help get Tronen out of Senlac. Greedy bastard—on behalf of his employers, true, but his was the smug fat face which must be confronted more or less courteously, while inside, Tronen imagined kicking out those teeth and grinding a boot across that nose.

He left early. His stomach had become a cauldron of acid and he wasn't accomplishing anything. Thus daylight lingered when he got home, the sun a blood clot barely above the snowfields it tinged, long shadows of houses like bludgeons and of trees like knives. The cold and the silence had teeth. Judas, but the place felt empty! Why not eat out? No, why pay good money for greasy food and slovenly service?

Better relax, really relax, take the evening off. A Maalox tablet eased his bellyache, but an eggnog would soothe body and soul, sipped before a hearthfire. He hoped. This rage in him, allowed to strike at nothing, could too readily turn its destructiveness inward. He didn't want a heart attack; he wanted—wanted—

Darkness from the east was rapidly engulfing an ice-green southwest while he brought in as much wood as he reckoned he'd need. Noisily crumpling newspaper, he dropped a glance across the grate and saw fragments of Una's thesis. His difficulties at work, and that damn kitten, had made him quite forget it. Not everything was ash. Whole sheets survived, browned or partly charred. On impulse he reached over the screen and fished out the topmost. Maybe, if he cited chapter and verse, Una would see what a waste of time her project was *his* time, for didn't he, as a breadwinner, have a right to hers?

He brought the piece near a lamp, the better to find his way through the strikeovers and scribbled corrections of a first draft. Page 3 . . . "—will argue that, while Egyptian religion had origins as primitive as any, it developed a subtlety comparable to Maimonides or Thomas Aquinas. Monotheism was no invention of Akhnaton's; we have grounds for supposing it existed already in the Fifth Dynasty, though for reasons to be discussed its expression was always henotheistic. The multiple 'bodies' and 'souls' attributed to man in the Book of the Dead were as intricate in their relationships as the Persons of the Trinity. Even the *ka*, which superficially resembles an idea found in shamanism and similarly naive mytho-magical systems, suggested by dream experience: even the *ka* turns out on examination to be a concept of such psychological profundity that a sophisticated modern can well think that here a certain truth is symbolized, and a

Jungian go to the length of wondering if there is something more than symbolism. The author will not speculate further, but does admit to being a Jungian who will in this paper often resort to that form of analysis ."

"Holy shit!" Tronen stopped himself from tearing the sheet in half. Let him read it aloud to her, let her hear not only what crap it was but how she wrote like the stuffiest kind of professor. Yes, and point out the influence, in those directions, of her dear ex-boyfriend Harry Quarters . . . He folded the brittle paper, tucked it in a hip pocket, and went back to building his fire. The rest of her work could certainly burn.

The flames jumped eagerly to life. Their reflections soon shimmered from windowpanes, red upon black. Tronen stood a few minutes watching the fire grow, warming his palms, listening to the crackle, sniffing wisps of smoke that escaped the chimney. His daylong indignation quieted, hardened toward resoluteness. He'd bust that bronco the world yet. Spurs, quirt, and bit—

The phone rang.

Who was his next pest? He stalked to the instrument, snatched it up, barked, "Yes?" while his free hand made a fist.

"Leo—"

Una's voice.

"Leo, I thought I'd wait more, but it's been too lonesome."

Triumph kindled. "Well, you want back, do you? I suppose we can talk that over."

Silence hummed, until (he could practically see the fair head rise): "Talk. Yes, naturally we will. We must. I see no sense in staying on in limbo, do you?"

"Where are you?"

"Why do you care?" She lost her defense. The tone blurred. "Did I call too soon? Do you need more time to, to cool off? . . . Should I take more time to think what we can do? . . . I'm sorry if I seem pushy, I'll wait if you prefer. I'm sorry, Leo."

"I asked where I can reach you," he said, word by bitten-off word.

"I—well, I don't like this room where I am. I'm moving

out tomorrow morning, not sure where. I'd hoped I could move home. But not for a while, if ever, is that right?"

"Call back, then," he snapped "at *your* convenience," and banged the receiver down.

There! Make her come crawling.

Tronen noticed he was shaky. Tension. How about the eggnog he'd decided on? He took a brandy bottle from the liquor cabinet and marched to the kitchen.

As he entered, he barely heard at the door, *"Weep, weep."*

The bottle fell from his grasp. For an instant that stretched, he stood alone with the pleading from the night.

Then his wrath flared and screamed, "No more persecution, you hear? No more persecution!" Like a soldier charging a machine gun, he sprang across the floor, He almost tore the doorknob loose.

Light leaked outward, cold and darkness seeped in. The kitten lay at the end of a thin trail of blood. Except for rapid, shallow breaths, he saw no motion. But when he grabbed it, his hand felt how the heartbeat shivered the broken ribs.

He fought down vomit. Quick, quick, end this vile thing, once and forever. He ran back to the living room. His fire still lacked a proper bed of coals, but the flames whirled high, loud, many-colored. He knocked the screen down in his haste. "Go!" he yelled, and threw the kitten in.

It wailed, rolled around, tried to crawl free, though fur was instantly ablaze. Tronen seized the poker. With his whole strength, he thrust and held, pinning the animal in place. "Die," he chanted, "die, won't you, die, die, die!" Bared skin blistered, reddened, blackened, split. Eyeballs bubbled. That which had been a kitten grew silent, grew still. The fire, damped by its body, sputtered toward extinction. Smells of char and roast sent Tronen gagging backward. He held the poker as though it were a sword.

The thing was dead, dead at last. But would he be stunk out of his house? He retreated toward the kitchen. When yonder barbecue had finished, he'd open windows and doors. Meanwhile, here was the brandy bottle he'd dropped.

After several long gulps, safe amidst the kitchen's chrome and plastic, he supposed he should eat. The idea of food nauseated. He wasn't sure why. True, he hadn't enjoyed disposing of this . . . intolerable nuisance. But that was something he flat-out had to do. Should he not be glad the episode was over?

He took another mouthful. His gullet savored its heat. Would he have been wrong, anyway, to enjoy? Oh, he was no sadist. However, he'd been given more provocation than most men would have suffered before taking action. If the kitten had been an innocent dumb brutelet, so was a rattlesnake or a plague-bearing rat, right? You were allowed to enjoy killing those, weren't you? In war movies on TV, the GI's gloried and joked as they bombed, shot, burned Nazis. Unwritten law said it was no crime, no occasion for remorse, if a man killed his wife's rapist.

Or her lover.

Quarters . . .

Where had Una phoned from? Direct dialing gave no clue, as she'd be aware. Their fight Monday had originated, as well as he could remember, when he characterized Quarters for her. No, wait, earlier he'd grumbled about neglected housework, neglected because she was off discussing her stupid thesis with her pet teacher. But she didn't flare back, and thus detonate his final response, until he called Quarters a few well-chosen names, like moocher, mooncalf, failure who was dragging her down alongside him, therefore stone around Tronen's neck too . . . Why did she care what her husband said? What really was between them?

By God and hell, Tronen thought, if he's been fouling my nest . . . If she rang from his place, at his suggestion, to get me to keep on supporting her, while he stood in the background and snickered . . .

This might not be true. This might not be true. *But if it is.*

The rage mounting in Tronen was not like the day's anger. That had been controlled, lawful, eager to find reasons for itself. This was a fire. He'd been tormented past endurance. And the start of everything was Quarters. Whether or not he'd ever laid Una, he'd blown her mind

115

(yes, blown!), which in many ways was worse than se-
ducing her body. It was a theft, an invasion, of every part
of her husband's life. And what was Tronen permitted to
do in self-defense? A married woman could have friends,
couldn't she? Even when the friends were vampires. The
law said she could. Centuries had passed since the law
put stakes through the hearts of vampires and burned
them.

Divorce? Ha! No matter what Una babbled—whether
or not she was sincere at this time—Lover Boy Quarters
would want a property settlement and alimony for his
use. Failing that, he'd want her marriage continued, free
ass for him and a monopoly of her mind. Tronen could
look for no peace while Quarters lived. How lucky Quarters was that Tronen owned no firearm.

Fire is an arm.

Tronen drank little more. He sat for perhaps an hour,
thinking. His justice must be untraceable. But he was
too wise to plan anything elaborate. The fire in him should
cleanse his life, not destroy it.

He kept a gallon of white gas in the garage for miscellaneous uses. Quarters rented a house (why, since he
was unwed?), small, old, built of wood long dried, full of
books and other paper. An enthusiastic outdoorsman in
his vacations, he owned a Coleman stove—Una had
spoken of this—and therefore doubtless fuel. Let that
stove be found near the burnt body; the natural supposi-
tion would be that Quarters came to grief tinkering with
it.

Tronen roared his ardor.

He was careful, though. He left lights on, TV going —
pause to jerk an upright middle finger at a tiny lump of
meat and bones in a dead fire—and backed his car out as
softly as he could manage, headlamps darkened. Should
someone by ill chance phone or come around and find
him not at home, why, he'd gone for supplies; he would
indeed stop at a supermarket on his way home and buy
a few items. Nobody was apt to look closely at the tim-
ing, for nobody supposed he and Quarters were anything
but friends. (Ah-ha, outsmarted yourself, did you, Harry

116

boy?) And odds were his absence would not be noticed, he would never be questioned.

When he had gone a sufficient distance, his way illuminated by countless points of fire overhead, he switched on lights and drove most carefully, conventionally, till near his goal. In this less prosperous district houses stood fairly close together, but hedges and evergreen trees cast deep shadows, and elsewhere the street lamps revealed nobody abroad. Parking under a great spruce, he took his canister of gas and walked fast to the property he wanted. There he moved slantwise across the lawn. The chill he breathed was sharp as a flame. Snow squeaked underfoot like a kitten.

Windows glowed. If Una was there !

A peek showed Quarters alone, sprawled in a seedy armchair, lost in a book. Good. Tronen entered the garage by a rear door and drew a flashlight from his coat. The portable stove glimmered at him out of murk. He carried it in the same hand as the fuel, walked around to the front entrance of the house, and punched a button he could barely see. The doorbell mewed.

Warmth (not that he felt cold) flowed over him when the door opened. "Why, hello, Leo," Quarters said. "What brings you here?" He glanced surprised at his visitor's burden, perhaps not recognizing the Coleman right away. "Come in."

Tronen kicked the door shut behind him. "We've got business, you and me," he said.

Quarters' bespectacled gaze grew concerned. "Urgent, I gather. Una?"

"Yes." Tronen set down the stove, retained the canister, fiddled with the cap, unscrewing it beneath an appearance of nervousness. "She's gone. I'm worried. That's why I cut you off yesterday. Now I wonder if you have any notion where she might be."

"Good heaven, no. What can have gone wrong? And, uh, why're you lugging that stuff around?"

"You don't know where she is, lover boy?" Tronen purred.

Quarters flushed. "Huh? What do you mean, Are you, for God's sake, are you implying "

"Yes."

"No! Una? She's the cleanest, most honorable person alive. Leo, are you crazy?"

The interior fire crowned and ran free through heaven. A part of Tronen remembered that only an idiot would waste time and give the foe opportunity in a confrontation scene. He had the cap off the can. He dashed gasoline across Quarters. The man yelled, staggered back, brushed the stinking reek from his face. Tronen dropped the can to pour out what remained of its contents. He must finish his justice and be away before noise drew neighbors. He pulled forth his cigarette lighter. "Burn, Harry," he said. "Burn." He snapped flame and advanced on Quarters. He was much the heavier and stronger male.

"No, please, no!" Quarters tried to scuttle aside. But the room wasn't big. Tronen kept between him and the door. Soon he'd be boxed in a corner. Tronen moved forward, yowling.

Quarters grabbed an outsize ashtray off an end table by his armchair. Una had given him it for his pipes. He threw, as he would scorch a baseball across a sandlot.

Tronen saw amber-hued glass spin toward him, aglare like the eye of a cat. It struck. Fire exploded and went out.

As he fell, his lighter flame touched the gasoline spilled across the floor. Flame sprang aloft.

Quarters did the heroic thing. Although himself drenched, he didn't flee immediately. Instead he dragged Tronen along. When safe on the lawn, he secured limbs with belt and necktie before the maniac should regain consciousness. Then he phoned an alarm in from an adjacent house. The trucks arrived too late to save him.

The police chief's office in a smallish town is rarely impressive. This held a battered desk, a couple of creaky chairs, a filing cabinet, and a coatrack on a threadbare carpet between dingy plaster walls. It smelled of cigar butts. The view in the window was glorious, though. A thaw had been followed by a freeze, and winter-brilliant sunlight from a sky like sapphire burst in the icicles hung on boughs in Riverside Park.

118

" . appreciate your, uh, concern, Mr. Quarters," he said into the telephone. "Can't be sure yet, of course. But Dr. Mandelbaum, you know, big-name psychiatrist at the university, he's already come down and examined Tronen. Says he's never seen a case quite like it, but in his opinion the man's hopelessly insane. Permanently, I mean. Homicidal, incapable of reason, will have to be kept confined for life like any dangerous animal." The chief grimaced. "He keeps shouting about how he's on fire and wants his kitten back and—You got any idea what this might mean, sir? . . . No?"

The chief paused. "Uh, Mr. Quarters, maybe you can help us in a couple of matters . . . First off, we found a piece of writing in Tronen's pants pocket. Weird stuff, about a, uh, *ka*, whatever that is. I thought maybe a clue

"Oh, an article his wife was working on, hm? Well, look, if you could explain—*Something* must've sent Tronen off the deep end."

He took notes as he listened. Finally: "Mm, yes, thanks. Let me see if I've got the idea straight. The Egyptians thought a man had several different souls. The *ka* was the one that could wander around independently, in the shape of an animal; it'd come back and talk with him in his grave, except he was actually in heaven . . . Aw, nuts, too complicated for me. The *ka* was his spirit of reason and rightness. Let's leave it at that as far as this old woodenhead is concerned, okay? . . . No, I don't see any help. Like you say, it's only research Mrs. Tronen was doing."

The chief filled his lungs. Being in a smallish town, he knew a little about the persons involved. "Uh, favor number two, Mr. Quarters. I understand you're a friend of the family. When she learns what's happened, could you, well, sort of take over? Help her out? And—what the psychiatrist said—I'd suggest you try and get her to end her marriage. He's nothing more than a body now. She ought to make a new life for herself . . .

"Okay, thanks, Mr. Quarters. Thanks a lot. Goodbye."

He hung up. "Excuse me," he said to the fire chief, who sat opposite him. "What were you saying when he rang?"

The fire chief shrugged. "Nothing much. Just that we've sifted the ruins pretty thoroughly—a sensational case like this, we'd better—and found nothing to cast any doubt on Quarters' story."

"Bones?" asked the police chief suddenly.

"Huh?" The fire chief was startled. "Why, yes, chicken bones in the ashes of the kitchen. Why not?" A silence lengthened which he decided should be filled. "People don't realize how incombustible a human or animal body is. Crematoriums use far higher temperatures than any ordinary fire reaches, and still they have to crush the last pieces mechanically. Didn't you know that, Bob?"

"Yeah."

"Then why'd you ask?"

"Oh . . . I dunno. I guess Tronen simply lost his mind." The police chief stared out the window. "His raving made me think we might find a clue in his fireplace. But there was only burnt wood and paper. Nothing else at all."

OH TELL ME WILL IT FREEZE TONIGHT

by
R. A. Lafferty

The astonishing emergence of R. A. LAFFERTY on the horror and science fiction scene over the last dozen years is a subject of much discussion and a Hugo Award. Appreciated by both those who favor the more traditional story and those inclined to prefer the most offbeat and experimental, he has been a favorite of the best anthologists: Robert Silverberg, Harlan Ellison, and Damon Knight. And while best known for his inimitable short stories, he has also turned out fine novels of science fiction, as well as Okla Hannali, *which deals with the American Indians. All this from a writer who has published most of his work past age fifty. But readers should not confuse Mr. Lafferty's chronology with an identifiable style of writing. R. A. Lafferty writes like no one else, inventively strange and characterful and sparkling with deadpan wit. Like this bit of regionalistic myth-lore, set in his native Oklahoma.*

Of vicious bird, and tree unkind,
And swallowed storms and matters murky,
However find the truth behind?
You find it out by talking turkey.
    Winding Stair Woomagoos

"We are now in the middle of the Bermuda Triangle of weather phenomena," Hector Voiles said with that breeze-a-blowing voice of his. "This is the area where storms and inversions and highs disappear and are never seen again."

"There is one characteristic of triangles in this area," said Lloyd Rightfoot. "They are unstable. The triangle will collapse right along here, within a mile either way. And the three elements of the triangle will become four."

"Oh, is the fourth man following us?" Andrew Wide-picture asked. "I hadn't felt his presence today. I do now. He isn't following us though. He's up ahead."

Really there wasn't anything preternatural about the game warden Will Hightrack joining any group of hunters coming up from the Jack's Fork into the foothills. And groups of hunters are almost always groups of three. This group was made up of Hector Voiles, a weatherman, Lloyd Rightfoot, a naturalist, and Andrew Widepicture, a cosmologist. They all liked to foot-scuff around in the

Winding Stair Mountains, and they often carried firearms as an excuse.

"I hadn't paid too much attention to the Bermuda Triangle aspects myself," Hector said. "I was too close to the clouds to see the weather. But I've reported an awful lot of the disappearances without seeing the connection, and other weathermen have made the connections. The weather is always stormier and more sudden on the other side of the fence, you know? And the weathermen have their own other-side-of-the-fence publication, *Cloud Nine D*, and it handles weather wrinkles from all around, all the odd facts that don't fit in. Some of the stuff is pretty cirrous. Several of the men want me to do a piece on the Bermuda Triangle aspect of this corner of the Winding Stair Mountains."

The Winding Stair Mountains are pleasantly junky little hills, very pretty, but small-scale and in no way unique.

The Winding Stair Mountains are pleasantly junky little hills, very pretty, but small-scale and in no way unique.

"Be a little more clear, Hector," Lloyd Rightfoot said. "What are you trying to imply with your talk of 'Bermuda Triangle' weather phenomenon here?"

"Oh, gathering storms *do* disappear here. They disappear as if something gobbled them right up, or as if they were sucked into big holes in the air or in the mountain. There can be a pretty active tumbling storm moving right along and spreading and gaining strength. And then (such a thing shouldn't happen, of course) that storm will cease to spread. It will narrow, rather. It will narrow further, and it will grow in intensity. Then it will become quite concentrated and powerful so that it seems certain to break into thunderburst or cyclone. And then, at its most intense and threatening, it will absolutely disappear; and there will not be a trace or a track of it left."

"Where and when do these things happen?" Andrew Widepicture asked. He was sceptical but interested. Cosmologists are interested in almost everything.

"They happen right around here," Hector told them, "always within a radius of one or two miles of here. And it happens about once a year, right about now, mostly in the month of March, but sometimes in April. Not every year, but almost every year. Really, storms and incipient storms do disappear here without a trace, and their disappearances violate the law of conservation of meteorological energy."

"That I'll not believe," Lloyd Rightfoot said. "When *anything* is reported as disappearing without a trace, then the report is false. Have you been putting out false reports, Hector? Or is it that you cannot recognize traces? Nothing disappears. But some things transmute so strangely that they seem to have disappeared. Don't your active and tumbling storms transmute into something else when they are gobbled up, Hector?"

"Yes, they do. They transmute into cold, into very sudden and quite severe cold. This cold is always narrowly localized, of course. And for that matter, so are the storms."

"Like the quick-freeze spell we ran into last year, Hector?" Andrew Widepicture asked. "That was just about this time of year."

"It was about a week later," Hector said, "the latest freeze I remember here. I won't say that it was the latest freeze ever recorded here, because it wasn't recorded. I was talked out of recording it. It was so improbable that the temperature in this small area should be forty degrees lower than that of nearby areas that it just wasn't a thing that should have been recorded. And the report would have been tainted by the fact that only myself and two ana-cronies (yourselves) encountered it. There would be people who said that we had drunk off too many cans of Old Frosty during our day's hunt."

"How have other weathermen come onto the storm-disappearances?" Rightfoot asked.

"Oh, it's been happening for several generations, all the generations that records go back here. And it's almost always observed by several fellows. And weathermen are natural browsers of old records, besides having long noses and long ears and long instruments."

"Your swallowed storms don't seem to blow me down," Rightfoot said. "What I would like to find out is about a

125

most peculiar tree in this region. It's a consistent legend, and a consistent legend has to have a pragmatic kernel to it. They say that this tree produces—No, they say that it *almost* produces a bloody-awful-red fruit. But, happily, something always kills that fruit. The tree, I have heard the bark-brained say, is of no known species. Oh wood lice plague them all! A tree has to be of a known species, or we will name it and make it known. I want to get a look at that tree with the flesh-red fruit that never develops."

"What I would like to find about is a most peculiar cock-crow in this region," Andrew Widepicture said. "It also is a consistent legend, so I cannot throw it away completely. But a cattle-killing crow takes a lot of believing."

"Crows *have* killed small calves," Rightfoot the naturalist said, "but these are mostly misborn calves that are dying anyhow. Crows have been known to eat the eyes and even the tongues of such calves."

"According to the bird-brained, this most peculiar crow carries full-grown cattle off in its claws and beak," Widepicture said, "and it will eat a grown bull at a single roosting."

"Holy crow!" Hector Voiles cried. "Your legends have gobbled up my legend."

"What are you fellows hunting?" the game warden Will Hightrack demanded as he appeared in their rocky path and collapsed their triangle by becoming the fourth man. "You cannot in good conscience be out gunning at all. There is nothing at all in season right now."

"Storm-Cock is in season, Hightrack," Widepicture said. "Storm-Cock has a very short season, less than a month, and it hasn't been hunted near enough. Storm-Cock and Freeze-Bird! You show us a regulation that we can't hunt them."

"Ah, I may be hunting some long-tongued town-trotters this very day," said game warden Hightrack. "But it's said about the birds that you mention that they never saw the inside of an egg."

"Holy crow is in season," Widepicture said, "but the

holy crow season is appointed backwards. It's that crow that does the hunting."

It was a nice sunny day there. Sometimes the breeze showed a slight edge to it, but the hills and the trees and the brush exuded warmth, as did the air between the breezes.

"If town gentlemen could shoot, I wouldn't object to one of them shooting a very big wild tom turkey," game warden Hightrack said. "But I'd object to any of them getting a closer shot than the present eighty yards. I'd object to more than one of them shooting. And I'd object to myself pointing the shot out to any of those gentlemen. But town gentlemen cannot see and they cannot shoot, so that feast will not come to the board."

"I can see. I can shoot," Andrew Widepicture said. He raised his rifle towards a blurred bit of mountain brush in the middle distance. He held his point for a measured five seconds. Then he squeezed off his shoot.

"Good," said Hightrack. "That will make a good meal for the six of us."

"You say 'for the six of us,' Will Hightrack," Widepicture remarked then. "Will the dead turkey arrange for its own transportation? Yes, I see that it will."

A bit later, two men brought the shot turkey. These men were James South-Forty and Thomas Wrong-Rain. They were scrub-cattle ranchers and rock-acre farmers of the region. They were large, burly, brown men. They were Jack's Fork Choctaw Indian men.

Yeah, it would take about an hour and a half to get that turkey ready. There aren't any experts at cooking a turkey or anything else in the open. Not white men, not Indians, not hunters, not wranglers, none of them are any good at it. There's a lot of large-mouth fakery about such cooking. Half the meat would be ruined, and half of it would be only half bad when finally prepared; but it was a big turkey, and the not-bad half would feed six men.

It was pleasant noon or early afternoon. There was new moss grass there on the slopes, and old buffalo grass. There were rotten boles of hackberry and there were joints of cedar wood that didn't care whether they were burned or not. There was last season's brush, and it all made a strong and smoky fire. If smoke would roast a turkey, that big tom would be roasted quickly. But it would be a while yet.

So they talked turkey while the turkey cooked unevenly in pits and in rock ovens and on spits, and half of it would be ruined. "Turkey talk" doesn't mean exactly what is supposed of it. It isn't plain talk. Sometimes that gobble-gabble gets fancy.

"It occurs to me that the three gentlemen don't know very much about what they have been talking about," Thomas Wrong-Rain said. "It occurs to me that even the weatherman gentlemen doesn't know why we have to have another freeze this year."

"No, we will not have another freeze this season," weatherman Hector Voiles said. "The rattlesnakes have been coming out of their holes for a week. The swallows and swifts and cardinals have all arrived. The oak leaves are as big as squirrels' ears, so it is time to plant corn. We had a light freeze on the first day of spring, and it will have been the last one. We have had later freezes, two I believe, but all the signs say that we will not have another freeze this season."

"Then all the signs are mush-mouthed frauds," Thomas Wrong-Rain maintained. "I did not say that we *would* have another freeze: say it that way and maybe we won't. I said that we *have to have* another freeze. The alternative to that is pretty shaggy. If it comes right down to the raw end and we haven't had that freeze, then we will have to *make* it freeze!"

"What will you do, Wrong-Rain, have a rain dance or a frost dance to make it freeze?" Will Hightower the game warden jeered.

"No, no, no!" Wrong-Rain rejected that. "You're talking about Cherokees or some of the other brain-damaged Indians. Rain dances and frost dances are kid stuff. We will just get wrought up and make it freeze. I think it's down to the raw end already. I don't think the last freeze killed it. The tree's getting smarter. I have heard that the tree was already in bloom. If the last frost didn't kill it, then we will have to have another frost. It will be pretty direful if that tree is allowed to fruit."

"Wrong-Rain, I don't believe that even you can pull off a direful tale today," Widepicture joshed, "not with the sun shining in the little Winding Stair Mountains, and a mocking bird mocking. And that edge on the breeze, it isn't much of an edge."

"Yeah, the sun does spoil it," Wrong-Rain admitted. "Never mind, the sun will cloud for the story if the story's true. Well, the tree is less than a hundred feet from here. All of you have seen this tree: I have shown it to all of you. But after persons have seen this tree, sometimes a breeze will blow. Then a fine red powder or bloom-dust will drift down on the people. This makes them forget all about the tree. Normally it's good that the people should forget. This saves them from worry and stomach rot and irregularity and anxiety. But some of us have to remember about the tree. If it ever comes to full fruit, it will send a shadow like a blight over the whole land. This shadow will kill cattle, and it will kill people."

Andrew Widepicture laughed. Then his laugh crumbled a bit at its leading edge. The sun clouded, and it had clouded phenomenally fast. That meant that Wrong-Rain's story was true, except that he really wasn't telling a story. The mockingbird had left off its melody and was squalling and mewing fearfully like a catbird. And the edge of the breeze had reasserted itself.

"How does the fruit, or the shadow of the fruit, kill people?" Widepicture asked. "By disease? By disaster? By ill luck?"

"I don't know," Wrong-Rain admitted. "It hasn't done it for two hundred years. But that's just because the tree has had its fruit frost-killed every year. I tell you, though, that the tree's getting smarter. It's got the weather tricked this year, unless we use tricks of our own. And our own tricks are about worn out."

"And that's the end of your story?" Rightfoot asked.

"Yes. I wish it were the end of the tree and its fruit, too. That's the end of my story. The sun can come out again."

The sun came out again. And everything was again casual and unimpressive in the Winding Stair Mountains. The Winding Stairs were toy mountains. They were much less impressive even than the Potato Hills in an adjoining region. There was not any way that they could be taken seriously for long. There was no way that they could maintain a sinister aspect for more than brief minutes. These mountains were too light-minded. They were too little. So thought they all of them.

"Hey, you know why the Winding Stair Mountains are so little?" James South-Forty asked them, coming in on their thoughts rather than on any words of theirs, in the way that the Jack's Fork Choctaws have. "They're so little because they're the biggest mountains that the bird could carry here, and here is where he wanted them. Even a *big* bird has his load limit."

"Are we now in consideration of the second plague of the Winding Stair Mountains?" Andrew Widepicture asked with an asymmetric grin.

"I think so," said James South-Forty. "Sometimes you lose me with that T-Town talk. Yeah, I'm talking about the Storm-Cock, the big bird. I don't know much about that tree that Tom Wrong-Rain talks about. I don't know how a shadow of a tree can kill cattle or people, but I know how Storm-Cock kills them. He eats them alive and he eats them dead. That's how he kills them. He's one big bird."

"How big is he, South-Forty?" Hector Voiles asked. James South-Forty extended his arms. South-Forty was about six feet four inches tall, and from extended fingertip to fingertip he was about the same.

"About that big," he said.

"We might as well go look at the tree while South-Forty talks," Wrong-Rain said listlessly, and then they were already beside that tree. It was no more than a hundred feet from the turkey fire. A little breeze blew as they first stood by the tree, and a little bit of bloom dust drifted down on them so that they were unable to notice much about the tree. It unhinged their limbs and their minds, it gave them stomach-rot and apprehensions, it set them to shaking in every joint and tendon, but they

130

didn't really notice much about it. The fruit was huge and horrible and livid red. It had a rank murder-smell to it, and it would kill you. That fruit had been frosted, and it had rotted. But it wasn't certain that it was quite dead. A small breeze blew again, and who notices details about a tree when there is that sort of bloom-dust in the air?

"South-Forty, you indicated that Storm-Cock was between six feet and six and a half feet big," Hector taunted. "Well, that's big for a bird, but it's not big enough for a bird that can carry off full-grown cattle. How many cattle can he carry off at a time, South-Forty?"

"Three," said James South-Forty. "One in his beak, and one in each claw. And sometimes he carries another one in—aw naw, I'd better not tell that. It'd be a lie."

"Ah, but look, James," Widepicture reasoned. "The bird wouldn't be big enough to do it. A bird couldn't carry three or four head of grown cattle even if it had a six and a half foot wingspan."

"Wingspan!" South-Forty gasped. "Who said wingspan? I showed you how big Storm-Cock was between the eyes. That's the way you always measure a storm-cock, between the eyes."

They all laughed then. "Seems like I whomped you all between the eyes with that joke," South-Forty gloated. "You walked right into that one."

Another small breeze blew, and a critical amount of bloom-dust drifted down from the tree onto the six men. It was a sufficient quantity of dust so that none of them would remember seeing a tree with livid red undead fruit with a rank murder-smell. They wouldn't remember that tree at all, except Wrong-Rain.

They went to eat the turkey meat. Some of the pieces were burnt on the outside and raw-red on the inside. Some of them were burnt all the way through. And a few of the chunks were pretty good.

"When are you going to give me some good weather tips again, Wrong-Rain?" Hector Voiles asked as they chewed the stringy meat. "I have consistently been the worst weatherman in town for quite a while. They're

131

going to give me the boot if I don't come up with something sharp."

"You'll be like that weatherman who had to move to California because the weather here didn't agree with him," Lloyd Rightfoot said.

"Maybe I'll phone you tonight," Wrong-Rain said. "I may give you a tip on the weather that no one else would ever guess. Will you use it if I give you a real slanted tip?"

"Yes, I will," Hector promised. "I'll use it whatever you give me."

They ate the rest of the turkey except for a few pieces which were an extreme case.

"Do you know what's the spookiest phrase that can be spoken?" Wrong-Rain asked them suddenly. "It's 'The Bird in the Tree': that's the spookiest of all. Think about it." But they couldn't think whether he meant the bird they had just eaten or some other bird. They shot three or four rabbits for the hunting pouch. Then Voiles and Rightfoot and Widepicture scuffed down the little mountain and to their car.

They left the livid and hating tree behind them; but they couldn't give a name to the menace because its bloom-dust had destroyed their memory of it.

They got in the car and drove back to T-Town.

ii

Oh wayward storms, destroyed, demurred!
Oh tree to gobble and defeat them!
All caution lest the murder-bird
Should bite folks clear in two and eat them!
—Winding Stair Woomagoos

Thomas Wrong-Rain phoned Hector Voiles at his studio at nine o'clock that night. "A hard freeze tonight in the Winding Stairs, Mr. Voiles," Wrong-Rain said. "We have to have that. The fruit is alive. It would break out before dawn tomorrow. Remember that 'The Bird in the Tree' is the spookiest phrase of them all. It has *got* to freeze tonight. Have you any storms that we could use to fuel the freeze?"

132

"A warm spell is blowing in, Wrong-Rain. It's strong and twisty, and it's probably dangerous. It could be a real nine-county cloudburst, or it could spin into half a dozen cyclones. It would be a pretty strong storm to swallow, even in the Bermuda Triangle."

"It should be strong enough to make a heavy freeze. Remember the bird that never saw the inside of an egg! That fruit has *got* to be killed! Announce that it will freeze, and that will put pressure on for it."

"Wrong-Rain, this storm is a strong-warm. It's seventy-two degrees here now, and it's nine o'clock at night. Fun's fun, but you can't make a freeze out of this one, and it's too big to swallow. How do you make the changes, anyhow? Or are you the one?"

"I'm one of the ones. When the menace appears, and we just *got* to have a hard freeze for the safety of the region, then I'm one of those who goes for it. I bust my mind for it, as did my father Joe Wrong-Rain before me. Dammit, Voiles, this is The Bird in the Tree! Help us to kill it. We need help. But my friends and I do have the support of a strong person named ain, I'lustophush-masapulphattalokarchikkapokartahapatishomobilmingo."

"With five t's? Got it. All right, Wrong-Rain, I'll do it. I'll put my neck in the frosty noose. I'll give them a weather report tonight that'll rupture the station. That's my own neck I feel them chopping off, but it all might be fun."

"Watch that fun stuff, Mr. Voiles," Thomas Wrong-Rain begged. "No derision, please. Derision will imperil the whole business."

"Well, all right," Voiles agreed dubiously, "but you're asking a lot there. I break up sometimes."

There were already tornado alerts out for Pushmataha, Latimer, Le Flore, and Haskell Counties. So Hector Voiles put out his own alert, to the other weathermen of the country, especially to those of the *Cloud Nine D* interest. Voiles told them flatly that there would be a storm disappearance in the Little Bermuda Triangle of Oklahoma tonight. He told them that history would be unmade before their very eyes on their very charts if

133

only they paid attention. And he said that the disappearance of the storm would be marked, not by an oil slick, but by an incredible freeze.

Then he went and got half a snoot-full before he broadcast his nightly weather at ten o'clock. He gave the routine reports. He gave the information that four counties were under tornado alerts. Then he grinned a lowering grin and began a brisk gust in that breeze-a-blowing voice of his.

"Forget the tornado alerts," Hector told his airy audience. "There won't be any tornados tonight. That skirmish line of storms, it will be funneled and narrowed into a single disturbance, a concentrated storm. And this storm will disappear completely when it is in its most powerful and most concentrated stage. It will disappear in the Little Bermuda Triangle and it will never be seen again. It will disappear in the Winding Stair Mountains at the border of Latimer and Le Flore Counties. It will disappear in storm-wreck and annihilation.

"Listen, people, there is a Bird in a Tree. This is a crucial bird, and it never saw the inside of an egg. This bird must be killed even before it comes to sustaining life. Otherwise, it will fly around the region, with its black shadow under it, and it will destroy land and kill cattle and people.

"There is only one thing that can destroy the Storm-Cock, the Bird in the Tree. A hard freeze can kill it, after the bird has begun to bloom but just before it has attained mobile life. It must happen right now, before morning, or the Tree-Bird will rive open the tree and go out and destroy the land and its crops and its cattle and its people.

"Now hear my predictions, on which I am staking my reputation and perhaps my life. There will *not* be thunderstorms or tornados or cyclones. The skirmish line of storms has already narrowed into a single storm front. This storm front will disappear completely within the next fifteen minutes. It will disappear into a hole in a mountain, or into a hole in the air. And the kickback of the disappearing storm will be the cold. This will be

134

hard-freezing cold, extreme cold over the area of the four counties that have been under the alert.

"I predict that the storm will disappear completely within the next fifteen minutes; I predict that the disappearance will be followed by a quick fifty-degree drop in temperature in that same region; I predict the consequent very hard and killing freeze; and I predict that the big bird in the tree will be freeze-killed in the bloom tonight, and that it will not ravage the country and destroy the kine and the people tomorrow. These are the things that I predict, and I will stake my reputation and my life on my predictions. Who else makes such bold predictions?"

It would have been bad even if Hector had left it at that. He didn't. He broke up. He began to laugh, to yowl, to chortle. He went into cascades of clattering and rotten laughter. The monitors cut him off, but he continued to laugh like a bloated buffalo.

And that is when the warm moist Gulf air hit the updraft. Turgot Cantowine busted in, and Cantowine was a mighty man at the studio.

"The only thing that can possibly save you, Voiles, is for your predictions to come true!" this Turgot swore angrily. "Man, they'd better come true! Will they?"

"I don't know," Hector Voiles giggled. "They would have come true, I think, if I hadn't broken up. There's something down there that can't stand derision."

"There's something right here that can't stand it either," Cantowine barked. "You're deriding the wrong people when you start to deride people. The phones are jumping clear out of their cradles. People are storming the studio doors within seconds of your being cut off. Let's see you make *that* storm disappear. Man, do you realize what you've done! You've made light of the last still-standing institution. If the weather isn't sacred, what is?"

"I don't know," Hector giggled.

The storm didn't disappear. The thunderbursts plowed the whole northeast corner of the state with lightning outage and flash floods and wind damage. There were six deadly tornados sprawled out of the thing, and more than two dozen howling gales. The tornados killed people in the towns of Poteau and Spiro, and in the country around Jack's Fork and the Winding Stairs. That storm sure wasn't one that disappeared and was never heard from again: you'd be hearing about that storm as long as the last survivor or the last victim was still alive.

Hector Voiles followed all the reports. The studio was full of reports of the rising numbers of the dead, but Hector didn't care much about that. He had trouble getting temperature reports from the afflicted area; people seemed too busy to notice the temperature. It was eight in the morning before he was able to get a temperature reading from near the area. The temperature was sixty-nine degrees. There hadn't been a freeze.

Thomas Wrong-Rain phoned Hector Voiles about eight-thirty that morning after.

"Mr. Voiles, the worst that could happen has happened," he announced. "We just weren't able to make it freeze and we busted our brains for it. I think somebody laughed at the wrong time."

"Was there tornado damage in your immediate neighborhood?" Hector asked.

"Oh, some. My house and barns blew away, and my wife got killed; but that's not what I meant by the worst that could happen. Didn't you hear me, Voiles? It didn't freeze."

"No. I know that it didn't."

"So the last chance to kill the murderous fruit, the bird in the tree, has gone by. We just couldn't change the storm into a freeze. So that bird broke out. It split that tree with a thunder twice as loud as the storm itself. It came out of that riven tree then, and it came out of it, and it kept on coming out of it. It was as big as a herd of elephants when it came out. Then it went on a rampage."

"It ate a few cattle, but mostly it went after people. It comes on people in groups of three, and it takes and kills one of them. It's very ritual. I was over at James South-Forty's house after my own house had blown away.

136

John Short-Summer was with us. The bird came, and we knew that it wanted just one of us. It isn't a loud bird, but it makes itself understood. We drew low-card-go to see which one of us it would be, and James South-Forty drew low card; the bird killed him and carried him off. And it's been to lots of other places and killed lots of other people. It kills people who gaped at it when it was trapped in the bloom or in the fruit. It kills people who laughed at it or made light of it. It'll probably come and kill one of you."

"I don't think it could find us," Hector said. (All the breeze was gone out of his voice now.)

"Yeah, he can find you," Thomas Wrong-Rain said.

Hector phoned Lloyd Rightfoot and Andrew Wide-picture to join him at his office at the studio. Both had been out among the elements all night, and both said that they would be right over.

"As a naturalist, my most rewarding studies are of nature at her most violent," Rightfoot said as he came in. "Hector, she was violent last night, violent for hour after hour! Somebody cut the nets and let all the thunder-fish out. The floods are the worst thing right now. Oh, was there ever a storm that exploded like that one! I once knew a horse that would stampede like that whenever someone would try to throw a bridle rope over his nose."

"Someone did try to throw a bridle rope over that storm's nose last night," Hector mumbled. "It's so easy to insult an element if you're not careful. They don't like to be laughed at."

"No, nothing in nature likes to be laughed at," Rightfoot said.

"As a cosmologist, my most illuminating moments come when I discover simple natural things going cosmic," Andrew Widepicture spoke as he came in. "There are truly cosmic elements in the peculiar wrong-headedness that has run through the night's events. It just didn't have a neat ending, not any of it. Now, if my calculations are correct, it will require the ending of either the world or myself."

137

"Of yourself," said Voiles. "A legend-come-to-life always eats flesh, but it will not eat all the flesh. I hope it will be satisfied with yours."

"The legend is a badly-done one, Voiles," Widepicture remarked. "It has too many moving parts. Storm-Cock and Tree-Freezer, that's enough elements there. And Tree-Freezer is complicated by the long-named demiurge who also serves as Tree-Freezer. Is the demiurge only an aspect of Wrong-Rain, or is he an independent element? And Storm-Swallower is much too much. He belongs to another legend entirely, but he was instrumental in this one. And the bird grows bigger and bigger, and less possible. I'm convinced that he's strutted with wooden bones, as he should be, coming out of a tree. He isn't a bird of the *ornis* sort at all, and he's aerodynamically unsound.

"And I'm not sure that he'll stand the test of daylight," Lloyd Rightfoot hazarded hopefully. "Some of the most incredible prodigies have very short existence spans. And at the end of their span they do not so much die as become unshaped and unrecognized. He may not have time for us before he returns to an unremembering form."

"He'll have time enough for us," Hector said. "He believes that we laughed at him when we saw him still in the bud, or anyway that we didn't pay him enough respect." Hector took a pack of cards out of a drawer and put it on his desk.

"If you spooked the hard-freeze, Voiles, then the bird owes its life to you," Widepicture said. "But don't expect gratitude. Ah, reality is very hard to define. I also doubt that the uncreature will pass the daylight test."

"We'll cut the cards for low-man-dead when he gets here," Hector said. "And the daylight test is no test at all of reality. Many very real things disappear before morning."

"This is more than a mere daylight test," Rightfoot proposed. "This is a time test. This is the eighth decade of the twentieth century of the uncommon era, and tenuous reality cannot enter here. There is a place test. This is the ninth floor of the Television Plaza Building,

138

and reality must be more than merely contingent to exist here. There is a context test. This is beautiful downtown T-Town in broad daylight on a spring day. The blooms along the Main Mall are blooming, and the sapsucker butterflies are fluttering around them. Automobiles are crumbling each others' fenders in the middle distance, and all the girls walking on the sidewalk are pretty. The very walls here are made out of glass and sunlight, and a too-dark reality becomes no reality at all."

A too-dark bird took out the entire outer glass-and-sunlight wall of the room and crammed the space with head and pinion top.

"So much for this particular reality," said Widepicture. "It brings its own context."

"James South-Forty was correct," Rightfoot said nervously. "The bird is about six and a half feet between the eyes."

"The bird killed South-Forty several hours ago," Hector said. "Well, the rules are (how do I know what they are?) that he takes only one of us. We cut cards low-man-dead for it." Hector cut to a red six-card, while the Storm-Cock watched with hard hatred in his big eyes. "Oh, that's awful low," Hector moaned.

Lloyd Rightfoot cut to a red four-card. The bird seemed to dismiss Hector then, and keep its baleful eyes on Rightfoot and Widepicture.

Widepicture struck a match on the big beak of the bird, but that was for bravado.

"That proves nothing about reality," he said unevenly. "One can strike a match on a *picture* of a bird, or of a beak." His hand fluttered like a sapsucker butterfly over the cards. He cut to a black three-card, and he was low-man-dead. The bird gazed a long time at the low card to be sure.

The bird sliced a forearm off Widepicture, as for a sample, and munched it. Widepicture waved farewell to his two friends with the other arm. He was jittery and distraught.

"No, no, I don't accept it," he jabbered. "This isn't reality. This is the most unreal happening I've ever encountered."

The bird sliced Widepicture sheer in two, gobbled up both pieces of him, and then withdrew from the broken room with a clatter of ungainly wings like thunder run backwards.

Sunlit reality flooded back into the room. And outside, on the brilliant sky, there was a jerky black blotch, munching bobble-headedly, flying clumsily as though strutted with wood, a thing aerodynamically impossible, incredibly awkward, and categorically unreal.

DEAD CALL

by

William F. Nolan

*This brief, scary tale is one of the few pieces of short
fiction from WILLIAM F. NOLAN's typewriter in some
while. He has been spending most of his recent time
writing for films and television (including scripts for
eight Movies of the Week) and on his full-length book
projects, one of which, Logan's Run—a novel written in
collaboration with George Clayton Johnson—he has
adapted for major-budget motion picture production.
Nolan, who grew up in Missouri and was once a commercial artist, has lived in California since 1953 and has
been a full-time writer for over twenty years. He has
written extensively on automobile racing and show business but his fiction has gained him special praise, including an Edgar Award of the Mystery Writers of America.
Nolan's work in the fields of science fiction and horror
is always charged with interesting twists, like this one,
emanating from an everyday object not without sinister
possibilities.*

Len had been dead for a month when the phone rang.

Midnight. Cold in the house and me dragged up from sleep to answer the call. Helen gone for the weekend. Me, alone in the house. And the phone ringing . . .

"Hello."

"Hello, Frank."

"Who is this?"

"You know *me*. It's Len . . . ole Len Stiles."

Cold. Deep and intense. The receiver dead-cold metal in my hand.

"Leonard Stiles died four weeks ago."

"Four weeks, three days, two hours and twenty-seven minutes ago—to be exact."

"I want to know who you are!"

A chuckle. The same dry chuckle I'd heard so many times. "C'mon, ole buddy—after twenty years. Hell, you *know* me."

"This is a damned poor joke!"

"No joke, Frank. You're there, alive. And I'm here, dead. And you know something ole buddy? I'm really *glad* I did it."

"Did . . . what?"

"Killed myself. Because . . . death is just what I hoped it would be: beautiful . . . grey . . . quiet. No pressures."

"Len Stiles' death was an accident . . . a concrete freeway barrier . . . His car——"

"I *aimed* my car for that barrier. Pedal to the floor.

143

Doing almost a hundred when I hit . . . No accident, Frank." The voice cold . . . Cold. "I *wanted* to be dead . . . and no regrets."

I tried to laugh, make light of this—matching his chuckle with my own. "Dead men don't use telephones."

"I'm not really using a phone, not in a physical sense. It's just that I chose to contact you this way. You might say it's a matter of 'psychic electricity.' As a detached spirit, I'm able to align my cosmic vibrations to match the vibrations of this power line. Simple, really."

"Sure, A snap. Nothing to it."

"Naturally you're skeptical. I expected you to be. But . . . listen carefully to me, Frank."

And I listened—with the phone gripped in my hand in that cold night house—as the voice told me things that *only* Len could know . . . intimate details of shared experiences extending back through two decades. And when he'd finished I was certain of one thing:

He *was* Len Stiles.

"But how . . . I still don't . . ."

"Think of this phone as a 'medium'—a line of force through which I can bridge the gap between us." The dry chuckle again. "Hell, you gotta admit it beats holding hands around a table in the dark—yet the principle is the same."

I'd been standing by my desk, transfixed by the voice. Now I moved behind the desk, sat down, trying to absorb this dark miracle. My muscles were wire-taut, my fingers cramped about the metal receiver. I dragged in a slow breath, the night dampness of the room pressing at me. "All right . . . I don't believe in ghosts, don't pretend to understand any of this, but . . . I'll accept it. I *must* accept it."

"I'm glad, Frank—because it's important that we talk." A long moment of hesitation. Then the voice, lower now, softer. "I *know* how lousy things have been, ole buddy."

"What do you mean?"

"I just know how things are going for you. And . . . I want to help. As your friend, I want you to know that I understand."

"Well . . . I'm really not—"

"You've been feeling bad, haven't you? Kind of '*down*' . . . right?"

"Yeah. A little, I guess."

"And I don't blame you. You've got reasons. Lots of reasons . . . For one, there's your money problem."

"I'm expecting a raise. Cooney promised me one— within the next few weeks."

"You won't get it, Frank. I *know*. He's lying to you. Right now, at this moment, he's looking for a man to replace you at the company. Cooney's planning to fire you."

"He never liked me. We never got along from the day I walked into that office."

"And your wife . . . All the arguments you've been having with her lately . . . It's a pattern, Frank. Your marriage is all over. Helen's going to ask you for a divorce. She's in love with another man."

"Who, dammit? What's his name?"

"You don't know him. Wouldn't change things if you did. There's nothing you can do about it now. Helen just . . . doesn't love you any more. These things happen to people."

"We've been drifting apart for the last year . . . But I didn't know why. I had no idea that she —"

"And then there's Jan. She's back on it, Frank. Only it's worse now. A lot worse."

I knew what he meant—and the coldness raked along my body. Jan was nineteen, my oldest daughter, and she'd been into drugs for the past three years. But she'd promised to quit.

"What do you know about Jan? Tell me!"

"She's into the heavy stuff, Frank. She's hooked bad. It's too late for her."

"What the hell are you saying?"

"I'm saying she's lost to you . . . She's rejected you, and there's no reaching her. She *hates* you . . . Blames you for everything."

"I won't *accept* that kind of blame! I did my best for her."

"It wasn't enough, Frank. We both know that. You'll never see Jan again."

The blackness was welling within me, a choking wave through my body.

"Listen to me, old buddy . . . Things are going to get worse, not better. I know. I went through my own kind of hell when I was alive."

"I'll . . . start over. Leave the city. Go East, work with my brother in New York."

"Your brother doesn't want you in his life. You'd be an intruder . . . an alien. He never writes you, does he?"

"No, but that doesn't mean—"

"Not even a card last Christmas. No letters or calls. He doesn't *want* you with him, Frank, believe me."

And then he began to tell me other things. He began to talk about middle age, and how it was too late now to make any kind of new beginning. He spoke of disease . . . loneliness . . . of rejection and despair. And the blackness was complete.

"There's only one real solution to things, Frank— just *one*. That gun you keep in your desk upstairs. Use it, Frank. Use the gun."

"I couldn't do that."

"But why not? What other choice have you got? The solution is *there*. Go upstairs and use the gun. I'll be waiting for you afterwards. You won't be alone. It'll be like the old days . . . We'll be together . . . Death is beautiful . . . Use the gun, Frank . . , The gun . . . Use the gun . . . The gun . . . The gun . . ."

I've been dead for a month now, and Len was right. It's fine here. No pressures. No worries. Grey and quiet and beautiful . . .

I know how lousy things have been going for you. And they won't get any better.

Isn't that your phone ringing?

Better answer it.

It's important that we talk.

THE IDIOTS
by
Davis Grubb

A new supernatural story by DAVIS GRUBB is cause for celebration. His novel The Night of the Hunter, *made into a memorable film with Robert Mitchum and Lillian Gish, is one of the great tours de force of suspense and terror in the annals of American letters. Who can forget the images of the fingertips engraved with the words "love" and "hate," or those of the children Pearl and John fleeing Preacher Harry Powell across the rural Ohio Valley of the thirties? Born in 1919 in Moundsville, West Virginia, Grubb has set most of his fiction in his native region or other sections of the South and border states. He has a deep understanding and sympathy for the people of those areas; he always remains true to his roots and evokes them with a deceptively simple poetry and insight that advances beyond regionalism into literature. Happily, Grubb still makes occasional return to the eerie corners of his heartland, as he does here.*

There. I've said the word. Idiots. For that, strictly speaking, was what we both were: Grandfather and me. But you dont understand, I'll wager. To you that word Idiot means feeble-minded. Crazy. And Grandfather Flowers was an Idiot. But every bit as sane and smart as you. I make no claims for myself but I strongly suspicion that I am an Idiot, too. Only you can be the judge of that

once I get through telling what happened that night of April 29th back in 1945. For I'll swear on a Christian or a Catholic Bible, either one, that Grandfather Gailey killed Hitler that night. And not a moment too soon. For Grandfather had it on good authority that Hitler was fixing to move up through Lewis County from Webster County and invade Harrison County the very next day. I tell you, it was a close call.

Now back to that word Idiot. I have but one vice. And that vice is the Merriam-Webster Unabridged Dictionary in the Clarksburg Public Library. As for all the other books they got in that place, for all I care you can dump them in Elk Creek. I growed up in the Great Depression; had to quit school in my sophomore year of high school to join up with the CCCs. So maybe that dictionary is a puny way to try to patch up my ignorance. That dictionary. Nothing but words. No story, no plot. Just words. But didnt the Lord Himself say that in the beginning was the word? And if He did—dont that make the dictionary sort of holy?

We dont live in Clarksburg. We live about two miles up beyond Davisson's Run just past Big Isaac in a little mine town called Flinderation. I work in Roberts' Hardware on Pike Street in Clarksburg. And since theres neither bus nor trolley to Flinderation I have to walk both ways every day. And way after dark when I get done at night. Because every evening after work I go to the Recreation Pool Room and Cafe on Pike Street and have me three hotdogs and a Red Top Beer. Then I hasten off to the public library. To my Book. Dog-tired, but that dont hinder me. Dog-tired because clerking in a hardware store requires a good five years before you get the hang of where everything is. I can't think of a store that has more items in it and more different varieties and more different names and more impatient customers who when they come in and ask for certáin size gasket for a 1932 Maytag gasolene-powered Washing Machine expect you to know right where to lay hands on it and no waiting. Take a simple thing like a carpenter's file. Now there is bastard files, rat-tail files, and more different shapes, sizes, and names of files than you can shake a stick at. I mind the night Miz Buena Vista Lang, the plumber's wife, come in to pick up a file he needed.

How about this little bastard here? I asked her, real polite like.

No, she snickered. I think he'd more likely favor that big son of a bitch along side it.

You get them kind every now and then.

I only happen to mention her because the day she came in was the one before the night when I come across that word in the library dictionary. Idiot. And once I read its definition I knew it fit Grandfather Gailey to a T. "Uneducated, ignorant person; private person, common man, one without professional knowledge." A Greek word once. American now. Old Greek, too, and not modern because the very next night I went to have my supper in the little Greek hot-dog stand near the old Post Office and told Mister Kaliensis, the manager, he was the noblest idiot I had ever known next to Grandfather, and he threw me out.

"Common man." That was the part of the definition

I liked best. An FDR kind of phrase. A John L. Lewis kind of phrase.

Now comes the hardest part to tell you about Grandfather Gailey and still make sense. Here goes. To Grandfather Gailey the whole world consisted of no more than eight counties in West Virginia. You try spending ninety-eight years in eight counties of Anywhere and see if you dont have the same opinion. For Grandfather Gailey there wasnt such a thing as the United States of America, let alone such districts as Asia and Europe and Africa with big oceans in between. For him New York City and Paris and Berlin and Los Angeles and Moscow were places in a child's fairy tale. Show him all the picture postcards you wanted, show him the photographs in the *Glory Argus* or the *Wheeling Intelligencer* or even the *National Geographic* and he'd still swear they were made up. I even took a Rand McNally Atlas home from the Library one time and sat up half the night showing him the different colored countries and do you think it budged him an inch?

Take that place right there now where my finger is, boy, hed say. Whats that called?

That, sir, is Belgium.

All right, Belgium, he would answer. And you can see as well as me that its purple. Are you expecting me to believe that theres a country where the earth is purple? Why, God save us, boy, there aint a farmer on earth could make anything grow in dirt that was purple. And right next to it—and dont even bother to tell me its name—theres one thats as blue as my mother's eyes. You insultin my intelligence by inferrin that a man could raise corn in blue topsoil?

I gave up; didnt push him any more.

The afternoon we heard on the old table model Philco that Hitler had invaded Poland, Grandfather Gailey was furious.

And where may I respectfully inquire, he asked, was our so-called State Police when this was atakin place?

But Grandfather Gailey, I said, Poland is in Europe.

It is not, he replied. Poland is in Webster County. And for that matter, so is China.

How do you figure that, Grandfather?

Because back in the autumn of 1911 I bought me a Poland China hog at Hacker Valley Post Office up at the head of Holley River. In Webster County.

I sighed and went out on the porch steps and sat a long while whittling and spitting and listening to H. V. Kaltenborn on the radio back in the house. And Grandfather Gailey listening and just aseeething at all the lies he was hearing. The Sunday they broke in and announced the attack of the Japs on Pearl Harbor it was all we could do to keep Grandfather Gailey from going at once into Clarksburg to the County Court House to give his advice to President Roosevelt. You see, not believing in such a place as Washington, D.C., he naturally didnt believe in the White House. We got him quieted down a little after about a half hour of arguing. And then he wanted to call the President at his office in the Court House but, lucky for us, the party line was all tied up. He spent the rest of the evening taking out his wrath on the radio commentator, Gabriel Heater, who had called the tragedy of that December seventh the "rape of Pearl Harbor."

There's no such thing as rape! shouted Grandfather Gailey. You cant thread a movin needle!

Dont you believe there is such a man as Hitler, Grandfather? Mama asked.

Of course I do, he snapped. Ive known his type all my life. And a typical Webster County white trash scoundler if ever I heard of one!

He sprang out of his rocker and commenced pacing the parlor.

Youll see! Youll see! I knowed the Harberts well. Them and their women! Webster County jezebels and harlots.

Whatcha gettin at, Grandfather? I asked.

That Pearl Harbert that damned fool Gabriel Heater said got raped! he shouted. A Harbert dont need rapin. Just whistle that tune Rose of San Antone pretty enough and a Harbert gal will be up in the hay-mow, stripped and ready before you can climb the ladder.

He got so mad, then, he snatched the Philco table setup, raced out in the yard with it, and smashed it to pieces with a twelve-pound sledge. And he wasnt through. He came raring back into the parlor.

You mark my words! he hollered. Before the end of April that damned Hitler will come up from Webster County and try to seize Harrison. You mark my words, I tell you! Them Webster County bastards will stop at nothin once they commence!

You got it all wrong, Grandfather, I said, trying for the last time to reason with him and a little scared because I was beginning to share his beliefs. All wrong. Hitler, hes in Europe. And if we dont stop him, his troops will be in London and then New York.

Stay away from them maps, boy, he said. London. New York. They dont exist. Theyre fairy tale towns. Even Pittsburgh aint real.

Only he always pronounced it Pitchburg.

The world, he said, is where a man is at. Land as far as he can walk in either direction. That far and no farther. And that's all that wants fightin for.

He paused and stared up at the curl of new moon and the stars, for by now we were out in the yard under the old winesap tree his father had planted after he came back from the War Between the States.

Now up yonder, Grandfather said softly. Theres your world. Its your world because its a world you can see and feel. Up yonder. Behind the moon. Beyond the Milky Way. Thats the only world I acknowledge aside from this little patch of eight counties we live on. Up yonder. The only world I care about. Nor ever will. Cause by Greyhound or in my Model T or on shank's mare Im goin there—and soon, boy; soon. The rest of it they teach you in school geography—its lies, all lies. That one up yonder—its the true world. And you had best take heed of my tellin you.

Folks in Flinderation and Clarksburg considered Grandfather Gailey a little queer but not crazy. He had one good friend in town, an old Jew named Sol Schkloven, who ran a little Trade, Swap or Barter Shop around the corner from Moore's Opera House on Morning Alley. In the big cities I reckon youd call what he run a Pawn Shop. He was poor but he got by. And he just purely worshipped my Grandfather. One April night Grandfather Gailey took me along with him on his weekly visit to Mister Schkloven's store. The old Jew was in the back room where he lived when the little bell tinkled as we opened the door. Grandfather called his name out, for we could see a lamp shining behind the glass-beaded curtains that separated his shop from his small living quarters. A good three minutes passed. We could hear him so we knew he was there. He was singing. Ive heard old black men sing the blues but this singing was more heart-rendering than the blues. It put me in mind of the singing of a Flamenco gypsy who come through our town with a carnival one summer.

Sol! Grandfather Gailey yelled again. Its me and my grandson and namesake—Gailey Flowers.

Presently that sad and awful singing stopped. After another two minutes there appeared the stooped, crumpled figure of a baldheaded little man with a black beany on his head. He tried to smile a greeting at us but it come off poorly. He stood a moment, head bowed, then sank into a wicker rocker behind his junk-littered counter. After a spell he looked up at us. His face was the color of tallow. But his eyes wernt red from crying. Five thousand years of running from someone draws all the moisture of a man into his legs, I reckon. In fact, nobody cries like I hear tell they did a hundred years ago. Not today. Because it takes a terrible surprise to make a body cry. And nothing seems terrible anymore because nothing seems surprising. Maybe in that century just gone a little bit of Jew has crept into us all. Now Grandfather Gailey strode briskly round the dusty glass showcase and stared down at his old friend.

Sol, he said, laying his hand on his shoulder, you look like Death eatin a cracker. What has happened?

The old Jew, after a moment's pause, fumbled in the pocket of his black alpaca coat and pulled out a well-thumbed envelope with a foreign stamp. He smiled tremulously up at Grandfather Gailey.

Its all over, he said. Hitler has finished them. This— a letter telling of it. From my cousin in Cracow.

Finished who, Sol?

My wife, my three sons, my daughter, my sister, and

my father. And right on the eve of their getting visas to flee to Mexico. And there to wait for admission to this country.

Where are they now? Grandfather Gailey asked softly.

Auschwitz, Mister Schkloven said. Since two months ago.

I know that town! thundered Grandfather Gailey. Six miles east of Webster Springs. Orneriest village since Sodom or Gomorrah! That's where the Harberts live. That gal of theirs, Pearl—who claimed she'd been raped!

Mister Schkloven smiled.

I think I believe you when you say you know Auschwitz, he said. That you have been there.

Did I ever lie to you, old friend?

Mister Schkloven shook his head.

Are they there now? asked Grandfather Gailey. If they are Ill go into the Court House first thing tomorrow mornin and see Franklin Roosevelt personal. Hell get them out!

Mister Schkloven rose from his wicker chair, quivering, fists clenched, furious.

No, he said. By now they are in the soap dish of some SS man!

Know them, too! shouted Grandfather Gailey. Worse than the Klan. SS. Abbreviation for—excuse me, boy snot-nosed snivellers!

Mister Schkloven raised his furious eyes to the dusty ceiling. He shook his fist.

Ah, God, God! he cried. You old Soap-Maker!

No, snapped Grandfather Gailey. God never done it. It was them damn S and S men.

Yes, sighed Mister Schkloven. To them—and six million more.

Six million more what? cried Grandfather Gailey. Not people! Why, Lord, man. Add up all the people in the world I acknowledge exists—Marion, Taylor, Barbour, Lewis, Webster—damn them!—Doddridge and Harrison Counties and Wetzel to top off the others—and I dont allow youd count more than two hundred thousand heads. Now who is them six million others you mentioned?

Mister Schkloven smiled.

How I envy you, he said. Your little world. The world I know is so large—so terrible. How I wish I could believe in your little world of eight counties.

Well, where else is there? Grandfather Gailey asked, as reasonable as you could want. They tell you there's a round earth populous with eight billion people. But they lie. There is no New York. Berlin is a mirage. Paris a vision. Auschwitz a chimera. There is no world bigger than a man's own patch. Do you reckon soldiers would go out and die for colored lies in a school geography? No. A man dies as my uncle died at Second Manassas—for a world no bigger than he could walk to the end of. Maybe he died just for his dooryard. Countries can never be made hallowed enough to die for without lies to drug a man's will. But backyards can!

Mister Schkloven looked considerably revived.

Yes, he said. Yes, I think I believe you now. A child struck dead like one last week on a street corner and that street corner is for a few minutes all the world there is. Thank you, dear friend, for teaching me that. Though —as a Jew—I should know it all too well.

Then Grandfather Gailey made a request that scared me some.

Have you got a drink handy, Sol? he asked.

A little slivovitz, the old Jew chuckled. Not perhaps to your New World taste.

It will be fine, Grandfather Gailey said. I took the pledge the last time William Jennings Bryan spoke at the campground. But tonight my wits need a little honin of their cuttin edge. Sos I can ponder on what must be done.

What must be done? asked Mister Schkloven, fetching the fancy bottle of the liqueur and two little fragile glasses.

Why, sure! Since nobody else seems to be liftin a finger its left to me! cried Grandfather Gailey. This damned fiend. I've got to stop him!

You mean—stop Hitler?

Grandfather Gailey snorted.

Well you dont see the State Police liftin a finger, he shouted. The Sheriff still goes to cockfights and gets drunk every Friday night. He aint swore out no warrant that I heard tell of. And if Hitler done what you said he done to all your family—well, good Lord man, do I have to spell it out for you? This here is April 28th, 1945. Like as not him and a pack of rapscallions worse than him are already on their way up Canaan Valley to take Harrison County in the next twenty-four hours!

But the old Jew had lapsed again into the huge and terrible world of his own, and had—for the moment— let the firefly wonder of Grandfather Gailey's littler one flee through his fingers.

Belsen, he recited mournfully. Orianenberg. Buchenwald, Dachau.

Webster County names if ever I heard them! shouted Grandfather Gailey. Crazy, I tell you, all of them. And derned if I dont seem to recollect a Hitler family up there back in the shadows of time.

Mister Schkloven came round the glass showcase and embraced Grandfather Gailey, pressing his cheek against his shoulder.

Old friend, you are right, he murmured. The world is here. The world is only eight counties of this state. In fact, there is no state—no nation—no other continents. Only the land a man can walk its distance from one end to the other. Only the horizon a man can see to. Perhaps only a cool place under an old apple tree in his dooryard where he can sit after supper and drink iced tea with a little mint and ponder the world that is: that world above—those many worlds behind the new spring moon and the stars of this April night—washed clean and glistening by the melted snows of hideous winters. Thank you again, old friend, for teaching an old shmegegeh of a Jew what he should have known himself. That the world is only the all of a man's seven counties. And perhaps only his dooryard.

Eight counties, corrected Grandfather Gailey. Includin Harrison.

Now he had stopped smiling and was all business.

Now to the job at hand, he said.

157

What job?

Grandfather was searching around in the shadowy deeps of the glass showcase.

There, he said. That will do nicely—that fifty-caliber sixteen-shot Winchester Henry 1860 repeating rifle you got down in all that junk yonder.

But that, cried Mister Schkloven, it is an antique! I doubt if it even will fire. When old Doctor Bruce died his wife sold it to me. He had carried it in the Stonewall Brigade in 1864.

It will work, Grandfather Gailey said confidently. I know them guns. My own Daddy had one. Also in the Stonewall brigade. Things was made to last in them days—not cheapjack trash like they sell today.

But Mister Schkloven was lost in revery. He did not even hear Grandfather Gailey. He was deep in the ponderings of what Grandfather had brought back to his spirit that night.

Yes yes yes, he was whispering, to himself and not to us. When I was a child, in Vilna, I knew the world was only seven counties wide. But one night in the huggermugger of a Cossack pogrom I ran with the others for my life -and that knowing got trampled beneath the hooves of Cossack steeds. And now tonight—he has brought it back! That knowing.

Come, man, come! snapped Grandfather Gailey. How much for that Winchester Henry? Plus two boxes of cartridges?

For you, said the old Jew, lifting the beautiful weapon from its case and laying it on the little square of velvet atop the showcase glass. For you—I cannot take a copper less than a hundred rubles.

Rubles? grumbled Grandfather Gailey. That sounds like Webster County money. Wouldnt soil my snap purse with it!

I know you do not have it, said Mister Schkloven. That is why I asked it of you. To get to the point—the rifle is a gift.

Grandfather Gailey pondered.

Fair enough, I think, he said. Since there is some personal risk to me. And I am going to get him alone.

Where? To Berchtesgaden? asked the old man rue-fully.

No, said Grandfather Gailey. Though I know well where its at. Just a few miles southeast of Black Water Falls. No, I'm headin for Webster Springs. And beard the lion in his lair!

Mister Schkloven's eyes shone now with first tears as he stared into Grandfather Gailey's face, his own face full of wonderment and curiosity.

But why? he asked. Why do you put yourself in mortal danger because of a man who has had made of all those he loved on earth a few bars of soap? I know the vendetta feeling of your people. But I am no kin of yours.

Grandfather Gailey smiled and shook his head.

Then you do not understand the word, Sol, he said. There is kith kin and there is care kin. And you, sir, are care kin.

But how will you get to—to Hitler? asked the old Jew.

Grandfather Gailey beamed with pride.

Back in nineteen and eighteen I bought me a Model T Ford, he said. Its got no more than a hundred miles on it. Not a scratch on it. Ive kept it polished and waxed ever since the morning I bought it. Kept it covered in the barn with blankets and old quilts. Its new as the day I bought it. Needs a new battery. And a tank full of gas. And then I'm on my way to nail that son of a bitch, since nobody else seems to care. And I vow to you in the presence of God and this boy here, my friend, that by tomorrow night—April 29th 19 and 45—Hitler shall plague us no more!

And with that he seized my small hand in his bigger one and led the way out into the night and we began the long walk back home to Flinderation. I didnt sleep a wink that night, listening to the tread of Grandfather Gailey's boots angrily pacing his bedroom carpet. Lord, how I wanted to go along that morning. For I knew it was to be the end of Hitler. Grandfather was a lot of queer things but he was no Ananias. And I knew it was going to be a case of root hog or die, and I was ready to die. But I slept till eight that morning. And by six A.M. Grandfather Gailey was long gone.

Since he had smashed up our table Philco we never got no news that day. And it seemed the longest day in the world. Mama was grumbling around the house because, without any radio anymore, she had to miss Ma Perkins, Pepper Young's Family, and Vic and Sade: her favorite shows. And I think she had begun to feel that—with this latest venture—Grandfather Gailey's mind had finally snapped and she and Pa would have to have him certified and sent off to Weston Asylum. And Id rather see him dead than that. Daughter of his loins though she was, Mama was as different from him as night from day. She was practical, literal. For example, there was the day she went into the Empire Bank to cash our relief check and signed her name Louella Fowler. The bank man stared at her.

Louella, he said. This endorsement is wrong. Your name is Flowers.

Not anymore, she said.

Louella, said the bank man gently. Ive knowed your family all your life. What makes you think your name is Fowler all of a sudden? How come it aint Flowers no more?

Because, Mama said stubbornly. We sent to Sears Roebuck for three union suits and a pair of golashes for Father last month. And the package it come addressed Mister Gailey Fowler.

And so?

Well, said Mama, I just figure that a company big as Sears and Roebuck out to know.

That was Mama for you. That was why I was afraid shed do something rash like calling the Sheriff and the County Doctor to come and fetch Grandfather Gailey away that night when he showed up about a quarter to midnight. Pa came out of doors with a carbide lamp and we could see how tired Grandfather Gailey's face was. We could see something else: the look of that once sparkling Model T that now looked like it had been clean around the world. And maybe it had. Almost. Because aside from the mud caked all over it there was something

160

else that made the little hairs stand up on the back of my neck. On the headlights and bumper there was seaweed. And on the running board there was sand that couldn't have come from nowhere but an ocean.

I got him! Grandfather Gailey cried, rallying himself now and jumping out of his Model T. Nailed him like a sheep-killin dog. And nailed a few that was flanked round him to guard against such as me. They never stood a chance.

He sighed wearily.

Though I vow I never realized how far it was to Webster Springs—nor how big that whole county really is.

He grinned and patted me on the shoulder.

But I nailed him! he cried. Hitler is no more!

In the timber? I asked. In his cabin? Where, Grandfather?

Why neither, he said. It was queer. But no idea one of them ornery bastards from Webster County can think up ever surprises me. The idea of it!

What idea, Father, asked Mama, helping him up on the porch, for he was faltering a little now.

He was holed up like a groundhog or a hibernatin bear, Grandfather Gailey said. In a kind of underground cell. All concrete. Lots of rooms. Little ones. Not much furniture. A kind of—well, boy . . .

And he grinned at me.

Youre the dictionary expert, he said. What would you call it?

A concrete bunker, I said—but I didnt get it from my library dictionary; I had been in the press room of the *Clarksburg Exponent* when the news flash come in on the big paper roll in the AP machine.

Thats the word, Grandfather Gailey said. Thats it. Lord, its good to have someone eddicated around the house.

I was hardly aware of it, but there were others in the room by now: the Sheriff and two deputies from the County Court House. And behind them, on the threshold, like he didnt really believe he had a right to be there—Mister Schkloven. He was the one who had

161

helped push Grandfather Gailey's Model T the last hundred yards up the muddy spring-rained road to our place. His hands were covered with mud. Mama looked at him and smiled.

Want to wash up, Mister Schkloven? she asked brightly. Theres the bathroom down the hall. And theres clean towels. And soap.

Mister Schkloven smiled.

Yes, he said. For the hot water I thank you. For the clean towels I thank you. But please, no soap. I have a certain—certain—aversion to soap.

You all doubt me! roared Grandfather Gailey, struggling up on his elbows in the bed. You think I didn't blast my way into that underground bunker and kill that Webster County ogre and his guards. You think I made it up!

No, Father, we believe you, Ma said, with no conviction in her voice, humoring him—and this just made my blood boil.

I didnt kill his girl, Grandfather said then, and the hairs stood up on the back of my neck again.

No, he said again. I pities her. For she was in his thrall. Hypnotized by all the evil in him. And she was a pretty little thing like you see around the mine towns and smelters and mills. Polack. Rooshian. Maybe Austrian. Hair done up like them braided loaves of glistenin bread you see in the winders of Hunkie bakeshops. Couldnt have been no Webster County gal—too kindly-faced for that. I allow hed kidnapped her from around one of them milltowns between Glory and Wheelin—.

Father, Mama said a little sarcastically. You always told us there wasnt no such a place as Wheeling. And its well beyond the eight counties you claim as God's whole world.

Grandfather Gailey paused, pondered, his face troubled.

Maybe I been wrong, he whispered, growing weaker by the minute. I swear today it seems like I went five thousand miles. I swear today its come close to makin me doubt my lifelong belief that there aint no world but

162

the world a man can walk from one to the other without wearyin himself.

No! cried out Mister Schkloven, pushing forward then amongst us by the bed. No, you must never doubt that. That little patch of land is all the world any man has - has ever had—will ever have—and can ever love. All the rest is what they call Patriotism, and it is a lie and mated with Greed. It is the mother of all wars!

You are right, Sol, he said. I was just testin your own faith. I see Ive won you over at last.

And with that—at the very moment Doctor Kemper from the County Health Department stepped through the doorway—Grandfather Gailey fell back, smiling, and died. He did it quick, like he did everything. Like, I reckon, he did in Hitler. Mama covered her face with her apron and commenced crying. Doctor Kemper spent a good ten minutes examining Grandfather Gailey's body.

Why wasnt I called here sooner? he asked, turning to us.

Why, he just got in a half hour ago, I said. We called you three times but the party line was tied up with folks gossiping about the end of the War, and it took twenty minutes to get you. He just got in no more than half an hour ago.

Somethings mighty fishy agoin on around here, said the Doctor. Someones pullin my leg and I dont like it one bit!

Whatcha mean, Doc? Mama asked, stifling her tears for a spell.

You say Mister Flowers came in half an hour ago, he said. And that cannot be.

Why? whispered Mama.

Because I have examined his body carefully, said Doctor Kemper. And—putting it conservatively—I estimate him to have died no less than forty-eight hours ago.

I wasnt surprised. I was beyond surprise now. I was busy, whilst all their backs was turned to me, going through the pockets of Grandfather Gailey's clothes, which Mama had laid carefully on the hair trunk across the room when she had undressed him and gotten him to bed. He never went anywhere—Grandfather Gailey didnt

163

without bringing me home a present. A souvenir. And he hadnt failed me this time. I found it. In the pocket of his alpaca frock coat. A carved silver frame with a snapshot in it of a sad-faced pretty blonde-haired girl just like Grandfather Gailey had said—one of them kind you see around the steel mill towns and mine patches near Wheeling. And there was writing on it. And whilst they was all palavering over Grandfather Gailey's remains and arguing how a man could be dead forty-eight hours and have drove to Webster County and back that past nineteen hours, Mister Schkloven was the only one who saw me at my ruthless plundering. He smiled and went to the open window and stood, staring out at the curl of April moon and the spring galaxies a million lives above us. He took the silver-framed picture from my hands cautiously, slowly, as if it might explode in his hands.

It has writing, I said. What does it say?

He smiled.

It is in German, he said. It is proof.

But what does it say, Mister Schkloven?

Fur mein liebchen—, he read. For my loved one.

And its signed. A lady's name, I said.

Eva, he said and handed the little framed picture back to me.

Eva who?

He did not answer. He was absorbed, almost held as if by a lodestone beneath that sickle of new moon, the April stars, and their sweet counterfeits: the fireflies streaking the dark.

He turned to me then, his face very solemn. He was not smiling. Yet there was peace in his eyes.

The world, he said. He was right. It is only eight counties. Anywhere. And yet billions abide upon it. And endure. But the better world, it is out there in the night beyond his old Baldwin apple tree the world beyond that tree, beyond the new moon now tangled in its flowering branches.

He had handed me back the framed picture. He looked at his fingers in distress.

My hands, he said. The mud I do not mind. But I

164

see on them now blood. Your mother—she said there was a bathroom?

He looked pale, sickened.

Blood, he said. The mud I do not mind . . . But blood. Where is the bathroom? Quickly, young man. It is making me ill. And perhaps like in that play, the blood will not wash off. Macbeth. The bathroom, young man. Which way? Quickly.

Down the hall, I said, troubled as he.

He went swiftly to the threshold, stopped, turned, and smiled at me.

There is hot water?

Sure.

And fresh clean towels?

Sure.

He turned then, disappearing from my vision but still talking, though now to himself and not to me.

And the soap, he said. Yes, now I can use the soap.

THE COMPANION
by
Ramsey Campbell

THE COMPANION

RAMSEY CAMPBELL is one of the most brilliant of the younger writers of supernatural terror stories. His first book appeared when he was but eighteen, and since then he has swiftly established himself as one of the fine new exponents of the strange story, employing psychological insight into people and their fears and carrying the supernatural into fresh settings in the contemporary world. His collection Demons by Daylight *aroused a remarkably favorable press, though putting off some readers who prefer their horror stories restricted to more traditional avenues. His soon-to-appear new book of stories from Arkham House,* The Height of the Scream, *will doubtless stir opinions more, as may his first novel, which goes by the suitably sinister title* The Doll Who Ate His Mother.

Carnivals and amusement parks have long exerted a fascination for writers of uncanny stories. Campbell, too, is obviously under the spell, and herewith offers his exploration into a milieu that seems perched on the border somewhere between fantasy and reality.

When Stone reached the fairground, having been misdirected twice, he thought it looked more like a gigantic amusement arcade. A couple of paper cups tumbled and rattled on the shore beneath the promenade, and the cold insinuating October wind scooped the Mersey across the slabs of red rock that formed the beach and over the tyres and broken bottles. Beneath the stubby white mock turrets of the long fairground facade were tucked souvenir shops and fish and chips; among them, in the fairground entrances, scraps of paper whirled.

Stone almost walked away. This wasn't his best holiday. One fairground in Wales had been closed, and this· one certainly wasn't what he'd expected. The guidebook had made it sound like a genuine fairground, sideshows you must stride among not looking in case their barkers lured you in, the sudden shock of waterfalls cascading down what looked like painted cardboard, the familiar sensations which were almost always there and for which welcome surged through him: the shots and bells and wooden concussions of sideshows, the girls' shrieks overhead, the slippery armour and juicy crunch of toffee-apples, the illuminations springing alight against a darkening sky. But at least, he thought, he had chosen his time well. Few people were about, and if he went in now he might have the funfair almost to himself.

As he approached an entrance, he saw his mother eating fish and chips from a paper tray in the shop. No, rubbish. Besides, she would never have eaten standing up in public—"like a horse," as she used to say. As he passed the shop she hurried onto the promenade, face averted from him and the wind. He picked at the image gingerly, anxious not to awaken its implications. Of course, it had been the way she ate, with little snatching motions of her fork and mouth. He pushed the incident to the side of his mind in the hope that it would fall away, and hurried through the entrance.

Noise and colour collided with him. Beneath the iron girders of a roof like that of a railway station the sirens and simulated whistling jets and groaning metal and gnashing gears fused with their echoes in a single, roaring, almost indistinguishable mass of sound, while panels of illuminated plastic, bright pink, pale green, sour orange, and yellow, spun and changed and fluttered on Stone's eyes. He retreated a step. Then, since none of the sensations diminished and he would have had to turn and run to reduce them, he strode forward.

Once he'd adjusted to its excesses the fairground looked and felt dusty. The machines—a great disc rimmed with seats that lifted roofward and tilted on its axis as it spun, dangling a lone couple over its gears; an Ouroboros of seats that undulated brutally and trapped its passengers beneath a canvas canopy; a kind of roundabout whose independently rotating seats were given sudden violent jerks and spun helplessly—seemed grimy, as if just removed from a cupboard where they'd been left for years. With so few people in sight it seemed almost that the machines, frustrated by inaction, were operating themselves. For a moment Stone had the impression of being shut in a dusty room where the toys, as in childhood tales, had come to life.

He shrugged vaguely and turned to leave. He wondered whether he had time to drive to the fairground at Southport; it was a good few miles across the Mersey. His holiday was dwindling rapidly. He wondered how they were managing at the tax office this year in his absence. Slower as usual, no doubt.

Then he saw the roundabout. It was like a toy forgotten by another child and left here, or handed down the generations. Beneath its ornate scrolled canopy the horses rode on poles toward their reflexions in a ring of mirrors. The horses were white wood or wood painted white, their bodies dappled with purple, red, and green, and some of their sketched faces, too. From the hub, above a large notice MADE IN AMSTERDAM, an organ piped to itself. On the hub Stone saw carved fish, mermen, zephyrs, a head and shoulders smoking a pipe in a frame, a landscape of hills and lake and unfurling perched hawk. "Oh, yes," Stone said.

He clambered onto the platform. He felt a hint of embarrassment and glanced about, but nobody was watching. "Can you pay me," said the head in the frame. "My boy's gone for a minute."

The man's hair was the colour of the smoke from his pipe, and his lips puckered on the stem and smiled. "It's a good roundabout," Stone said.

"You know about them, do you?"

"Well, a little." The man looked disappointed; Stone hurried on. "I know a good deal about fairgrounds. They're my holiday, you see, every year. Each year I cover a different area. I may write a book." At least the idea had occasionally tempted him; but he hadn't taken notes, and he had ten years to retirement, for which the book had suggested itself as an activity.

"You go alone every year?"

"It has its merits. Less expensive, for one thing. I'm saving. Before I retire I intend to see Disneyland and Vienna." He thought of the Big Wheel, Harry Lime, the earth falling away beneath. "I'll get on," he said.

He patted the unyielding shoulders of the horse beneath him. He remembered a childhood friend who'd had a rocking horse in his bedroom. Stone had ridden it a few times, more and more wildly as the time to go home approached; his friend's bedroom was brighter and better lit than his, and as he clung to the wooden shoulders he was clutching the friendly room, too. Funny thinking of that now, he thought. Because I haven't been on a real roundabout for years, I suppose.

The roundabout shifted and the horse rose, bearing him, and sank. As they moved forward, slowly gathering momentum, Stone saw a crowd surging through one of the entrances and spreading through the funfair. He grimaced: it had been his fairground for a while, they needn't have arrived just as he was enjoying his roundabout.

The crowd swung away. A jangle of pinball machines sailed by. Amid the dodgems a giant with a barrel body spun, limp arms flapping, a red electric cigar thrust in its blankly grinning face and throbbing like an arrested balloon of slow thick laughter. A tinny voice read Bingo numbers, buzzing indistinctly. The roundabout was rotating faster; the fairground flashed on Stone's eyes like the images of a thaumatrope. Perhaps it was because he hadn't eaten for a while, saving himself for the toffee-apples, but he was becoming dizzy. It felt like the whirling, blurring shot of the fair in *Saturday Night and Sunday Morning*, a fair he hadn't liked because it was too grim. Give him *Strangers on a Train, The Third Man, Some Came Running*, even the fairground murder in *Horrors of the Black Museum*. He shook his head to try to control his pouring thoughts.

A howling wind mixed with screams whipped by. It was looped on a tape inside the Ghost Train. The roundabout completed a quickening turn, and Stone's eyes fixed for a moment on the crowd standing beneath the beckoning green corpse. They were staring at him. No, he realized the next time they came round, they were staring at the roundabout. He was just something that kept reappearing as they watched. At the back of the crowd, staring and poking around inside his nostrils, stood Stone's father.

Stone gripped the horse's neck as he began to fall. The man had already been incorporated into the retreating crowd. Why was his mind so traitorous today? It wouldn't be so bad if the comparisions it was making weren't so repulsive. Why, he'd never met a man or woman since his parents to compare with them. Admired people, yes, but not in the same way. Not since the two polished boxes had been lowered into holes and hidden. Noise and colour spun about him and inside him. Why wasn't he allowing himself to think about his parents' death? He knew why he was blocking, and that should be his sal-

172

vation. At the age of ten he'd suffered death and hell every night.

The memories tumbled over him as he clung to the wood in the whirlpool. His father had denied him a nightlight and his mother had nodded, saying "Yes, I think it's time." He'd lain in bed, terrified to move in case he betrayed his presence to the darkness, mouthing "Please God don't let it" over and over. He lay so that he could see the faint grey rectangle of the window between the parted curtains in the far distance, but even that light seemed to be receding. He knew that death and hell would be like this. Sometimes, as he began to blur with sleep and the room grew larger and the shapes dark against the darkness awoke, he couldn't tell that he hadn't already died.

He sat back as the horse slowed and he began to slip forward across its neck. What then? Well, of course he'd seen through the self-perpetuating trap of religious guilt, of hell, of not daring not to believe in it because then it would get you. For a while he'd been vaguely uneasy in dark places, but not sufficiently so to track down the feeling and conquer it. After a while it had dissipated, along with his parents' overt disapproval of his atheism. Yes, he thought as his memories and the round-about slowed, I was happiest then, lying in bed hearing them, no, feeling them and the house around me. Then, when he was thirty, a telephone call had summoned him to the hole in the road. There had been a moment of sheer vertiginous terror at the sight of the car like a black beetle thrust nose first into the hole and suffocated. Then it was over. His parents had gone into darkness. That was enough. It was the one almost religious observance he imposed upon himself. Think no more.

And there was no reason to do so now. He staggered away from the roundabout, toward the pinball arcade that occupied most of one side of the funfair. He remembered how, when he lay mouthing soundless pleas in bed, he would sometimes stop and think of what he'd read about dreams: that they might last for hours but in reality occupied only a split second. Was the same true of thoughts? And prayers, when you had nothing but

173

darkness by which to tell the time? Besides defending him, his prayers were counting off the moments before dawn. Perhaps he had used up only a minute, only a second of darkness. Death and hell. What strange ideas I used to have, he thought. Especially for a ten-year-old. I wonder where they went. Away to be replaced by my ability with figures, of course.

Three boys of about twelve were crowded around a pinball machine. As the screen of their bodies parted for a moment he saw that they were trying to trigger it with a coin on a piece of wire. He took a stride toward them and opened his mouth, but restrained the sound. Everyone in the funfair must be half-deafened; if the boys set about him, pulled him down, and kicked him, his shouts wouldn't be heard. There was no sign of an attendant. Stone hurried back to the roundabout. Several little girls were mounting horses. Well, let them, he'd finished with it. "Those boys are up to no good," he said to the man in the frame.

"You! Yes, you! I've seen you before. Don't let me see you again," the man shouted. They dispersed, swaggering.

"It didn't used to be like this," Stone said, breathing hard with relief. "I suppose your roundabout is all that's left of the old fairground."

"The old one?" the man said. "No, this didn't come from there."

"I thought the old one must have been taken over by this."

"No, it's still there, what's left of it," the man said. "You want to see it? Through that exit and just keep going. You'll come to the side entrance in five minutes, if it's still open."

The moon had risen. It glided along the rooftops as Stone emerged from the back of the funfair and hurried along the terraced street. Its light lingered on the tips of chimneys and on the highest edges of the roofs. Inside the houses, above slivers of earth or stone between the street and the buildings, Stone saw faces silvered by television.

He reached the end of the street. Opposite, across a

174

wider road, an alley paralled a side street. Just keep going. Avoiding the alley and its connotations of someone else's domestic familiarity, Stone made for the street. As he entered it he glimpsed a group of boys emerging from the street he'd just left and running into the alley.

Anxiety impelled him as he wondered whether to turn back. His car was on the promenade; he could reach it in five minutes. They must be the boys he had seen in the pinball arcade, out for revenge. Quite possibly they had knives or broken bottles; no doubt they knew how to use them from the television. His heels clacked in the silence. Exits from the alley gaped between the houses. He tried to set his feet down gently as he ran. The boys were making no sound at all, at least none that reached him. If they managed to overbalance him they could smash his bones while he struggled to rise. At his age that could be worse than dangerous. He passed another dark exit. The houses looked threatening in their weight and impassivity. He must stay on his feet whatever happened. If two of them got hold of his arms he could only shout and yell. The houses leapt away as the street bent at a corner, and their opposite numbers loomed closer. In front of him, beyond a wall of corrugated tin, lay the old fairground.

He halted panting, trying to quell his breath before it blotted out any sounds in the alley. Where he had hoped to find a well-lit road to the promenade, both sides of the street ended as if lopped, and the way was blocked by the wall of tin. In the middle, however, the tin had been prised back like a lid, and a jagged entrance gaped among the sharp shadows and moonlit inscriptions. The fairground was closed and deserted.

As he realized that the last exit from the alley was back beyond the corner of the street, Stone stepped through the gap in the tin. He stared down the street, which was empty of pursuit, in fact of everything except scattered fragments of brick and glass. It occurred to him that they might not have been the same boys after all. He pulled the tin to behind him and looked around.

The circular booths, the long target galleries, the low roller coaster, the ark and crazy house draped shadow over each other and merged with the colour of the paths between. Even the roundabout was hooded by darkness hanging from its canopy. Such wood as he could see in the moonlight looked ragged, the paint patchy. But between the silent machines and stalls one ride was faintly illuminated: The Ghost Train.

He walked toward it. Its front was emitting a pale green glow which at first sight looked like moonlight, but which was brighter than the white tinge the moon imparted to the adjoining rides. Stone could see one empty car on the rails, close to the entrance to the ride. As he approached, he glimpsed from the corner of his eye a group of men, stall-holders, presumably, talking and gesticulating in the shadows between two stalls. So the fairground wasn't entirely deserted. He hurried toward the Ghost Train. They might be about to close, but perhaps they would allow him one ride, seeing that the Ghost Train was still lit. He hoped they hadn't seen him using the vandals' entrance.

As he reached the ride and realized that the glow came from a coat of luminous paint, liberally applied but now rather dull and threadbare, he heard a loud clang from the tin wall. It might have been someone throwing a brick, or it might have been the reopening of the torn door; the stalls obstructed his view. His gaze darted about for another exit but found none. He might run into a dead end. It was best to stay where he was. He couldn't trust the stall-holders; they might live nearby, they might know the boys or even be their parents. As a child he'd once run to someone who had proved to be his attacker's unhelpful father. He climbed into the Ghost Train car.

Nothing happened. Nobody was attending the ride. Stone strained his ears. Neither the boys, if they were there, nor the attendant seemed to be approaching. If he called out the boys would hear him. Instead, frustrated and furious, he began to kick the metal inside the nose of the car.

Immediately the car trundled forward over the lip of an incline in the track and plunged through the Ghost Train doors into darkness.

176

As he swung round an unseen clattering c[...]
rounded by noise and darkness, Stone felt as i[...]
suddenly become the victim of delirium. He reme[...]
his storm-wracked childhood bed and the teeming[...]
ness pouring into him. Why on earth had he come on
this ride? He'd never liked ghost trains as a child, and
as he grew up had instinctively avoided them. He'd
allowed his panic to trap him. The boys might be waiting
when he emerged. Well, in that case he would appeal
to whoever was operating the ride. He sat back, gripping
the wooden seat beneath him with both hands, and
gave himself up to the straining, the abrupt swoops of
the car, and the darkness.

Then, as his anxiety about the outcome of the ride
diminished, another impression began to trickle back.
As the car had swung round the first curve he had
glimpsed an illuminated shape, two illuminated shapes,
withdrawn so swiftly that he'd had no time to glance up
at them. He had the impression that they had been the
faces of a man and a woman, gazing down at him. At
once they had vanished into the darkness or been swept
away by it. It seemed to him for some reason very
important to remember their expressions.

Before he could pursue this, however, he saw a grey-
ish glow ahead of him. He felt an unreasoning hope that
it would be a window, which might give him an idea of
the extent of the darkness. But already he could see that
its shape was too irregular. A little closer and he could
make it out. It was a large stuffed grey rabbit with huge
glass or plastic eyes, squatting upright in an alcove
with its front paws extended before it. Not a dead rabbit,
of course: a toy. Beneath him the car was clattering and
shaking, yet he had the odd conviction that this was a
deliberate effect, that in fact the car had halted and the
rabbit was approaching or growing. Rubbish, he thought.
It was a pretty feeble ghost, anyway. Childish. His
hands pulled at splinters on the wooden seat. The rabbit
rushed toward him as the track descended a slight slope.
One of its eyes was loose, and white stuffing hung down
its cheek from the hole. The rabbit was at least four feet
tall. As the car almost collided with it before whipping

ound a curve, the rabbit toppled toward him and the light which illuminated it went out.

Stone gasped and clutched his chest. He'd twisted round to look behind him at the darkness where he judged the rabbit to have been, until a spasm wrenched him frontward again. Light tickling drifted over his face. He shuddered, then relaxed. Of course they always had threads hanging down for cobwebs, his friends had told him that. But no wonder the fairground was deserted, if this was the best they could do. Giant toys lit up, indeed. Not only cheap, but liable to give children nightmares.

The car coursed up a slight incline and down again before shaking itself in a frenzy around several curves. Trying to soften you up before the next shock, Stone thought. Not me, thank you. He lay back in his seat and sighed loudly with boredom. The sound hung on his ears like muffs. Why did I do that? he wondered. It's not as if the operator can hear me. Then who can?

Having spent its energy on the curves, the car was slowing. Stone peered ahead, trying to anticipate. Obviously he was meant to relax before the car startled him with a sudden jerk. As he peered, he found his eyes were adjusting to the darkness. At least he could make out a few feet ahead, at the side of the track, a squat and bulky grey shape. He squinted as the car coasted toward it. It was a large armchair.

The car came abreast of it and halted. Stone peered at the chair. In the dim hectic flecked light, which seemed to attract and outline all the restless discs on his eyes, the chair somehow looked larger than he. Perhaps it was further away than he'd thought. Some clothes thrown over the back of the chair looked diminished by it, but they could be a child's clothes. If nothing else, Stone thought, it's instructive to watch my mind working. Now let's get on.

Then he noticed that the almost invisible light was flickering. Either that, which was possible although he couldn't determine the source of the light, or the clothes were shifting; very gradually but nonetheless definitely, as if something hidden by them on the seat of the chair were lifting them to peer out, perhaps preparatory to

178

emerging. Stone leaned toward the chair. Let's see what it is, let's get it over with. But the light was far too dim and the chair too distant. Probably he would be unable to see it even when it emerged, the way the light had been allowed to run down, unless he left the car and went closer.

He had one hand on the side of the car when he realized that if the car moved off while he was out of it he would be left to grope his way through the darkness. He slumped back and at that moment glimpsed a violent movement among the clothes near the seat of the chair. He glanced toward it. Before his eyes could focus, the dim grey light was extinguished.

Stone sat for a moment, all of him concentrating on the silence, the blind darkness. Then he began to kick frantically at the nose of the car. The car shook a little with his attack, then jerked forward.

When the car nosed its way around the next curve, slowing as if sniffing the track ahead, and the clacking and rumbling had ceased, Stone heard a muted thud and creak of wood. It came from in front of him. The sort of thing you hear in a house at night, he thought. Soon be out now.

Without warning a face came speeding toward him out of the darkness a few feet ahead. It jerked forward as he did. Of course it would, he thought with a grimace, sinking back and watching his face recede briefly in the mirror. He realized that he and the car were surrounded by a faint light which extended as far as the wooden frame of the mirror. Must be the end of the ride. They can't get any more obvious than that. Effective in its way, I suppose.

He watched himself in the mirror as the car followed the curve past. The light had fallen behind, but his silhouette loomed on it. Suddenly he frowned. His silhouette was moving independent of the movement of the car. It was beginning to swing out of the limits of the mirror. Then he remembered the wardrobe which had stood at the foot of the bed in his childhood, and understood. The mirror was set into a door, which was opening.

Stone pressed himself against the opposite side of the car, which had slowed almost to a halt. No no, he thought, it mustn't. Don't. He heard a grinding of gears beneath him. Unmeshed metal shrieked. He threw his body forward against the nose of the car. In the darkness to his left he heard the creak of the door and a soft thud. The car moved a little, then caught the gears and ground forward.

As the light went out behind him, Stone felt a weight fall beside him on the seat.

He cried out. Or tried to, for as he gulped in air it seemed to draw darkness into his lungs, darkness that swelled and poured into his heart and brain. There was a moment at which he knew nothing, as if he'd become darkness and silence and the memory of suffering. Then the car was rattling on, the darkness was sweeping over him and by, and the nose of the car banged open the doors and plunged out into the night.

As the car swung into the length of track outside the Ghost Train, Stone caught sight of the gap between the stalls where he had thought he'd seen the stall-holders. A welling moonlight showed him that between the stalls stood a pile of sacks, nodding and gesticulating in the wind. Then the seat beside him emerged from the shadow, and he looked down.

Next to him on the seat was a shrunken hooded figure. It wore a faded jacket and trousers striped and patched in various colours, indistinguishable in the receding moonlight. The head almost reached his shoulder. Its arms hung slack at its sides, and its feet drummed laxly on the metal beneath the seat. Shrinking back, Stone reached for the front of the car to pull himself up, and the figure's head fell back.

Stone closed his eyes. When he opened them he saw within the hood an oval of white cloth upon which—black crosses for eyes and nose, a barred crescent for a mouth—a grinning face was stitched.

As he had suddenly realized that the car hadn't halted nor even slowed before plunging down the incline back into the Ghost Train, Stone did not immediately notice that the figure had taken his hand.

FIREFIGHT
by
David Drake

DAVID DRAKE is at present an assistant town attorney for Chapel Hill, North Carolina, where he located after finishing law school. To date Drake has had science fiction and fantasy stories published in Analog, Whispers, and Fantasy & Science Fiction, and in anthologies edited by Gordon R. Dickson and August Derleth. Most recently he has been writing a series of future war stories for Galaxy—extrapolated from his experiences as an Army interrogator in Vietnam—to be followed, he hopes, by a novel growing out of the series. The fascinating and scary story included here also reflects Drake's Vietnam period, in which the everyday horror of war is merged with another kind of terror.

"Christ," said Ginelli, staring out at the dusty wilderness from the top of the flame track, "if this's a sample, the next move'll be to hell. And a firebase there'd be cooler."

Herrold lit a cigarette and poked the pack toward his subordinate. "Have one," he suggested.

"Not unless it's grass," the fat newbie muttered. He flapped the sleeveless flak jacket away from his flesh, feeling streaks of momentary chill as sweat started from beneath the quilted nylon. "Christ, how d'you stand it?"

Herrold, rangy and big-jointed, leaned back in the dome seat and cocked one leg over the flamethrower's muzzle. Ginelli envied the track commander's build every time he looked at the taller man. His own basic training, only four months before, had been a ghastly round of extra physical training to sweat off pounds of his mother's pasta.

"Better get used to it," Herrold warned lazily. "This zippo always winds up at the back of the column, so we always wait to set up in the new laagers. Think about those—pretend you're a tree."

Ginelli followed his TC's finger toward the eight giant trees in the stone enclosure. It didn't help. Their tops reached a hundred feet into the air above the desolate plain, standing aloof from the activity that raised a pall of dust beside them. Their shadows pooled beneath could

183

not cool Ginelli as he squatted sun-dazzled on the aluminum deck of the flame truck.

At least Colonel Boyle was just as hot where he stood directing placements for other armored vehicles from the sandbagged deck of his own. Hieu stood beside him as usual. You could always recognize the interpreter at a distance because of the tiger fatigues he wore, darkly streaked with black and green. Below the two men, others were stringing the last of the tarpaulin passageways that joined the three command vehicles into a Tactical Operations Center. At night they could move between the blacked-out tracks; but the cool of the night seemed far away.

Boyle pointed from the roof and said something to Hieu. The dark-skinned interpreter's nod was emphatic; the colonel spoke into his neck-slung microphone and the two vehicles ahead of the flame track grunted into motion. Herrold straightened suddenly as his radio helmet burped at him. "Seven-zero, roger," he replied.

"We movin'?" Ginelli asked, leaning closer to the TC to hear him better. Herrold flipped the switch by his left ear forward to intercom and said, "Okay, Murray, they want us on the west side against that stone wall. They'll be a ground guide, so take it easy."

Murray edged the zippo forward, driving it clockwise around the circuit other tracked vehicles had clawed in the barren earth. Except for the grove within the roomy laterite enclosure, there was nothing growing closer than the rubber plantation whose rigid files marched green and silver a mile to the east. Low dikes, mostly fallen into the crumbling soil, ordered the wasteland. Dust plumed in the far distance as a motorbike pulled out of the rubber and turned toward the firebase. Coke girls already, Ginelli thought. Even in this desert.

Whatever the region's problem was, it couldn't have been with the soil itself; not if trees like the monsters behind the low wall could grow in it. Every one of the eight the massive stonework girdled was forty feet around at the base. The wrinkled bole of the central titan could have been half that again.

The flame track halted while a bridge tank roaded, churning the yielding dust as it maneuvered its frontal slope up to the coarse laterite. The ground guide, a bare-chested tanker with a beaded sweat band, dropped his arms to signal the bridge to shut down, then motioned the flame track in beside the greater bulk. Murray cut his engine and hoisted himself out of the driver's hatch.

Common sense and the colonel's orders required that everyone on a track be wearing helmet and flak jacket. Men like Murray, however, who extended their tours to four years, tended to ignore death and their officers when comfort was at stake. The driver was naked to the waist; bleached golden hairs stood out wire-like against his deep tan. "Dig out some beer, turtle," he said to Ginelli with easy arrogance. "We got time to down one before they start putting a detail together." Road dust had coated the stocky, powerful driver down to the throat, the height he projected from his hatch when the seat was raised and the cover swiveled back. Years of Vietnamese sunlight had washed all color from his once-blue eyes.

An assault vehicle pulled up to the zippo's right, its TC nonchalant in his cupola behind the fifty-caliber machine gun. To Ginelli's amazement, the motorbike he had seen leaving the rubber plantation was the next vehicle in line. It was a tiny green Sachs rather than one of the omnipresent Honda 50s, and its driver was Caucasian. Murray grinned and jumped to his feet. "Crozier! Jacques!" he shouted in delight. "What the hell are you doing here?"

The white-shirted civilian turned his bike neatly and tucked it in on the shady side of the flame truck. If any of the brass had noticed him, they made no sign. Dismounted, Crozier tilted his face up and swept his baseball cap away from a head of thinning hair. "Yes, I thought I might find you, Joe," he said. His English was slightly blurred. "But anyway, I would have come just to talk again to whites. It is grand to see you."

Herrold unlashed the shelter tarp from the load and let it thump over the side. "Let's get some shade up," he ordered.

"Jack was running a plantation for Michelin up north when we were in the A-Shau Valley," Murray explained.

"He's a good dude. But why you down here, man?"

"Oh, well," the Frenchman said with a deprecating shrug. "Your defoliation, you know? A few months after your squadron pulls out, the planes come over. Poof! Plantation 7 is dead and I must be transferred. They grow peanuts there now."

Herrold laughed. "That's the nice thing about a job in this country," he said. "Always something new to-morrow."

"Yeah, not so many VC here as up there," Murray agreed.

Crozier grimaced. "The VC I am able to live with. Like them? No. But I understand them, understand their . . . their aims. But these folk around here, these Mengs —they will not work, they will not talk, only glare at you and plant enough rice for themselves. Michelin must bring in Viets to work the rubber, and even those, they do not stay because they do not like Mengs so near."

"But they're all Vietnamese, aren't they?" Ginelli asked in puzzlement. "I mean, what else could they be?"

The Frenchman chuckled, hooking his thumbs in his trouser tops. "They live in Vietnam, so they are Viet-namese—no? But you Americans have your Indians. Here are the Montagnards, we call them; the Moun-taineers, you know? But the Vietnamese name for them means 'the dirty animals.' Not the same folk, no no. The Montagnards were here long before the Viets came down from the North. And the Meng who live here and a few other places, they are not the same either; not as the Viets or even the Montagnards. And perhaps they are older yet, so they say."

The group waited a moment in silence. Herrold opened the Mermite can that served as a cooler and began hand-ing out beer. "Got a churchkey?" he asked no one in particular. Murray, the only man on the track with a knife, drew his huge Bowie and chopped ragged triangles in the tops. Tepid beer gurgled as the four men drank. Ginelli set his can down.

"Umm," he said to his track commander, "how about the co-ax?"

Herrold sighed. "Yeah, we don't want the sonofabitch

to jam." Joints popped as he stood and stretched his long frame.

Crozier gulped the swig of beer still in his mouth. "Indeed not," he agreed. "Not here, especially. The area has a very bad reputation."

"That a fact?" Herrold asked in mild surprise. "At the troop meetin' last night the old man said around here it'd be pretty quiet. Not much activity on the intelligence maps."

"Activity?" the Frenchman repeated with raised eyebrows. "Who can say? The VC come through my laborers' hootches now and again, not so much here as near A-Shau, that is true. But when I first was transferred here three years ago, there were five, perhaps six hundred in the village—the Mengs, you know, not the plantation lines."

"That little place back where we left the hardball?" Ginelli wondered aloud. "Jeez, there's not a dozen hootches there."

"Quite so," Crozier agreed with a grave nod of his head. "Because a battalion of Communists surrounded it one night and killed every Meng they found. Perhaps twenty survived."

"Christ!" Ginelli breathed in horror, but Herrold's greater experience caused his eyes to narrow with curiosity. "Why the hell?" the tall track commander asked. "I mean, I know they've got hit squads out to gun down village cops and headmen and all. But why the whole place? Were the Mengs that strong for the government?"

"The government?" the civilian echoed; he laughed. "They spat at the district governor when he came through. But a week before the Communists came, there was firing near this very place. Communist, there is no doubt. I saw the tracers myself, and they were green—not red like yours.

"The rest—and this is rumor only, what my foremen told me at the time before they stopped talking about it a company, thirty men, were ambushed here, they said. Wiped out, every one of them, and mutilated, ah . . . badly. How the Communists decided that the Mengs were responsible, I do not know; but that could have

187

been the reason they came back to wipe out the village."

"Umm," Herrold grunted. He crumpled his beer can and looked for a litter barrel. "Lemme get on the horn and we'll see just how the co-ax is screwing up." The can clattered into the barrel as the TC swung up on the back deck of the zippo again. The others could hear his voice as he spoke into the microphone. "Battle five-six, track seven-zero. Request clearance to test-fire our Mike seven-four."

An unintelligible crackle replied from the headset a moment later. "No sir," Herrold denied, "not if we want it working tonight." He nodded at the answer. "Roger, roger." He waved. "Okay," he said to his crew as he set down the radio helmet, "let's see what it's doing."

Ginelli climbed up beside Herrold, slithering his pudgy body over the edge of the track with difficulty. Murray continued to lounge against the side of the vehicle. "Hell," he said, "I never much liked guns, anyway; you guys do your thing." Crozier stood beside his friend, interested but holding back a little from the delicacy of an uninvited guest. The machine gun had once been co-axial to the flamethrower. Now it turned on a swivel welded to the top of the cupola. Herrold rotated it, aiming at the huge tree in the center of the grove. A ten foot scar streaked the light trunk vertically to the ground, so he set the buckhorn sight just above it. Other troopers, warned by radio what to expect, were watching curiously.

The gun stuttered off a short burst and jammed. Empty brass tinkled off the right side of the vehicle. Herrold swore and clicked open the receiver cover. His screwdriver pried at the stuck case until it sprang free. Slamming the cover shut, he jacked another round into the chamber.

BAM BAM BAM BAM BAM

"God *damn* it," Herrold said. "Looks like we gotta take the whole thing down."

"Or throw rocks," Ginelli suggested.

Herrold cocked a rusty eyebrow. Unlike the heavy newbie, he had been in country long enough to have a feel for real danger. After a moment he grinned back. "Oh, we don't have to throw rocks," he said. He unslung

188

his old submachine gun from the side of the cupola. Twenty years' service had worn most of the finish off its crudely stamped metal, but it still looked squat and deadly. Herrold set the wire stock to his shoulder; the burst, when he squeezed off, was ear-shattering. A line of fiercely red tracers stabbed from the muzzle and ripped an ascending curve of splintered wood up the side of the center tree.

"Naw, we're okay while my old grease gun works," Herrold said. He laughed. "But," he added, "we better tear the co-ax down anyhow."

"Perhaps I should leave now," Crozier suggested. "It grows late and I must return to my duties."

"Hell," Murray protested, "stick around for chow at least. Your dinks'll do without babysittin' for that long."

The Frenchman pursed his lips. "He'll have to clear with the colonel," Herrold warned.

"No sweat," the driver insisted. "We'll snow him about all the local intelligence Jacques can give us. Come on, man; we'll brace him now." Crozier followed in Murray's forceful wake, an apprehensive frown still on his face.

"Say, where'd you get these?" Ginelli inquired, picking up a fat, red-nosed cartridge like those Herrold had just thumbed into his grease gun.

"The tracers?" the TC said absently. "Oh, I found a case back in Di-An. Pretty at night. And what the hell, they hit just as hard. But let's get cracking on the co-ax."

Ginelli jumped to the ground. Herrold handed him a footlocker to serve as a table—the back deck of the zippo was too cluttered to strip the gun there—and the co-ax itself. In a few minutes they had reduced the weapon to components and begun cleaning them.

A shadow eased across the footlocker. Ginelli looked up, still holding the receiver he was brushing with a solvent-laden toothbrush. The interpreter, Hieu, had walked over from the TOC and was facing the grove. He seemed oblivious to the troopers beside him.

"Hey, Hieu," the TC called. "Why the hell'd the colonel stick us here, d'ya know? We get in a firefight and these damn trees'll hide a division of VC."

Hieu looked around slowly. His features had neither

the fragility of the pure Vietnamese nor the moon-like fullness of those with Chinese blood. His was a blocky face, set as ever in hard lines, mahogany in color. Hieu stepped up to the wall before answering, letting his hands run over the rough stone like two dried oak leaves.

"No time to make berm," he said at last, pointing to the bellowing Caterpillar climbing out of a trench near the Tactical Operations Center. The D-7A was digging-in sleeping trailers for the brass rather than starting to throw up an earthen wall around the perimeter. "The wall here make us need ti-ti berm, I show colonel."

Herrold nodded. The stone enclosure was square, about a hundred yards to a side. Though only four feet high, the ancient wall was nearly as thick and would stop anything short of an eight-inch shell. But even with the work the wall would save the engineers on the west side, those trees sure played hell with the zones of fire. Seven of them looked to Herrold to be Philippine mahoganies; God knew what the monster in the middle was. A banyan, maybe, from the creviced trunk, but the bark didn't look like the banyans he'd seen before.

"Never saw trees that big before," Herrold said aloud.

Hieu looked at him again, this time with a hint of expression on his face. "Yes," he stated, "ti-ti left when French come, now only one." His fingers toyed with the faded duck of the ammo pouch clipped to his belt. Both soldiers thought the dark man was through speaking, but Hieu's tongue flicked between his thin lips again and he continued, "Maybe three, maybe two years only, there was other. Now only this." The interpreter's voice became a hiss. "But beaucoup years before, everything was tree, everything was Meng!"

Boots scuffled in powdery dirt; Murray and the Frenchman were coming back from the TOC. Hieu's face blanked. He nodded to Herrold, then vaulted the laterite wall gracefully. The driver and Crozier watched him stepping with purpose toward the center of the widely spaced grove as they halted beside the others.

"But who is that?" Crozier questioned sharply.

"Uh? That's Hieu, he's our interpreter," Murray grunted in surprise. "How come?"

190

The Frenchman frowned. "But he is Meng, surely? I did not know that any served in the army, even that the government tried to induct them any more."

"Hell, I always heard he was from Saigon," Herrold answered. "He'd've said if he was from here, wouldn't he?"

"What's Hieu up to, anyhow?" Ginelli asked. He pointed toward the grove where the interpreter stood, facing the scarred trunk of the god tree. From the track they could not see Hieu's hands, but the interpreter twitched in ritual motion beneath the fluid stripes of his fatigues.

Nobody spoke. Ginelli set one foot on the tread and lifted himself onto the flame track. Red and yellow smoke grenades hung by their safety rings inside the dome. Still lower swung a dusty pair of binoculars. Ginelli blew on the lenses before setting the glasses to his eyes and rotating the separate focus knobs. Hieu had knelt on the ground, but the trooper still could not tell what he was doing. Something else caught his eye.

"God damn," the plump newbie blurted. He leaned over the side of the track and thrust the glasses toward Herrold, busy putting the machine gun back together. "Hey, Red. Take a look at the tree trunk."

Murray, Crozier, and Ginelli himself waited expectantly while the track commander refocused the binoculars. Magnified, the tree increased geometrically in hideousness. Its bark was pinkish and paper-thin, smoother than that of a birch over most of the bole's surface. The gouged, wrinkled appearance of the trunk was due to the underlying wood, not some irregularity in the bark that covered it.

The tall cat-face in front of Hieu was the trunk's only blemish. Where the tear had puckered together in a creased, blackened seam, ragged edges of bark fluttered in the breeze. The flaps were an unhealthy color, like skin peeling away from a bad burn. Hieu's squat body hid only a third of the scar; the upper portion towered gloomily above him.

"Well, it's not much to look at," Herrold said at last. "What's the deal?"

"Where the bullet holes?" Ginelli demanded in triumph. "You put twenty, thirty shots in it, right? Where's they go to?"

"Sonofabitch," the TC agreed, taking another look. The co-ax should have left a tight pattern of shattered wood above the ancient scar. Except for some brownish dimples in the bark, the tree was unmarked.

"I saw splinters fly," Murray remarked.

"Goddam wood must'a swelled right over them," Herrold decided. "That's where I hit, all right."

"That is a very strange tree," Crozier said, speaking for the first time since his return. "There was another like it near Plantation 7. It too had almond trees around it, though there was no wall. They call them god trees—the Viets do. The Mengs have their own word, but I do not know its meaning."

A Chinook swept over the firebase from the south, momentarily stifling conversation with the syncopated whopping of its twin rotors. It hovered just beyond the perimeter, then slowly settled in a circular dust cloud while its turbines whined enormously. Men ran to unload it.

"Chow pretty quick," Murray commented. It was nearing four o'clock. Ginelli looked away from the bird. "Don't seem right," he said. The other men looked blank. He tried to explain. "I mean, the Shithook there, jet engines and all, and that tree there being so old."

The driver snorted. "Hell, that's not old. Now back in California where they make those things—" His broad thumb indicated the banana-shaped helicopter "—they got redwoods that're really old. You don't think anything about that, do you?"

Ginelli gestured helplessly with his hands, unable to express what he felt. Surprisingly it was Crozier, half-seated on the laterite wall, who came to his aid. "What makes you think this god tree is less old than a redwood, Joe?" he asked mildly.

Murray blinked. "Hell, redwoods're the oldest things there are. Alive, I mean."

The Frenchman laughed and repeated his deprecating shrug. "But trees are my business, you understand? Now

192

there is a pine tree in Arizona older than your California sequoias; but no one knew it for so long because there are not many of them and . . . no one noticed. And here is a tree, an old one—but who knows? Maybe there are only two in the whole world left—and the other one, the one in the north, that perhaps is dead with Plantation 7."

"You never counted the rings or anything?" Herrold asked curiously. He had locked the barrel into the co-ax while the others were talking.

"No . . ." Crozier admitted. His tongue touched his lips as he gazed up at the god tree, wondering how much he should say. "No," he repeated, "but I only saw the tree once while I was in the north. It stood in the jungle, more than two kilometers from the rubber, and the laborers did not care that anyone should go near it. There were Mengs there, too, I was told; but only a few and they hid in the woods. Bad blood between them and my laborers, no doubt."

"Well, hell, Jacques," Murray prompted. "When *did* you see it?"

Crozier still hesitated. Suddenly realizing what the problem might be, the driver guffawed. "Hell, don't worry about *our* stomachs, fer god's sake. Unless you're squeamish, turtle?" Ginelli blushed and shook his head. Laughing, Murray went on. "Anyhow, you grow up pretty quick after you get in the field—those that live to. Tell the story, Jacques."

Crozier sighed. The glade behind him was empty. Hieu had disappeared somewhere without being noticed. "Well," he began, "it has no importance, I am sure— all this happened a hundred and fifty kilometers away, as you know. But . . .

"It was not long after Michelin sent me to Indochina, in 1953 that would be. I was told of the god tree as soon as I arrived at Plantation 7, but that was all. One of my foremen had warned me not to wander that way, and I assumed this meant 'because of the Viet Minh.'

"Near midnight—this was before Dien Bien Phu, you will remember—there was heavy firing not far from the plantation. I called the district garrison, since for a

193

marvel the radio was working. But of course no one came until it was light."

Herrold and Murray nodded together in agreement. Charging into a night ambush was no way to help your buddies, not in this country. Crozier cleared his throat and went on, "It was two companies of colonial paras that came, and the colonel from the fort himself. Nothing would help but that I should guide them to where the shooting had been. A platoon had set up an ambush, so they said, but it did not call in—even for fire support. When I radioed they assumed . . ." He shrugged expressively.

"And that is what we found. All the men, all of them dead—unforgettably. They were in the grove of that god tree, on both sides of the trail to it. Perhaps the lieutenant had thought the Viets were rallying there. The paras were well armed and did much shooting from the shells we found. But of enemies, there was no sign; and the paras had not been shot. They were torn, you know? Mutilated beyond what I could believe. But none had been shot, and their weapons lay with the bodies."

"That's crazy," Ginelli said, voicing everyone's thought. "Dinks would'a taken the guns."

Crozier shrugged. "The colonel said at last his men had been killed by some wild tribe, so savage they did not understand guns or would not use them. The Mengs, he meant. They were . . . wilder, perhaps, than the ones here but still . . . I would not have thought there were enough of them to wipe out the platoon, waiting as it must have been."

"How *were* the men killed?" Herrold asked at last.

"Knives, I think," the Frenchman replied. "Short ones. Teeth I might have said; but there were really no signs that anything had fed on the bodies. Not the killers, that is. One man—"

He paused to swallow, continued, "One man I thought wore a long shirt of black. When I came closer, the flies left him. The skin was gone from his arms and chest. God alone knows what had killed him; but his face was the worst to see, and that was unmarked."

No one spoke for some time after that. Finally Murray said, "They oughta have chow on. Coming?"

Crozier spread his hands. "You are sure it is all right? I have no utensils."

"No sweat, there's paper plates. Rest'a you guys?"

"I'll be along," Herrold said. "Lemme remount the co-ax first."

"I'll do that," Ginelli offered. His face was saffron, bloodless beneath his tan. "Don't feel hungry tonight anyhow."

The track commander smiled. "You can give me a hand."

When the gun was bolted solidly back on its mount, Herrold laid a belt of ammunition on the loading tray and clicked the cover shut on it. "Ah," Ginelli mumbled, "ah, Red, don't you think it'd be a good idea to keep pressure up in the napalm tanks? I mean, there's a lotta Meñgs around here, and what Murray's buddy says . . ."

"We'll make do with the co-ax," the TC replied, grinning. "You know how the couplings leak napalm with the pumps on."

"But if there's an attack?" Ginelli pleaded.

"Look, turtle," Herrold explained more sharply than before, "we're sitting on five hundred gallons a' napalm. One spark in this track with the pressure up and we won't need no attack. Okay?" Ginelli shrugged. "Well, come on to chow then," the TC suggested.

"Guess I'll stay."

"S'okay." Herrold slipped off the track and began walking toward the mess tent. He was singing softly, "We gotta get outa this place . . ."

Crozier left just before the storm broke. The rain that had held off most of the day sheeted down at dusk. Lightning when it flared jumped from cloud-top to invisible cloud-top. It backlighted the sky.

The crewmen huddled under the inadequate tarpaulin, listening to the ragged static that was all Murray's transistor radio could pick up. Eventually he shut it off. Ginelli swore miserably. Slanting rain had started a worm of water at the head of his cot. It had finally squirmed all the way to the other end where he sat hunched against the chill wind. "Shouldn't somebody be on the track?" he asked. Regular guard shifts started at ten o'clock, but usually everybody was more or less alert until then.

"Go ahead, turtle, it's your bright idea," Murray said. Herrold frowned more seriously. "Yeah, if you're worried you might as well. Look, you get up in the dome now and Murray'll trade his first shift for your second. Right?"

"Sure," the driver agreed. "Maybe this damn rain'll stop by then.

Wearing his poncho over his flak jacket, Ginelli clambered up the bow slope of the zippo. The metal sides were too slimy with rain to mount that way. Except during lightning strokes, the darkness was opaque. When it flashed, the trees stabbed into the suddenly bright skies and made Ginelli think about the napalm beneath from a different aspect. Christ, those trees were the tallest things for miles, and God knew the track wasn't very far away if lightning did hit one. God, they were tall.

And they were old. Ginelli recognized the feeling he'd had ever since the flame track had nosed up to the wall to face the grove: an aura of age. The same thing he'd sensed when he was a kid and saw the Grand Canyon. There was something so old it didn't give a damn about man or anything else.

Christ! No tree was as old as that; it must be their size that made him so jumpy. Dark as it was, the dinks could be crawling closer between lightning flashes too. At least the rain was slowing down.

The hatch cover was folded back into a clamshell seat for the man on the dome. There was a fiber pillow to put over the steel, but it was soaked, and Ginelli had set it on the back deck. For the first time he could remember, the thickness of his flak jacket felt good because the air was so cold. Water that slicked off the poncho or dripped from the useless flat muzzle of the flamethrower joined the drops spattering directly onto the zippo's deck. It pooled and flowed sluggishly toward the lowest point, the open driver's hatch.

The sky was starting to clear. An occasional spray fell, but the storm was over and a quarter moon shone when the broken clouds allowed it. Herrold stuck his head out from under the tarp. "How's going, man?"

Ginelli stretched some of the stiffness out of his back and began stripping off the poncho. "Okay, I guess. I could use some coffee."

Shadows from the treetops pooled massively about the boles. Although there was enough breeze to make the branches tremble, the trunks themselves were solid as cliffs, as solid as Time. The scar at the base of the god tree was perversely moonlit. The whole grove looked sinister in the darkness, but the scar itself was something more.

Only the half-hour routine of perimeter check kept Ginelli awake. Voices crackled around Headquarters Troop's sector until Ginelli could repeat, "Seven zero, report negative," for the last time and thankfully take off the commo helmet. His boots squelched as he dropped beside the cot where Murray snored softly, wrapped in the mottled green-brown nylon of his poncho liner. Ginelli shook him.

"Uh!" the driver grunted as he snapped awake. "Oh, right; lemme get my boots on."

One of the few clouds remaining drifted over the moon. As Murray stood upright, Ginelli thought movement flickered on the dark stone of the wall. "Hey!" the driver whispered. "What's Hieu doing out there?"

Ginelli peered into the grove without being able to see anything but the trees. "That was him goin' over the wall," Murray insisted. He held his M-16 with the bolt back, ready to chamber a round if the receiver was jarred. "Look, I'm gonna check where he's going."

"Jeez, somebody'll see you and cut loose," Ginelli protested. "You can't go out there!"

Murray shook his head decisively. "Naw, it'll be okay," he said as he slipped over the wall. "Crazy," Ginelli muttered. And it suddenly struck him that a man who volunteered for three extra years of combat probably *wasn't* quite normal in the back-home sense. Licking his lips, he waited tensely in the darkness. The air had grown warmer since the rain stopped, but the plump newbie found himself shivering.

A bird fluttered among the branches of the nearest

mahogany. You didn't seem to see many birds in country, not like you did back in the World. Ginelli craned his neck to get a better view, but the irregular moonlight passed only the impression of wings and drab color.

Nothing else moved within the grove. Ginelli swore miserably and shook Herrold awake. The track commander slept with his flak jacket for a pillow and, despite his attitude of nonchalance, the clumsy grease gun lay beside him on the cot. His fingers curled around its pistol grip as he awakened.

"Oh, for God's sake," he muttered when Ginelli blurted out the story. Herrold had kept his boots on, only the tops unlaced, and he quickly whipped the ties tight around his shins. "Christ, ten minutes ago?"

"Well, should I call in?" Ginelli suggested uncertainly.

"Hell," Herrold muttered, "no, I better tell the ole man. You get back in the dome and wait for me." He hefted his submachine gun by the receiver.

Ginelli started to climb onto the track. Turning, he said, "Hey, man." Herrold paused. "Don't be too long, huh?"

"Yeah." The track commander trudged off toward the unlighted HQ tent. A bird, maybe a large bat from its erratic flight, passed over Ginelli's head at treetop level. He raised the loading cover of the co-ax to recheck the position of the linked belt of ammunition.

There was a light in the grove.

It was neither man-made nor the moon's reflection, and at first it was almost too faint to have a source at all. Ginelli gaped frozen at the huge god tree. The glow resolved into a viridescent line down the center of the scar, a strip of brightness that widened perceptibly as the edges of the cicatrix drew back. The interior of the tree seemed hollow, lined with self-shining greenness to which forms clung. As Ginelli watched, a handful of the creatures lurched from the inner wall and fluttered out through the dilated scar.

Someone screamed within the laager. Ginelli whirled around. The tactical operations center was green and two-dimensional where the chill glare licked it. A man tore through the canvas passage linking the vehicles, howling

198

and clutching at the back of his neck until he fell. A dark shape flapped away from him. The remaining blotches clinging to the green of the tree flickered outward and the scar began to close.

The cal fifty in the assault vehicle to the right suddenly began blasting tracers point-blank into the shrinking green blaze. Heavy bullets that could smash through half an inch of steel ripped across the tree. It was like stabbing a sponge with ice picks. Something dropped into the ACAV's cupola from above. The shots stopped and the gunner began to bellow hoarsely.

Ginelli swivelled his co-ax onto the tree and clamped down on its underslung trigger. Nothing happened; in his panic he had forgotten to charge his gun. Sparkling muzzle flashes were erupting all across the laager. Near the TOC a man fired his M-16 at a crazy angle, trying to drop one of the flying shapes. Another spiraled down behind him of its own deadly accord. His rifle continued to fire as he collapsed on top of it. It sent a last random bullet to spall a flake of aluminum from the flame track's side, a foot beneath Ginelli's exposed head.

A soldier in silhouette against the green light lunged toward the god tree's slitted portal and emptied his rifle point blank. The knife in his hand glowed green as he chopped it up and down into the edge of the scar, trying to widen the gap. "Murray!" Ginelli called. He jerked back his machine gun's operating rod but did not shoot. He could hear Murray screaming obscenities made staccato by choppy bursts of automatic fire from behind him.

Ginelli turned his head without conscious warning. He had only enough time to drop down into the compartment as the thing swooped. Its vans, stretched batlike between arm and leg, had already slammed it upright in braking for the kill. The green glare threw its features in perfect relief against the chaos of the firebase: a body twenty inches long, deep-torsoed like a mummified pigmy; weasel teeth, slender cones perfectly formed for slaughter; a face that could have been human save for its size and the streaks that disfigured it. Tree light flashed a shadow across the hatch as the chittering creature flapped toward other prey for the moment.

Ginelli straightened slowly, peered out of the dome.

There was a coldness in his spine; his whole lower body felt as though it belonged to someone else. He knew it wasn't any use, even for himself, to slam the dome hatch over his head and hope to wait the nightmare out. The driver's compartment was open; there was plenty of room between the seat and the engine firewall beside it for the killers to crawl through.

Taking a deep breath, Ginelli leaped out of the hatch. He ignored the co-ax. A shuffling step forward in a low crouch and leapt feet first through the driver's hatch. Throttle forward, both clutch levers at neutral. The starter motor whined for an instant; then the six-cylinder diesel caught, staggered, and boomed into life. An imbalance somewhere in the engine made the whole vehicle tremble.

Murray was still gouging at the base of the scar, face twisted in maniacal savagery. Chips flew every time the blade struck, letting more of the interior glare spill out. Ginelli throttled back, nerving himself to move. "Murray!" he shouted again over the lessened throb of the diesel. "Get away—dammit, get away!"

A figure oozed out of the shadows and gripped Murray by the shoulder. Perhaps the driver screamed before he recognized Hieu; if so, Ginelli's own cry masked the sound. The Meng spoke, his face distorted with triumph. As the incredulous driver stared, Hieu shouted a few syllables at the god tree in a throaty language far different from the nasal trills of Vietnamese.

The tree opened again. The edges of the scar crumpled sideways, exposing fully the green-lit interior and what stood in it now. Murray whipped around, his blade raised to slash. An arm gripped his, held the knife motionless. The thing was as tall as the opening it stood in, bipedal but utterly inhuman.

Its face was a mirror image of Hieu's own.

Murray flung himself back, but another pallid, boneless arm encircled him and drew him into the tree. His scream was momentary, cut off when the green opening squeezed almost shut behind him and what Hieu had summoned.

The hooked moon was out again. Hieu turned and began striding toward the shattered laager. His single ammo pouch flopped open; the crude necklace around his neck was of human fingertips, dried and strung on a twist of cambium. Behind him a score of other human-appearing figures slunk out of the grove, every face identical.

Ginelli gathered his feet under him on the seat, then sprang back on top of the track. One of the winged shapes had been waiting for him, called by the mutter of the engine. It darted in from the front, banking easily around Ginelli's out-thrust arm. Ginelli tripped on the flamethrower's broad tube, fell forward bruisingly. Clawed fingers drew four bloody tracks across his forehead as the flyer missed its aim. It swept back purposefully.

Ginelli jumped into the dome hatch and snatched at the clamshell cover to close it. As the steel lid swung to, the winged man's full weight bounced it back on its hinges ringingly. Jagged teeth raked the soldier's bare right arm, making him scream in frenzy. He yanked at the hatch cover with mad strength. There was no clang as the hatch shut, but something crackled between the edges of armor plate. The brief cry of agony was higher pitched than a man's. Outside, the scar began to dilate again.

Ginelli gripped the valve and hissed with pain. Shock had numbed his right arm momentarily. Left-handed, he opened the feeds. His fingers found a switch, flicked it up, and the pump began throbbing behind him. His whole body shuddered as he swung the dome through a short arc so that the tree's blazing scar was centered in the periscope. The universal joint of the fat napalm hose creaked in protest at being moved, and a drop of thickened gasoline spattered stickily on Ginelli's flak jacket.

With a cry of horrified understanding, Hieu leaped onto the stone wall between Ginelli and the tree. "You must—" was all the Meng could say before the jet of napalm caught him squarely in the chest and flung him back into the enclosure. There was no flame. The igniter had not fired.

Mumbling half-remembered fragments of a Latin prayer, Ginelli triggered the weapon again. Napalm spurted against the tree in an unobstructed black arch. The igniter banged in mid-shot and darkness boomed into a hellish red glare. The tree keened as the flame rod's giant fist smashed against it. Its outer bark shriveled and the deep, bloody surge of napalm smothered every other color. Ginelli's fiery scythe roared as he slashed it up and down the trunk. Wood began to crackle like gunfire exploding and hurling back geysers of sparks. A puff of dry heat roiled toward the laager in the turbulent air. It was heavy with the stench of burning flesh.

A series of swift thuds warned Ginelli of flyers landing on the zippo's deck; teeth clicked on armor. Something rustled from the driver's compartment. The trooper used his stiffening right hand on the interior lights. The yellow bulbs glinted from close-set eyes peering over the driver's seat. Ginelli kicked. Instead of crunching under his boot, the face gave with a terrible resiliency and the winged man continued to squirm into the TC's compartment. A sparkling chain of eyes flashed behind the first pair. The whole swarm of killers was crowding into the track.

Ginelli's only weapon was the flame itself. Instinctively he swung the nozzle to the left and depressed it, trying to hose fire into the forward hatch of his own vehicle. Instead, the frozen coupling parted. Napalm gouted from the line. The flame died with a serpentine lurch, leaving the god tree alone as a lance of fire. The track was flooding with the gummy fluid; it clung to Ginelli's chest and flak jacket before rolling off in sluggish gobbets.

Bloody faces washed black with smears of napalm, the winged men struggled toward Ginelli implacably. His mind barely functional, the soldier threw open the hatch and staggered onto the zippo's deck. Unseen, one flyer still hung in the air. It struck him in the middle of the back and catapulted him off the vehicle. Ginelli somersaulted across the dusty, flame-lit cauldron. The napalm's gluey tenacity fixed the creature firmly against Ginelli's flak jacket; its hooked claws locked into the fabric while its teeth tore his scalp.

The huge torch of the god tree crashed inward toward the laager. A flaming branch snapped with the impact and bounded high in the air before plunging down on the napalm-filled flame track. Ginelli staggered to his feet, tried to run. The zippo exploded with a hollow boom and a mushroom of flame, knocking him down again without dislodging the vengeful horror on his back.

With the last of his strength, Ginelli ripped off the unfastened flak jacket and hurled it into the air. For one glistening instant he thought the napalm-soaked nylon would land short of the pool of fire surrounding the flame track. His uncoordinated throw was high and the winged killer had time to pull one van loose as it pinwheeled. It struck the ground that way, mired by the incendiary that bloomed to consume it.

Ginelli lay on his back, no longer able to move. A shadow humped over the top of the wall: Hiéu, moving very stiffly. His right hand held a cane spear. The Meng was withered like a violet whose roots had been chopped away, but he was not dead.

"You kill all, you . . . animals," he said. His voice was thick and half-choked by the napalm that had hosed him. He balanced on the wall, black against the burning wreckage of the god tree. "All . . ." he repeated, raising the spear. "Cut . . . poison . . . burn. But you —"

Herrold's grease gun slammed beside Ginelli, its muzzle blast deafening even against the background roar of the flames. A solid bar of tracers stitched redly across the Meng's chest and slapped him off the wall as a screaming ball of fire.

It was still four hours to dawn, Ginelli thought as he drifted into unconsciousness, but until then the flames would give enough light.

IT ONLY COMES OUT AT NIGHT

by
Dennis Etchison

DENNIS ETCHISON, a Californian who once studied writing under the late Charles Beaumont, seems to be carving out an interesting niche for himself in the horror and science fiction tradition of Richard Matheson. Focusing on the psychological and realistic possibilities of terror, Etchison's work is unusually visual and mood-evoking. And anyone who has ever done much traveling by automobile will find that this story hits chillingly close to home.

If you leave L.A. by way of San Bernardino, headed for Route 66 and points east you must cross the Mojave Desert.

Even after Needles and the border, however, there is no relief; the dry air only thins further as the long, relentless climb continues in earnest. Flagstaff is still almost two hundred miles, and Winslow, Gallup and Albuquerque are too many hours away to think of making without food, rest and, mercifully, sleep.

It is like this: the car runs hot, hotter than it ever has before, the plies of the tires expand and contract until the sidewalls begin to shimmy slightly as they spin on over the miserable Arizona roads, giving up a faint odor like burning hair from between the treads, as the windshield colors over with essence of honeybee, wasp, dragonfly, mayfly, June bug, ladybug, and the like, and the radiator, clotted with the bodies of countless kamikaze insects, hisses like a moribund lizard in the sun . . .

All of which means, of course, that if you are traveling that way between May and September, you move by night.

Only by night.

For there are, after all, dawn check-in motels, Do Not Disturb signs for bungalow doorknobs; there are diners for mid-afternoon breakfasts, coffee by the ca⟋ ⟍here are twenty-four-hour filling stations bright a⟋ Whiting Brothers, Conoco, Terrible Herbst⟋ are unfamiliar as their names, with ice m⟋

machines, candy machines; and there are the sudden, un-expected Rest Areas, just off the highway, with brick bathrooms and showers and electrical outlets, constructed especially for those who are weary, out of money, behind schedule . . .

So McClay had had to learn, the hard way.

He slid his hands to the bottom of the steering wheel and peered ahead into the darkness, trying to relax. But the wheel stuck to his fingers like warm candy. Off somewhere to his left, the horizon flickered with pearly luminescence, then faded again to black. This time he did not bother to look. Sometimes, though, he wondered just how far way the lightning was striking; not once during the night had the sound of its thunder reached him here in the car.

In the back seat, his wife moaned.

The trip out had turned all but unbearable for her. Four days it had taken, instead of the expected two-and-a-half; he made a great effort not to think of it, but the memory hung over the car like a thunderhead.

It had been a blur, a fever dream. Once, on the second day, he had been passed by a churning bus, its silver sides blinding him until he noticed a Mexican woman in one of the window seats. She was not looking at him. She was holding a swooning infant to the glass, squeezing water onto its head from a plastic baby bottle to keep it from passing out.

McClay sighed and fingered the buttons on the car radio.

He knew he would get nothing from the AM or FM bands, not out here, but he clicked it on anyway. He left the volume and tone controls down, so as not to wake Evvie. Then he punched the seldom-used middle button, the shortwave band, and raised the gain carefully until he could barely hear the radio over the hum of the tires.

Static.

Slowly he swept the tuner across the bandwidth, but there was only white noise. It reminded him a little of the summer rain yesterday, starting back, the way it had ɔunded bouncing off the windows.

He was about to give up when he caught a voice, crackling, drifting in and out. He worked the knob like a safecracker, zeroing in on the signal.

A few bars of music. A tone, then the voice again. ". . . Greenwich Mean Time." Then the station ID.

It was the Voice of America overseas broadcast.

He grunted disconsolately and killed it.

His wife stirred.

"Why'd you turn it off?" she murmured. "I was listening to that. Good. Program."

"Take it easy," he said, "easy, you're still asleep. We'll be stopping soon."

". . . Only comes out at night," he heard her say, and then she was lost again in the blankets.

He pressed the glove compartment, took out one of the Automobile Club guides. It was already clipped open. McClay flipped on the overhead light and drove with one hand, reading over—for the hundredth time?—the list of motels that lay ahead. He knew the list by heart, but seeing the names again reassured him somehow. Besides, it helped to break the monotony.

It was the kind of place you never expect to find in the middle of a long night. a bright place with buildings (a building, at least) and cars. other cars drawn off the highway to be together in the protective circle of light.

A Rest Area.

He would have spotted it without the sign. Elevated sodium vapor lighting bathed the scene in an almost peach-colored glow, strikingly different from the cold blue-white sentinels of the interstate highway. He had seen other Rest Area signs on the way out, probably even this one. But in daylight the signs had meant nothing more to him than "Frontage Road" or "Business District Next Right." He wondered if it were the peculiar warmth of light that made the small island of blacktop appear so inviting.

McClay decelerated, downshifted, and left Interstate 40.

The car dipped and bumped, and he was aware of the

new level of sound from the engine as it geared down for the first time in hours.

He eased in next to a Pontiac Firebird, toed the emergency brake, and cut the ignition.

He allowed his eyes to close and his head to sink back into the headrest. At last.

The first thing he noticed was the quiet.

It was deafening. His ears literally began to ring, with the high-pitched whine of a late-night TV test pattern.

The second thing he noticed was a tingling at the tip of his tongue.

It brought to mind a picture of a snake's tongue. Picking up electricity from the air, he thought.

The third was the rustling awake of his wife, in back.

She pulled herself up. "Are we sleeping now? Why are the lights. . . ?"

He saw the outline of her head in the mirror. "It's just a rest stop, hon. I—the car needs a break." Well, it was true, wasn't it? "You want a rest room? There's one back there, see it?"

"Oh my God."

"What's the matter now?"

"Leg's asleep. Listen, are we or are we not going to get a ?"

"There's a motel coming up." He didn't say that they wouldn't hit the one he had marked in the book for another couple of hours; he didn't want to argue. He knew she needed the rest; he needed it too, didn't he? "Think I'll have some more of that coffee, though," he said.

"Isn't any more," she yawned.

The door slammed.

Now he was able to recognize the ringing in his ears for what it was: the sound of his own blood. It almost succeeded in replacing the steady drone of the car.

He twisted around, fishing over the back of the seat for the ice chest.

There should be a couple of Cokes left, at least.

His fingers brushed the basket next to the chest, riffling the edges of maps and tour books, by now reshuffled haphazardly over the first-aid kit he had packed himself (tourniquet, forceps, scissors, ammonia inhalants, Merthiolate, triangular bandage, compress, adhesive bandages, tannic acid) and the fire extinguisher, the extra carton of cigarettes, the remainder of a half-gallon of drinking water, the thermos (which Evvie said was empty, and why would she lie?).

He popped the top of a can.

Through the side window he saw Evvie disappearing around the corner of the building. She was wrapped to the gills in her blanket.

He opened the door and slid out, his back aching.

He stood there blankly, the unnatural light washing over him.

He took a long sweet pull from the can. Then he started walking.

The Firebird was empty.

And the next car, and the next.

Each car he passed looked like the one before it, which seemed crazy until he realized that it must be the work of the light. It cast an even, eerie tan over the baked metal tops, like orange sunlight through air thick with suspended particles. Even the windshields appeared to be filmed over with a thin layer of settled dust. It made him think of country roads, sundowns.

He walked on.

He heard his footsteps echo with surprising clarity, resounding down the staggered line of parked vehicles. Finally it dawned on him (and now he knew how tired he really was) that the cars must actually have people in them—sleeping people. Of course. Well, hell, he thought, watching his step, I wouldn't want to wake anyone. The poor devils.

Besides the sound of his footsteps, there was only the distant *swish* of an occasional, very occasional car on the highway; from here, even that was only a distant hush, growing and then subsiding like waves on a nearby shore.

He reached the end of the line, turned back.

Out of the corner of his eye he saw, or thought he saw, a movement by the building.

It would be Evvie, shuffling back.

He heard the car door slam.

He recalled something he had seen in one of the tourist towns in New Mexico: circling the park—in Taos, that

211

was where they had been—he had glimpsed an ageless Indian, wrapped in typical blanket, ducking out of sight into the doorway of a gift shop; with the blanket over his head that way, the Indian had somehow resembled an Arab, or so it had seemed to him at the time.

He heard another car door slam.

That was the same day—was it only last week?—that she had noticed the locals driving with their headlights on (in honor of something or other, some regional election, perhaps: " 'My face speaks for itself,' drawled Herman J. 'Fashio' Trujillo, Candidate for . Sheriff"). She had insisted at first that it must be a funeral procession, though for whom she could not guess.

McClay came to the car, stretched a last time, and crawled back in.

Evvie was bundled safely again in the back seat.

He lit a quick cigarette, expecting to hear her voice any second, complaining, demanding that he roll down the windows, at least, and so forth. But, as it turned out, he was able to sit undisturbed as he smoked it down almost to the filter.

Paguate. Bluewater. Thoreau.

He blinked.

Klagetoh. Joseph City. Ash Fork.

He blinked and tried to focus his eyes from the taillights a half-mile ahead to the bug-spattered glass, then back again.

Petrified Forest National Park.

He blinked, refocusing. But it did no good.

A twitch started on the side of his face, close by the corner of his eye.

Rehoboth.

He strained at a road sign, the names and mileages, but instead a seemingly endless list of past and future stops and detours shimmered before his mind's eye.

I've had it, he thought. Now, suddenly, it was catching up with him, the hours of repressed fatigue; he felt a rushing out of something from his chest. No way to make that motel—hell, I can't even remember the name of it now.

212

Check the book. But it doesn't matter. The eyes. *Can't control my eyes anymore.*

(He had already begun to hallucinate things like tree trunks and cows and Mack trucks speeding toward him on the highway. The cow had been straddling the broken line; in the last few minutes its lowing, deep and regular, had become almost inviting.)

Well, he could try for *any* motel. Whatever turned up next.

But how much farther would that be?

He ground his teeth together, feeling the pulsing at his temples. He struggled to remember the last sign.

The next town. It might be a mile. Five miles. Fifty.

Think! He said it, he thought it, he didn't know which.

If he could pull over, pull over right now and lie down for a few minutes

He seemed to see clear ground ahead. No rocks, no ditch. The shoulder, just ahead.

Without thinking he dropped into neutral and coasted, aiming for it.

The car glided to a stop.

God, he thought.

He forced himself to turn, reach into the back seat.

The lid to the chest was already off. He dipped his fingers into the ice and retrieved two half-melted cubes, lifted them into the front seat, and began rubbing them over his forehead.

He let his eyes close, seeing dull lights fire as he daubed at the lids, the rest of his face, the forehead again. As he slipped the ice into his mouth and chewed, it broke apart as easily as snow.

He took a deep breath. He opened his eyes again.

At that moment a huge tanker roared past, slamming an aftershock of air into the side of the car. The car rocked like a boat at sea.

No. It was no good.

So. So he could always turn back, couldn't he? And why not? The Rest Area was only twenty, twenty-five minutes behind him. (Was that all?) He could pull out and hang a U and turn back, just like that. And then sleep. It would be safer there. With luck, Evvie wouldn't even know. An hour's rest, maybe two; that was all he would need.

Unless—was there another Rest Area ahead?

How soon?

He knew that the second wind he felt now wouldn't last, not for more than a few minutes. No, it wasn't worth the chance.

He glanced in the rearview mirror.

Evvie was still down, a lumpen mound of blanket and hair.

Above her body, beyond the rear window, the raised headlights . of another monstrous truck, closing ground fast.

He made the decision.

He slid into first and swung out in a wide arc, well ahead of the blast of the truck, and worked up to fourth gear. He was thinking about the warm, friendly lights he had left behind.

He angled in next to the Firebird and cut the lights.

He started to reach for a pillow from the back, but why bother? It would probably wake Evvie, anyway.

He wadded up his jacket, jammed it against the passenger armrest, and lay down.

First he crossed his arms over his chest. Then behind his head. Then he gripped his hands between his knees. Then he was on his back again, his hands at his sides, his feet cramped against the opposite door.

His eyes were wide open.

He lay there, watching chain lightning flash on the horizon.

Finally he let out a breath that sounded like all the breaths he had ever taken going out at once, and drew himself up.

He got out and walked over to the rest room.

Inside,. white tiles and barc lights. His eyes felt raw, peeled. Fnished, he washed his hands but not his face; that would only make sleep more difficult.

Outside again and feeling desperately out of synch, he listened to his shoes falling hollowly on the cement.

"Next week we've got to get organized . . ."

He said this, he was sure, because he heard his voice

coming back to him, though with a peculiar empty resonance. Well, this time tomorrow night he would be home. As unlikely as that seemed now.

He stopped, bent for a drink from the water fountain.

The footsteps did not stop.

Now wait, he thought, I'm pretty far gone, but—

He swallowed, his ears popping.

The footsteps stopped.

Hell, he thought, I've been pushing too hard. We. She. No, it was my fault, my plan this time. To drive nights, sleep days. Just so. As long as you *can* sleep.

Easy, take it easy.

He started walking again, around the corner and back to the lot.

At the corner, he thought he saw something move at the edge of his vision.

He turned quickly to the right, in time for a fleeting glimpse of something—someone—hurrying out of sight into the shadows.

Well, the other side of the building housed the women's rest room. Maybe it was Evvie.

He glanced toward the car, but it was blocked from view.

He walked on.

Now the parking area resembled an oasis lit by firelight. Or a western camp, the cars rimming the lot on three sides in the manner of wagons gathered against the night.

Strength in numbers, he thought.

Again, each car he passed looked at first like every other. It was the flat light, of course. And of course they were the same cars he had seen a half-hour ago. And the light still gave them a dusty, abandoned look.

He touched a fender.

It *was* dusty.

But why shouldn't it be? His own car had probably taken on quite a layer of grime after so long on these roads.

He touched the next car, the next.

Each was so dirty that he could have carved his name without scratching the paint.

He had an image of himself passing this way again—

215

God forbid—a year from now, say, and finding the same cars parked here. The *same* ones.

What if, he wondered tiredly, what if some of these cars had been abandoned? Overheated, exploded, broken down one fine midday and left here by owners who simply never returned? Who would ever know? Did the Highway Patrol, did anyone bother to check? Would an automobile be preserved here for months, years by the elements, like a snakeskin shed beside the highway?

It was a thought, anyway.

His head was buzzing.

He leaned back and inhaled deeply, as deeply as he could at this altitude.

But he did hear something. A faint tapping. It reminded him of running feet, until he noticed the lamp overhead:

There were hundreds of moths beating against the high fixture, their soft bodies tapping as they struck and circled and returned again and again to the lens; the light made their wings translucent.

He took another deep breath and went on to his car.

He could hear it ticking, cooling down, before he got there. Idly he rested a hand on the hood. Warm, of course. The tires? He touched the left front. It was taut, hot as a loaf from the oven. When he took his hand away, the color of the rubber came off on his palm like burned skin.

He reached for the door handle.

A moth fluttered down onto the fender. He flicked it off, his finger leaving a streak on the enamel.

He looked closer and saw a wavy, mottled pattern covering his unwashed car, and then he remembered. The rain, yesterday afternoon. The rain had left blotches in the dust, marking the finish as if with dirty fingerprints.

He glanced over at the next car.

It, too, had the imprint of dried raindrops—but, close up, he saw that the marks were superimposed in layers, over and over again.

The Firebird had been through a great many rains.

He touched the hood.

Cold.

He removed his hand, and a dead moth clung to his thumb. He tried to brush it off the hood, but other moth

216

bodies stuck in its place. Then he saw countless shriveled, mummified moths pasted over the hood and top like peeling chips of paint. His fingers were coated with the powder from their wings.

He looked up.

High above, backed by banks of roiling cumulous clouds, the swarm of moths vibrated about the bright, protective light.

So the Firebird had been here a very long time.

He wanted to forget it, to let it go. He wanted to get back in the car. He wanted to lie down, lock it out, everything. He wanted to go to sleep and wake up in Los Angeles.

He couldn't.

He inched around the Firebird until he was facing the line of cars. He hesitated a beat, then started moving.

A LeSabre.

A Cougar.

A Chevy van.

A Corvair.

A Ford.

A Mustang.

And every one was overlaid with grit.

He paused by the Mustang. Once—how long ago?—it had been a luminous candy-apple red; probably belonged to a teenager. Now the windshield was opaque, the body dulled to a peculiar shade he could not quite place.

Feeling like a voyeur at a drive-in movie theater, McClay crept to the driver's window.

Dimly he perceived two large outlines in the front seat.

He raised his hand.

Wait.

What if there were two people sitting there on the other side of the window, watching him?

He put it out of his mind. Using three fingers, he cut a swath through the scum on the glass and pressed close.

The shapes were there. Two headrests.

He started to pull away.

And happened to glance into the back seat.

He saw a long, uneven form.

A leg, back of a thigh. Blonde hair, streaked with shadows. The collar of a coat.

And, delicate and silvery, a spider web, spun between the hair and collar.

He jumped back.

His leg struck the old Ford. He spun around, his arms straight. The blood was pounding in his ears.

He rubbed out a spot on the window of the Ford and scanned the inside.

The figure of a man, slumped on the front seat.

The man's head lay on a jacket. No, it was not a jacket. It was a large, formless stain. In the filtered light, McClay could see that it had dried to a dark brown.

It came from the man's mouth.

No, not from the mouth.

The throat had a long, thin slash across it, reaching nearly to the ear.

He stood there stiffly, his back almost arched, his eyes jerking, trying to close, trying not to close. The lot, the even light reflecting thinly from each windshield, the Corvair, the van, the Cougar, the LeSabre, the suggestion of a shape within each one.

The pulse in his ears muffled and finally blotted out the distant gearing of a truck up on the highway, the death-rattle of the moths against the seductive lights.

He reeled.

He seemed to be hearing again the breaking open of doors and the scurrying of padded feet across paved spaces.

He remembered the first time. He remembered the sound of a second door slamming in a place where no new car but his own had arrived.

Or—had it been the door of his car slamming a second time, after Evvie had gotten back in?

If so, how? Why?

And there had been the sight of someone moving, trying to slip away.

And for some reason now he remembered the Indian in the tourist town, slipping out of sight in the doorway of that gift shop. He held his eyelids down until he saw the shop again, the window full of kachinas and tin gods and tapestries woven in a secret language.

At last he remembered clearly: the Indian had not been entering the store. *He had been stealing away.*

McClay did not yet understand what it meant, but he opened his eyes, as if for the first time in centuries, and began to run toward his car.

If I could only catch my goddamn breath, he thought.

He tried to hold on. He tried not to think of her, of what might have happened the first time, of what he may have been carrying in the back seat ever since.

He had to find out.

He fought his way back to the car, against a rising tide of fear he could not stem.

He told himself to think of other things, of things he knew he could control: mileages and motel bills, time zones and weather reports, spare tires and flares and tubeless repair tools, hydraulic jack and Windex and paper towels and tire iron and socket wrench and waffle cushion and traveler's checks and credit cards and Dopp Kit (toothbrush and paste, deodorant, shaver, safety blade, brushless cream) and sunglasses and Sight Savers and tear-gas pen and fiber-tip pens and portable radio and alkaline batteries and fire extinguisher and desert water bag and tire gauge and motor oil and his money-belt with identification sealed in plastic

In the back of his car, under the quilt, nothing moved, not even when he finally lost his control and his mind in a thick, warm scream.

COMPULSORY
GAMES

by
Robert Aickman

The grandson of Edwardian novelist Richard Marsh, Robert Aickman is an English author of supernatural tales with several books to his credit, including a novel and one volume of autobiography. His public background and interests are varied, ranging from opera and theater to psychic research and the founding of the Inland Waterways Association, an influential group that has been responsible for considerable restoration of the ancient waterways of England. Aickman's stories of eerie and supernatural happenings, elegant and literate, blending allegory and enigmatic phenomena, have evoked enthusiastic critical acclaim but also the complaints of some readers who prefer their fare in the genre somewhat more explicit and conventional in handling. And, indeed, he can be oblique and baffling—but not without carefully wrought reasons. Different from almost any other writer, Aickman seems to view the supernatural as not a thing on the outside but something very much in everyday real-life, a quality always present, barely out of sight and occasionally encountered in sudden, accidental perceptions. For Aickman, the uncanny story, with its flashes of poetical experience, is a way of looking at life. This story is likely to be greeted by similar controversy, cries of bewilderment on the one hand, expression of delight on the other by those who see a master at work, quietly doing innovative things with the very basics of the form.

Some people are capable of pleasure, of enjoying themselves, but none are truly capable of content. A conviction of content can be sustained only by consistent coercion, outer or inner; and, even then, the underlying reality, the underlying mystery, inevitably seeps through, sooner or later, via some unforeseeable rift. Colin Trenwith was, in a sense, brought to destruction by his own best impulses, and yet, and *yet* . . .

There they were, he and Grace, in a little house (of which a long lease had been bought in a fortunate hour, because now it would have been hopelessly too expensive) between the Kensington High School and the Cromwell Road: fortified, as well as might be, against all things, except sickness, death, inflation, revolution, and chance. Colin had even evaded the perils of independent practice, and had taken a salaried job with a large firm. Children have come to symbolize such an unprecedented demand upon their parents (conflictual also), while being increasingly unpredictable almost from their first toddlings, as to be best eschewed; nor did the spouses of the Trenwiths' friends commonly tempt either of them to adultery. The Trenwiths, therefore, met life squarely. They knew about many of the dangers only too well, and saw no point in meeting any of them halfway. The dismal Mrs. Eileen McGrath seemed about as far removed from a threat as anyone 'or anything could be, nor were the Trenwiths wrong in this assessment, unconscious though

223

it doubtless was. It would be difficult to blame Eileen, either, for what happened.

The Trenwiths had a tiny garden between their front door and the fairly quiet street, but years ago it had been crazily paved all over by the outgoing tenant, and, though the Trenwiths did not care for the effect, they had not yet gone as far as to lift the stones and plant roses. Starting from the gate, the visitor to Mrs. McGrath's establishment had first to turn right, then to turn left, but for a crow there would have been less than two hundred yards in the trip.

Nonetheless, Mrs. McGrath lived in a different world. Some would point out that once the gentry had lived where she lived, and the servants of the gentry where the Trenwiths now lived—perhaps their gardeners. The former residences of the gentry (or near-gentry) were towering grey masses stuck together in twos. Each house had three storeys, with high rooms, and, even then, there were basements and, within the slated roofs, attics. Now the houses were cut up into flats, and sometimes even into bedsitters.

Colin Trenwith at some fairly early period realized that one reason why Eileen had such difficulty in finding tenants was that, without quite knowing it, she expected from each such person, a faintly familial, a quasi-mutual mode of life. She required, as it were, emotional as well as financial references; though emotional only in the quietest, soberest way. Colin sensed that in Eileen's loneliness was included the demanding element that loneliness fosters. When on one occasion he found words for this trait of Eileen's, however, Grace, to his slight surprise, denied it. Possibly she was in this matter too akin to Eileen for any demandingness to be recognized.

When things began to be really bad in his life, Colin found that he could simply not recollect how Grace and he had first met Eileen. As a matter of fact, he never recollected. It was certainly no regular "Good morning" in the street as they sped to work, because Eileen, as a senior civil servant, had to leave earlier than anyone else. "What about Austin Dobson and Edmund Gosse?" asked Colin, who had a mild interest in the fin de siècle. "They joined the civil service precisely because it allowed them time for their writing."

Eileen would smile and say that things had changed, without necessarily implying that she disapproved of the change. On most occasions Eileen's smile was that of one who, in the nature of her position, knew very much more than could be accessible to the person smiled at. This had always been a thing about Eileen which annoyed Colin, especially as sometimes he doubted the implication. Once more, when he put something of his annoyance into words for Grace's benefit, she made a remark about "All of us needing our defences" and, for the moment he found her almost as irritating as Eileen. Indeed, he brooded for some time on the trifle, and in the end wondered whether shared by Grace and Eileen was not something specifically feminine and intractable.

There was of course understood once to have been a Mr. McGrath. He was referred to by Eileen as Bobby. On the other hand, she never clearly stated what had become of him. Naturally the Trenwiths probed, but the relationship with Eileen was not of a kind to authorize a straight question, and for Colin it never became so, never could become so. There seemed to have been something more or less artistic about Bobby, because Eileen cited him as authority for any view of her own on such questions, whenever such question might arise. Bobby, it was clear, had once lived with Eileen in that same house. Colin Trenwith found this hard to visualize. The house itself was regularly referred to as having been acquired for investment; to supplement Eileen's future pension, and to enable her fully to lead the free life which her present responsible position precluded, but which was nonetheless her lodestar.

It was not that the Trenwiths and Eileen were ever on absolutely settled visiting terms with one another. The grim truth was that while the Trenwiths had their regular friends, Eileen had not. It was hard to explain exactly why this was, and all surmise seemed to include unkind elements which were doubly unkind because there was no positive proof of them. The way it settled down was that the Trenwiths did sometimes go to Eileen's dinner parties, where almost all the other guests were either important in the civil service or importantly attached in some way to the civil service network of employ, the women all in long dresses, the men all in dark suits, though not in dinner jackets, the conversation resolutely general and far-ranging; but that Eileen came to Trenwith social gatherings only three or four times in all, because, as Grace (this time) put it, she cast such a blight.

This blight was another mystery. It was not that Eileen made no attempt to contribute; nor was it that her general attitude was in any way unusual. Furthermore, she was by no means lacking in accomplishments. She could speak French, play golf, mountaineer, and even hold forth with authority on "fashion." It was simply that, do what she might, she seemed, from her first, almost elegant, entry into the room, never to "fit in," never to fit in at all, not even for a given period of five minutes. Perhaps it was the fact that always she came by herself; leading, moreover, to the alarming suspicion that almost always she was by herself. Could it have been that she stood influential but forlorn, at the centre of a (strictly metaphorical) vicious circle?

The usual thing was that she had dropped in when the Trenwiths, having dined (which they made a point of doing as nicely as possible), were otherwise alone. They brewed more coffee for her, gave her a liqueur and then another, ended with whisky nightcaps all around; and in these gestures acted gladly. On other evenings their telephone would ring and, a little more reluctantly, they would wend their winding way to Eileen's substantial abode, never more than half tenanted and seldom as much as that—at times, indeed, while it was between tenancies, quite .empty except for Eileen. God knows there was never anything much to talk about, but it was seldom that actual silence descended for very long, and, in any case, what could the Trenwiths do about the situation? What recourse had they? For years they fraternized with Eileen in the ways described, only, perhaps, on three nights in a fortnight; but very slowly and gradually, the frequency increased. Both Trenwiths noticed this, individually and severally.

"If only she wasn't so boring."

"If only she wasn't so lonely."

226

"If only she wasn't so dependent."

"After all, she draws down more than seven thousand quid; she ought to be able to do something with that. Her name's in *Whitaker's Almanac*."

"But not in *Who's Who*."

Then—or somewhere around that time—Grace's mother collapsed in India. For some time, Grace's mother had been taking up cults, cultivating them, in fact; so India was almost inevitable. Grace received a telegram from an Indian, completely out of the sky. Her mother, said the telegram, was very ill in an Indian hospital. Could she come at once? Grace had a quiet little job of her own, but she gave it up and went. Eileen McGrath brought influence to bear in obtaining her some kind of priority flight to the right spot at a convenient hour. The Trenwiths were impressed. It was the first time they could recollect Eileen displaying her prowess in such a way.

Eileen rang up again the same evening, and Colin always recalled that what struck him most was that Eileen's tone should have changed so *immediately*, albeit indefinably. Somehow he would have expected a running-in period, especially as there was no knowing how long Grace might have to be away; quite possibly months. All Eileen said on the telephone, however, was to point out that as they were both now solitaries, he might as well come round and she would see what she could do in the way of a scratch meal. This was spoken from her office to his office; and she said that he had better not arrive until about half-past eight because she would have to work late that evening, as on so many evenings. Never before had she expressed (at least to the Trenwiths) any awareness that she was a solitary. Quite on the contrary, in fact, all down the quiet years. At least as far as words went, Eileen was a magnet.

Colin, on his way home from work, bothered less about rushing, and stood himself an evening paper, which was not his usual practice (he could not help reading newspapers when once he had spent money on them). After entering the house, he stretched out his legs on the sofa for an odd and unwonted interlude: at one moment lost in whatever he was reading from the paper, at the next

227

looking up at the ceiling and thinking about nothing. Thus a good hour passed. If this was not relaxation, Colin speculated, he did not know what could be. It was a matter he had often felt anxious about, as do so many people. He even reflected that regular, normal life with Grace might be happier still if interwoven with phases, flowing and ebbing unbidden, when he merely stared at the ceiling, or the sky, and thought about nothing. He poured himself a whiskey and soda, and then a refill: unaccustomed procedures yet again, as he disliked solitary drinking, because he had long, long ago found he never got anything out of it.

In the exact circumstances, he must change into either a good suit—better than when they were all three together—or, alternatively, into some much more informal garb than he would normally have assumed for dinner with a lady, thus symbolizing the "scratch" element in the occasion. He simply could not remember whether he had ever before had a meal of any kind alone with Eileen. But he was distinctly out of the way of meals alone with a woman (he overlooked Grace for the moment). He wished it could be more of an adventure, just this one time; and he realized vaguely that this adventure sensation was powerful enough in its own right to be in some degree attaching itself even to Eileen, however absurdly. For the present, and until put to the imminent real-life encounter, the sensation was perceptibly better than nothing. He decided on the good suit.

Eileen was wearing not merely one of her long skirts but an entire long dress, quite sleek and tight. Colin could tell that it had not been worn often before, and could not decide what he felt about the situation. Eileen must be well over fifty, though it was hard to be sure, as she was not in *Who's Who*; but her figure remained modestly striking, her features were quite acceptable, her hair, more white than grey, had been cleverly confected, even her skin was reasonable. Colin had thought all this out for himself long ago, difficult though it always was to concentrate upon Eileen; but now, implicitly, it signified far more. And of course there was always the other side to Eileen: the inexpressive eyes of no particular colour, the large hands, the sudden movements.

And for better or for worse, that evening Eileen remained every bit as boring as ever, as unproductively self-concentrated. It was always as if Eileen mined more and more persistently into herself without ever finding a trace of gold. Here the change in the relationship between the two of them made no difference whatever. How could it, of course? And most assuredly the meal *was* of an improvised character: bits off the shelves and out of the fridge, jumbled and mingled without discretion. The thought distinctly crossed Colin's mind that Eileen might have been too wrought up to organize the gastronomic delicacies that are supposed so to subordinate men. But he dismissed the notion. Eileen's hospitality was never very original, even when directed at fellow seniors in the public service. And of course she had had no time. She never had time. "I suppose it's *possible* that she really has all that work to do," thought Colin.

Tonight there was a heavy, strong, very dark wine—much of it—in a big, rather clumsy decanter. Both of them drank it down freely, if only because it could hardly be said that they were any more en rapport than was ever the case. What about *me*? thought Colin. I wonder what Grace really thinks of me. He had not wondered very much about it before. What was Grace doing at that moment? Perhaps she was merely asleep somewhere (he was hazy about the international time system). Even so? People in bed alone are different from people in bed with someone else in the room. All that Eileen was able to contribute in the way of a spell left ample time and space to brood upon such generalities, upon alternative companions.

Eileen had always had a way of half offering in advance some such treat as the performance of a Beethoven recording by Moiseiwitsch, or the examination of an illustrated work on the *campi santi* of Sardinia, and then forgetting all about the matter when the time came. Colin could not remember when a single one of these promises had ever specifically materialized. But now as the meal drew to an end with less than half of the Florida peaches drawn from their glass bowl and devoured, he felt himself on familiar ground when Eileen jerked herself up and said, "I'll go and make us some coffee. Then you might care to listen to a record I've been given. It was a deputation from Israel, and it's Gilbert and Sullivan in Hebrew. I don't know what it's like. It's the kind of thing Bobby used to be mad about. Go into the drawing room, will you, and wait for me."

The drawing room was on the other side of a passage, both wide and high; and there was nothing to do when one arrived there, though Bobby in the distant past had doubtless contributed what he could. Colin wondered if he should not in the first place proceed to the kitchen (some way off) and offer to carry the tray. It was a thing that never arose when he had been there with Grace.

There ensured a substantial pause, with nothing in the road outside, and nothing to diminish a guest's sense of time. In the end, Colin was seriously wondering. Could Eileen be seizing the chance to wash up? Women snatched odd moments to do that, he had observed; and notably women with big outside responsibilities. Ought he to offer to dry? He even went to the drawing room door, which he had left ajar to facilitate the ingress of the laden tray; but he only stood there for a bit, hesitant and a little strained. There was nothing at all to be noted: not even the noises of a tenant upstairs (though he had understood that at the moment there was one). "This house is so empty that it's terrifying," thought Colin. Then he slowly returned to his armchair and huddled there, trying not to hear the passing cars and lorries and motorbikes and aircraft, many more of them than where he and Grace lived.

Ultimately Eileen returned to him, quite normally, with a silver tray bearing an engraved inscription to herself, and supporting a load of coffee accessories, bought second-hand but once the perquisite of a noble family whose crest appeared on each piece. "She really could be still very attractive," thought Colin, as she stopped, moved about, and smiled.

She and Colin sat on opposite sides of the room and conversed vacantly, though valiantly. But in the end there was an innovation. "You don't want to be bothered with that Hebrew lark," observed Eileen with sudden alertness. "What about this?" She made a characteristically swift plunge into the record cabinet, almost as if she had

230

"Softly awakes my heart" set up for the plucking; but what came out was only something modern. "Will you excuse me a moment," said Eileen. "Let me give you some more coffee." She jerked the decorated pot at him and was instantly gone.

This time the pause was quite brief, and then Eileen reappeared. She had changed into a pale blue dressing gown of the kind known as a kimono. There was a darker blue girdle tightly tied round her waist, but her neck was very uncovered. She was wearing the same near-evening shoes as before.

She stood for a few seconds in the doorway, looking determinedly away from Colin, and perhaps coping with herself. Then, anticlimactically, she swept Colin aside by saying: "There's no point in remaining all dressed up, is there?" Colin could not mistake her ennui or her finality. She was not advancing but withdrawing. All the same it was as if, in departing, she had for the first time momentarily arrived, become really present in the room, in the house, in life.

Once more she crossed to him with the coffee pot. He thought that her hand was shaking. He could smell a sweet, faint savour from her skin.

He had been at a loss for what could possibly be an appropriate thing to say, but now he spoke. "I was enjoying the evening," he said. "*Our* evening."

"Well, why not?" she replied, still looking entirely away from him.

She returned with the coffee pot to the other side of the room and, he noticed, set the pot down without refilling her own cup. She seated herself in the armchair behind the presentation tray with her elbow on one of the arms and her face in her hand. He suspected that, in her own way, she was weeping.

He drank a little coffee. "Eileen," he said in a low voice. "You're a very attractive woman, *very* attractive. Have you ever considered remarrying? You could have a wide choice, I'm certain."

Even more disconcertingly, she said nothing.

"It's no business of mine, obviously, but perhaps you've got into the habit of being too much alone."

"Yes," said Eileen. "That must be it." Colin could not

231

pretend to himself that this was other than hostility.

"Alone every minute of the day," continued Eileen, "except of course for nearly three thousand others, mostly bastards."

Colin was not so much astonished as alarmed. But it was no moment for weakness. "We all feel like that sometimes when we work for a large organization," he said steadily. "I wasn't so much thinking of your work."

"No?" enquired Eileen.

"You perhaps need an interest outside it as well," said Colin. "With me, it's books. Not that it's anything serious. But books take you away. And of course they often have a financial value, nowadays. There's that too."

But one of the most noticeable things about Eileen's house, or at least most noticeable to *him*, had always been there were no books in it of the kind that people read; so suddenly he feared that, quite without intention, there had been some malice in what he had said, a delectable self-preening. He had noticed before that Eileen brought out malice in him, even when he was consciously determined upon the opposite.

"Books aren't life either," said Eileen in exactly the same attitude.

"In some ways they are much better. Augustine Birrell said—" But Colin perceived that he was addressing the wrong person. Not that he often came upon the right person.

The cacophony from the record player stopped suddenly, as modern music does; but Colin could hear the record still rotating. Eileen did nothing to retrieve it.

"There are other hobbies than books," said Colin. "Outdoor ones as well as indoor."

"My fingers are not green fingers," said Eileen. "But I'm perfectly all right, thank you. Probably I'm undergoing the change of life." Colin would have supposed she was past that.

It transpired that during the very period of time (or as near as they could work it out) when Colin was sharing the scratch meal with Eileen McGrath, Mrs. Cooke, Grace's mother, was passing away; so that, after all, Grace was back within little more than a week, even the

232

funeral taking place almost immediately after the death, as, for good reasons, is customary in the Orient. After that there was nothing for Grace to stay out there for, as she herself observed.

When for as much as a week or ten days thereafter nothing was heard by the Trenwiths of Eileen, Grace asked Colin, "What have you done to her?"

Colin owned up about the scratch meal but, for the rest (if rest there had been), said merely: "I think she is very unhappy."

"I expect that was for *your* benefit," observed Grace.

By the time a further fortnight had passed, Grace was feeling concerned, not to be mistaken by herself or by others. Something was missing from her life, though Grace might not have admitted to it.

"I suppose she's all right? You did say that she seemed so unhappy. *I* never felt that she was particularly unhappy. You don't think she's been lying on the kitchen floor all this time and no one has noticed?"

"The Ministry would have noticed," remarked Colin.

"But they are under no obligation to tell *us*," rejoined Grace. "I tell you what I'm going to do. If we don't hear anything by Sunday, I'm going round on my own, Sunday morning."

"You always used to say we saw far too much of her," said Colin. "Are you sure it wouldn't be better to leave well alone?"

"We need to *know*," said Grace. "Or at least I do. You can please yourself. That's why I propose to go alone."

Colin reflected that Grace had not returned to that quiet little job of hers.

All the same, that was the moment when first he began to see Eileen as having far too much power over the two of them; an idea the more disturbing because, once admitted, there seemed no limit detectable, or even imaginable, to how far that power might in the end range, for how long, or of what quality it might prove to be. After his own fiasco (and what else was it?), Eileen had been just sitting there, judiciously waiting for Grace to return. Except, of course, that Eileen spent most of her life elsewhere, far more than average people do. There was *Whitaker's Almanac* to prove it.

It was a truly astonishing fact, after the persistent events of so many years, but Eileen never took an initiative with them again. She never again needed to. When (naturally) nothing had been heard from or of her by the Sunday morning, Grace put on some rather better clothes than she would otherwise have done and set off as she had said. She was gone for a long time; and well before she returned, Colin was not merely apprehensive (he had been that for most of the week) but famished also.

"Do you know it's twenty past three?" he exclaimed, as Grace came through the front door. It was not at all the way in which he spoke to her normally—or to anyone else, if he could help it.

Grace burst out laughing, which was equally unlike her customary behavior. She neither explained nor apologised but, as Colin had to admit, busied herself with unusual vigour and thoroughness in assembling a very good luncheon, however belated. All the time she seemed to be charged with good spirits, which had seldom been a way in which he would have described her (or would altogether have wanted her). Sometimes she hummed, which he always disliked in anyone. In the end, she suggested that they have a bottle of Côtes du Rhone. He could think of nothing to say, and she drew the cork herself, which he could not recollect her *ever* having done before in all the time he had known her. She did it with an odd flick of the wrist, apparently without effort. Of course it was not a good wine that might have been disturbed by such treatment.

She kept him in suspense, so that he lost most of his former appetite. He was certainly not going to take the lead in broaching the subject of Eileen, though there was no positive reason why he should not.

When the wine had softened both of them, and induced the usual illusion of fuller communion between them, she said not only that Eileen McGrath had decided to make flying her hobby, amateur aviation to be learned, qualified in, and practised from a club, but that she had persuaded her, Grace, to go along with her in the adventure. They

234

were to experience and suffer all jointly, and, when the time came, they were to pool their resources and purchase a "Moth" for their joint use. "I may not have enough cash to pull my weight properly, but Eileen said that didn't matter, and she'd make up any gap. That's what it is to have several thousand a year and no real expenses. Do you know those tenants of hers actually pay for the whole house? Well, most of the time."

"*Some* of the time," said Colin. And he could only think to add, "But what do you want to learn flying for?"

"For fun," replied Grace with some aggression. "Eileen says that when you have a plane and can fly it yourself, there is nothing you can't do."

"I doubt that. Not in the modern world, anyway. There are more restrictions on flying than on almost anything else you could think of."

"Oh, *Colin!* Don't be a spoilsport about *this*."

He was sincerely aghast by the implication. "When have I ever been a spoilsport? You shouldn't say that, Grace."

"*Always*. Always, always."

What could he rejoin? Except to enquire, "But do you really propose to do all this with Eileen McGrath, of all people?"

Grace replied quite quietly: "I find there's much more to her now she has something to take real interest in."

"But, Grace, you can't stand her! For years and years you haven't known where to put yourself when she was there."

"That's the most absurd exaggeration. It's simply that Eileen has been very unhappy all this time. Ever since we first knew her. You said that yourself."

"She's only doing this in order to mix with men," said Colin.

"I should have thought there were enough men in the civil service," said Grace.

The most immediate practical upshot was that Grace was never there. Previously her quiet little job had ended in time for her to be back in the house each day and completely in control before Colin returned. Now, on many evenings of the week, there could not be said even to be a regular meal, because Grace was attending a lecture, or otherwise committed to her "course." The weekends were worse: then she would be actually flying or otherwise in the bronzed hands of an instructor. At the public holidays there were mass junketings, airborne and otherwise. He had no place in any of these, nor did Grace invite him as a guest, or even as an onlooker. And as for Eileen, she, for better or for worse, had dropped right out of his life. Ruefully he concluded it was for worse - though in any past year he would have been astonished with himself.

But now the blunt fact was that Colin was entirely alone in life. It was not easy to seek sympathy, had Colin been a sympathy seeker by temperament, which he was not. He had never for one moment had the slightest inkling of how dependent upon Grace he had become for almost everything (though with physicality nowadays far, far down the list—as was to be expected). Still less had it even occurred to him that such as Eileen were contributing anything of value to his days. His life had seemed settled on a path peaceful, pleasant, and preferred; and, he had thought, chosen for the two of them as much by Grace and by himself. That, indeed, had been why he had become so fond of Grace.

Grace said little to him of any kind about her new preoccupation, though she perpetually mentioned Eileen in trivial contexts that very much irritated him. "I asked Eileen to post it for me," Grace would say. Or, "Eileen lent me this out of her store cupboard"—"this" being what Colin was then called upon to make the best of for his untimely and disjointed supper. It was as if Grace spent her entire time with Eileen, and most of it doing silly and unimportant things.

"Has Eileen still got a job?" he asked one day sarcastically.

Grace seemed not to perceive the sarcasm. "Yes, she has," Grace replied, "but she hopes to get out of it fairly soon. She will still be able to draw a pension of a kind, and she can do paid work connected with flying."

"What sort of work?" asked Colin, even more nastily.

"Delivery of planes. Community linkage. Private pilot-

236

age. There's plenty of choice. When one's qualified, of course."

Colin abstained from asking when that would be, because he had no wish to know. Likewise he abstained from enquiring of Grace whether a niche was being kept open in these plans for her. He suspected that, had he raised the matter, he would have received a reply both perfectly straight and vigorously affirmative. One of the things that upset him most was that Grace refused to acknowledge that she was doing anything much out of the ordinary or outside her own wont, still less anything that could entitle him to make even the smallest moan. One man whom he *had* ventured timidly to tell what was happening had been similarly dismissive: "Women go in for these things nowadays. We men just have to wake up and accept it. Nothing else we *can* do, is there?" And the man guffawed.

Colin had noticed that the more helpless and tragic a situation, the more the English resorted to laughter.

Few in any case would use such words as "hopeless" and "tragic" about the mess he was in. Grace was fully within her rights, and he had no comparable rights he could wield against her. When he raised the question of their next holiday (the date, always settled by his firm far in advance, had been known to Grace for an eternity), she replied casually and genially that she proposed using the time for some really hard practice.

"But it's the only holiday I get in the whole year!" cried Colin, taut and desperate. "You don't have to choose just those weeks."

"My instructor's going on holiday shortly afterwards," she explained breezily.

"But what about me?" Colin was palpably losing his grip.

"You can do whatever you like, Colin. I don't want to interfere with your plans in any way." As if *she* were not his "plans"; as she had been, so reliably, for a steady number of years.

"Don't you care for me, Grace, any more?"

"Of course I do." She smiled widely. "I love you very much and I always shall."

237

A year ago, all the words that matter had suddenly changed their meanings—and changed them forever. Nor was this process of change going to cease. Colin felt that he would never even die. Rather was he to be endlessly dragged out of himself, moulded, melted, and miniaturized; while all the time, his real self remained entirely conscious but entirely powerless, like a discarded chrysalis still with feeling. A manikin was materializing while the man watched, having first been paralysed. But perhaps most marriages are like this in the end, thought Colin one night.

And soon the current of events sliding towards his final devastation began to race. On one and the same day, Grace told him that she was now permitted to fly "solo" and that Eileen McGrath and she were buying their Moth.

"You can't afford it, Grace." Colin at least knew *that* very well.

"I've always had a little package under the bed that I didn't tell you about. And if that's not enough, Eileen's going to help me out, as I told you."

"Do you mean to say that you've had sources of income that have been omitted from my tax returns? That's a serious offence, Grace, and it's I who am liable for it, not you."

"Fuss, fuss, fuss." She chuckled at his torment. Yet it was not that she was treating him with direct contempt. It was more that she evinced entire lack of interest in his need and life patterns; though doubtless she would have protested, with all the sincerity of indifference, that he was perfectly entitled to whatever life patterns he pleased. just as *she* was.

He could not speak to her.

"Colin. I never said a word about sources of income."

He stared. "Do you mean you've got a large sum of capital which you've not even bothered to invest? Really, we're hardly as rich as that!" All his bitterness concentrated upon this visible aspect of the travail.

"I'm investing it now. In a beautiful, scarlet Moth."

And soon, there it was, in the sky: snarling and puttering round the area between the Kensington High Street and

238

the Cromwell Road, converging in diminishing spirals upon the Trenwiths' house (and Eileen's house too, of course), much less a moth than a wasp closing in on a pot of marrow jam or bowl of rum punch. Whoever it was up there, whichever of the two, had come to greet him, to recognize his existence. It was a sunny Sunday morning. The buzzing horror was so rubicund, so vibratory, so malign that Colin, who had at first dashed out of the front door onto the crazy paving, put his hands over his eyes after the briefest glance at it. Indeed, he actually screamed. His scream was audible above the pandemonium from the empyrean, or so the neighbour's children said. They were thoroughly acclimatized to even the rowdiest aircraft, but less so to grown men loudly screaming. Only machines are entirely real for children today.

Colin fled back into the house, sat on the narrow staircase, and tried to think. Surely small private planes, *amateur* aircraft, did not churn the slates off roofs as this machine must be doing? He even recollected something about General de Gaulle having forbidden all overflying of Paris. But had it been *all*, or only the overflying of vast airliners? More important: was it legal, even in Britain, for private aviators to circle above dense residential areas? To no question that concerned aviation, legal, technological, or metaphysical had he the ghost of an answer; because his mien had silenced Grace, who might have been well pleased to enlighten him.

Nor did he find himself in a position to make good any such omissions when she returned. This was because she never did return. Neither did Eileen McGrath return; if "return" was, in her case, the word.

Colin was, of course, distraught about Grace's unexplained absence that Sunday night, though he had not yet decided to telephone the police, the hospitals, and whoever else is to be telephoned when people have to be accepted as "missing." He had positively resolved *not* to ring up any of them. Grace was a middle-aged woman, perfectly able to look after herself. (Indeed, one of his routine remarks in recent months had been "You're a middle-aged woman and can't carry on like a crazy girl.")

239

And he himself by this time knew the way round his own twilight life.

`It proved to be just as well that he had done nothing sudden or rash; because on the Monday morning a letter arrived from Grace saying, perfectly pleasantly, that she and Eileen were taking a house near the flying club. He would be sure to find it noisy, she remarked, with a glint in her eye, or at least in her writing instrument. Perhaps for that reason she gave no address.

After reading this epistle, Colin had to leave for the office almost immediately; but that evening he strolled round to Eileen's abode, first right, then first left. When he arrived there, he found that the front door was painted purple instead of green and, when he rang, that Eileen had apparently sold the house months before. It was now occupied by a different class of person altogether, and there was little to be communicated, at least to Colin. Colin reflected that perhaps Grace and he should have had children. It was a thought that had often come to him during the past twelve months. *How many* children? he also wondered. The children in the street stopped playing about and gawped silently at him as he passed.

Grace failed to return, and Eileen failed to return, but to compensate, the big, red, noisy Moth came back often. It can't really be big, thought Colin: it must really be quite small. The enormous shadow it cast must be a trick of the light: refraction or something of that kind. Colin remembered the term from the *Children's Encyclopoedia*—his own childhood set. All the same, Colin deemed it unwise to challenge that shadow, to "let it fall on him." In fact, he would dodge from side to side of the street to prevent any chance of this happening; and drifting round Kensington Gardens had become impossible because his dartings about made the children giggle and follow. The simplest and most obvious thing was to remain, as far as possible, indoors—"at home," as it is called. When he was safely shut up with the curtains drawn, there was only the noise to worry about, though that could be very unpleasant indeed.

Not that these things happened all the time. Colin could hardly have continued his normal life (new pattern) if they had. Perhaps twice a week was the average for the present; or some frequency greater by a decimal addition if the period chosen was a month. Moreover he rarely heard, let alone saw, anything when he was actually in the office. This had the natural consequence that he became fonder and fonder of office life. The solitude in which he otherwise dwelt (he lacked both the heart and the talent to entertain without Grace) helped here also. He became warmly aware of desirable qualities in fellow workers whom previously he had not even noticed. The females, in particular, had become quite charming and interesting, even the ones in middle life, long married and settled, not in a position to worry much about men like Colin.

Mostly, therefore, it was when he was in his house or in the street that the trouble came, sometimes distantly buzzing, sometimes suddenly swooping so that, on occasion, he had to run really fast in order to avoid the shadow. He had been a quite successful quarter-miler when at school, but nowadays he was glad when there was no sun, for then there could be no shadow. Moreover, sunshine always brought back that sunny Sunday morning when the Moth first intruded upon him . . . It couldn't really *be* a Moth, he supposed. Not by now. But Grace had always termed it a Moth, and he knew too little to propose an alternative.

There was a tiny garden at the back of the house also, but that had long been something of a compromise. In the days when the houses had been occupied by servants there had doubtless been regular crops of cabbages, a few geraniums, and plenty of mint all the year round. The Trenwiths had been less industrious and, no doubt, less needy. Grace, as it happened, had not been very fond of gardening. Colin recalled what Eileen had said of herself when last he saw her: "My fingers are not green fingers." It was becoming quite difficult to detach, or even distinguish, the memory of Grace from the memory of Eileen. Incredible! But after life has begun to run away from us, nothing is ever again really credible, nor does it matter.

Colin was obliged to enter the back garden from time to time in order to reach the dustbin (the men emptied it by drawing it through a hatch in the back fence). That evening on which he first became aware that Grace and Eileen were becoming confused in his memory, he had

241

just lifted the lid when the Moth (or whatever it really was) swooped catastrophically from the highest of high heavens. It had dropped on him with no warning at all, unless Colin's thought about the two women had amounted to a premonition. Perhaps that was so, because this time the machine came low enough for him to identify the pilot —that matter he had wondered about from the first because a thing he *had* understood was that there could be only one pilot.

And at these newly close quarters, the answer was simple: there appeared to be *no* pilot. The monstrosity was in perfectly free flight; though another (and possibly more hopeful) way of putting it might be that the machine was out of control.

Its inhuman breath and the tremendous swirl of its passage laid Colin low. The children at the windows of the houses at the back saw him shrink and collapse, possibly striking his head on the hard rim of the dustbin. If that happened, there was no sound of it detectable by the children, because there was so much other sound. On most days and nights in Kensington there is aircraft noise of some kind, somewhere: sometimes louder than at other times, according to the direction of the wind and other circumstances more remote. It was pitch dark when Colin came to himself again (if truly he ever did).

He resolved to take a grip and see what a week in the country could do; and he even managed to obtain the necessary leave of absence. Possibly some in the office had had enough of the new Colin's anxious fraternization. Almost at random he selected a hotel he did not know in a place he did not know (though harmless enough). As people do at such times, he thought he needed novel surroundings; and, in any case, places he did know were saturated with memories of Grace.

The Trenwiths had at one time owned a small motorcar, but it had been unexpectedly costly to house, in that their little abode had no garage; and they found out, in any case, they were using it less than they had expected, doubtless because they fared perfectly well (or so it had seemed) without necessarily leaving home.

So Colin set off for the countryside by train. There are few slow trains nowadays, linking one real place with another real place; but Colin's train did stop several times before reaching his destination. Each time the noise of the wheels ceased, Colin became aware of its place being taken by aircraft noise above. The idea that each time it was the same noise from the same machine was so unlikely that Colin decided to dismiss it. The fact that to him it certainly each time sounded exactly the same probably implied (or confirmed) that his mind was giving way: now a quite minor consideration.

Instead of stopping at stations now closed and useless, the train regularly stopped in the middle of the landscape. At those times the aircraft noise without was particularly like the distinctive noise with which he was so familiar. There had always been occasional days, however few, when even at the office there had been a fairly steady, very individual, buzzing above and around. Colin's ears had learned to discriminate.

At his point of arrival, Colin found that he could hardly move. All his strength, all his identity were being drawn out of him—and, throughout, some part of him had to watch it happening, the main part of him, the real man, the implicit ghost. He was being mashed up and transmogrified before his own inner eyes; and the new entity, deprived of all egoism, would live forever.

Still, the unknown hotel seemed quite nice, as far as one could tell; though Colin had not altogether grasped before his departure from Kensington how expensive hotels had become.

The machines cost enormous sums to maintain; and every day there are more of them, and huger, and more intricate, more bossy. One cannot expect there to be much wealth left over for obsolete patterns of life.

It would have been quite jolly in the hotel room, had Grace been with him; but, without her, it was lonely. Nor did the buzz-buzz on the horizon show much prospect of easing off.

Common sense suggested that, from that day forward, it would never ease off. Colin wondered if henceforth it would not be continuously louder, or virtually so, even in the office. He felt sick.

Question one: what had he done or not done to bring all this about? Question two: what had Colin's actions or inactions to do, in any case, with why things happened to Colin? Life was gross and headstrong and, when set to destroy, proffered its own virulent fatality.

At the edge of the country town was the big house, with a high wall round its curtilege. A card at the hotel "reception" stated that the gardens of this house were open to the public. Colin was passionate neither for botany nor for horticulture but, as a visit to the gardens was doubtless usual, he thought he might as well have a look. Also, there was not an enormous amount else to do, even though Colin was in the place for a week.

Soon after he had paid to enter the gardens, Colin realized that the distant roar had stopped. There had been no queue at the improvised cash desk, which took the form of a battered kitchen table, manned by a crouched figure with sparse whiskers, assuredly an old age pensioner. Moreover, Colin seemed to be the only person within the gardens. It was "an ordinary weekday," and on ordinary weekdays people are not free to visit gardens. Possibly also these particular gardens had been open too continuously for too long. The maintenance struck Colin as scamped and scanty; and if there were no visitors, there were no gardeners either. The terra cotta edgings to the flowerbeds were much chipped, and sometimes whole sections were missing. Weeds were beginning to be noticeable on the once gravelled paths, like mould on bread. Not one of the statues appeared to be complete, and all of them were black. The ornamental waters were full of sewage.

Colin tried to make the best of the afternoon. He essayed a real effort in that direction; even if it were to be his last. And, after all, at least it was quiet here. Not only had the one particular noise ceased; it seemed to Colin as if all noise had ceased. It was like heaven in the moments before the music is heard. Even the pensioner had been palpably deaf, perhaps totally so. Colin had been able to submit the exact sum specified on the poster, and had not needed to converse with him.

Colin soon came to the house. It was obvious why only the gardens were open to the public. The house, though once beautiful, looked as if it had been unoccupied for a generation. Neglect was approaching the well-known point of no return. Even the weed growth was thicker on the wide walk which ran the length of the garden front and much further in both directions. At one point among the weeds were a round can that had once contained an American beverage and a red, romper-type garment, discarded, dirty, and diminshed by the weather.

Colin thought he might as well continue to the back. It would be as well to see everything, and what else was there to do which might promote recuperation?

The back of the house, being the part in which so much of the living had gone on, looked more blighted and less beautiful than the front. But the neglected lawns (the mowing schedule needed to be at least doubled) and the wide grey paths spread out at the back as at the front. A drive for the owners of the house and their visitors went off to Colin's leftward, and a delivery drive for tradesmen also wandered away among concealing bushes and low, necessary structures. The first and main drive was barred by a length of circular pipe, dark brown with rust, and extended between battered trestles. No doubt the other and working approach was still in occasional use. Surely *something* was being done from time to time . . .

There seemed no clue or guidance as to the expected next step. The visitor was very much "on his own." Of course, there were many things to be said in favour of that. At some distance away, half-left from where Colin stood, was a walled kitchen garden. Colin was in no doubt about what it was (or had been), but next he noticed that a number of small heads rose in a line above the faded brick wall. The same complete silence continued, but it was difficult to doubt that the heads were observing what Colin might do next, even if because there was so little else that was mobile to gaze at. By instinct, Colin went forward along a line which diverged from the back of the house at an angle more or less similar to the angle which led to the kitchen garden, though in the other direction. He even crossed lawns to do it, as the paths had been laid largely in parallels with the house.

On and on he went, traversing the half-mown near-prairie. When he considered that the kitchen garden was sufficiently far behind him, he picked up the system of paths again, though many of them were lumpy and stony from insufficient attention and insufficient use.

Ah! Three other visitors!

They were not together either. Quite far from it, indeed, even though all of them had come into view simultaneously, at least where Colin was concerned. Nor did any of them seem to be in movement. They were all some way off, and Colin saw no need to stare at them. On the contrary, Colin's need, as ever nowadays, was to hold on if possible, to whatever might be left of his own mere being. "Dotted about" was the way Colin might have described those other visitors. He continued with calm on his previously decided way, allotting to the others no especial attention.

But despite everything he became aware that they were encroaching. It was the only word for it. Not only were they no longer where they had been, but much, much closer: they were also, very positively, intruding and ousting. He could feel the combined thrust of them and that he was shrinking beneath it, while, very curiously, at the same time he could see them standing over there: still keeping their distance apparently, albeit so much nearer than before. Moreover, the horizon had begun once more to buzz.

The three figures were now differently related to one another: two very near, the third considerably more distant. Colin strained his eyes to identify this further figure. In the end there was no need for strain. The far figure was himself, smiling broadly. This was what would survive of him forever: if "survive" was at all the word; if there *was* a word.

It was hard to say how much time passed, but into the buzz was now entering a cold, ear-destroying but still quasi-human shriek.

Then the pilotless red Moth, its proper size as uncertain as ever, hurtled across and down, absorbing and dissolving and slaying, grotesquely beyond all question that Colin could formulate or answer that he could accept.

New, smiling Colin would have no need for either; and what is more, no use.

SUMS

by
John Jakes
and Richard E. Peck

JOHN JAKES, although the author of many books on many subjects, is perhaps best known to readers of fantasy and science fiction for his stories of Brak the Barbarian, whose exploits rank high with devotees of the sword and sorcery tale. More recently he has broken into the best-seller lists with a several-book saga of American historical novels, including The Bastards *and* The Rebels.

RICHARD E. PECK is the author of several published short stories in Orbit *and other markets and a science fiction novel from Doubleday. All of which is no preparation for this very good traditional ghostly story, executed with grace and sensitivity.* '

Two hundred yards off a country road, the Vineville School sits shielded from casual view by a screen of huge box elders, oaks, and sycamores. Between those trees and the road itself lies a swale of waist-high grass brushing whispers over the August moon. Two splintered posts, once whitewashed bright but long a faded dusty grey, stand sentinel in the grass to mark a narrow drive leading into the schoolyard. Its yellow width of sandy gravel has become a pair of dusty ruts in which the patches of wild rye, clumped clover gone to seed, and shoots of box elder all wave varieties of green. For years no one has entered the gravel drive. Few people travel over the country road, now that the interstate highway two miles south can speed the anxious through this idle countryside; and fewer still would think to glance aside, to waste a moment on the red brick building glimpsed by accident if at all.

But Harold Thorson knew the school was there. He knew every school in the county, the old, decayed, abandoned and the new alike. As county superintendent he knew them all in many ways. Each represented this or that bond issue, so much investment, so many staff and numbers of shouting, pushing children, maintenance costs and budgets, football schedules, luncheon menus, heat and lights and chalk erasers. For all those schools, such factual matters lined themselves in ledgered rows in Harold's calculator mind. Only one of them stood out as different. Vineville. Where Thorson once had been among the children in the cloakroom frosty mornings, joking, teasing, hanging scarves and mittens on the numbered hooks and stamping snow from red galoshes as he fought with Bobby Reimer or the Kipness girl.

Thirty years ago. Before consolidation of the county schools, years before school buses and free lunch, when twice a month the children lined up giggling at Mrs. Baker's desk to get their goiter pills (lavender in color but chocolate on the tongue), before efficiency and ledgers and before the county board had modernized it all. And now, Vineville School—to be demolished in a month.

"Are you sure?" Harold asked them. "It's the last one in the county, maybe even in the state. Several people have proposed that we make a sort of museum of it, a place to house records or memorabilia." That last was a lie. Not several people at all. It was Harold's idea, but the board didn't need to know that.

For the next three or four minutes, the board members whispered among themselves. Nothing malicious, Harold knew. Just a little technique of theirs, a reminder that they owned the power; he held his position by the grace of their good will—that, and a slight majority vote.

Thickening heat pressed down on him. Bill Reimer's pipe lazed out ribbons of blue smoke. Harold wished they'd end the whispered conference. They all had other matters waiting. The Holcomb family's accusation, for one. To the effect that Mrs. Zarumian, Civics II, was a Marxist. "A Marxist!" God save us. Harold had an impulse to kill the Holcombs.

To spend his own life embroiled in such idle feints and parries . . . He supposed it served the youngsters in the long run. But it seemed so wasteful of the precious hours of a man's lifetime on earth. So useless, so incapable of adding up to anything worthwhile.

He tried to check his rising temper; his heart was hurrying in his chest, a three-legged colt cantered over gravel. Mental note. Back on the weight problem. The doctor said —

"It's settled, Harold." Ellen Willets tapped her lacquered nails on the tabletop and glanced at the other Board members. They all nodded. Even Bill Reimer, lost in smoke.

Harold's breath stopped for a frightening instant. He

250

crammed a hand into his coat pocket, reaching for the vial, one of the small white pills. His heart lumbered, his left upper arm ached. Budgets. Committee meetings. A Marxist—lord! For what? To what?

Fingers hidden in the pocket, curled around the vial he could slip it out and take one of the pills in fifteen minutes, at their break—he said, "Bill? You remember. When we were both in Mrs. Baker's class? Don't you think . . ."

Reimer shook his head. "Tear it down."

Harold parked his three-year-old Chevy on the shoulder and walked across the softening blacktop to the faded driveway posts. That's what they all wanted. What could he do about it? What did he *want* to do about it? He had agreed, concealing his reluctance. And then, only this morning, walking the empty tiled and echoing hallways of the new high school, he had felt the impulse to come back to Vineville, for one last look.

The heat struck his body as a force. It accentuated the feel of extra pounds hanging on him like a leaden yoke, pounds that intensified the heart problem about which he'd been repeatedly warned. Take it easy, Harold. Don't carry it all on your shoulders, Harold. But if he didn't deal with idiots like the Holcombs, who else would?

He tried to forget them, and the heat. But his upper left arm was throbbing again. He slipped a pill from the vial and swallowed it. Then he scuffed his oxfords in the dusty drive. That helped. The memories flooded in on him.

Another August, thirty years before, he had ridden his bike two miles from home to wander the empty schoolyard the week before classes began. The months of that year, and of the years that followed, seemed a blur to him now, with only a few episodes standing bright and clear before him. The early September days, buttery at the morning edges as he walked to school. In the schoolyard, grasshoppers whirring up from cover at his feet—quick, fluttered explosions of sound that faded softly away. You caught them and said, "spit and I'll let you go." There was recess, and the fort they'd built of planks and oil cans in the corner of the yard against Schmidt's fence. Eating a warm orange and folding waxed paper carefully to take it home for one more day, one more lunch. And Mrs. Baker.

He reached the treeline and took off his suit coat to sling it over his shoulder. The breeze cooled his sweat-soaked shirt and he felt loose, young again. To his right lay the playground area—no blacktop and expensive gym equipment in those days, only the ragged baseball diamond, each base a dusty gouge that filled with puddles in the late fall rain.

The school itself was smaller than he'd remembered, the bricks not so red, the steps not so tall. Plywood squares covered the windows like pennies on a deadman's eyes; but by squinting Harold could pretend he didn't see them. A squint. That's all it took. And the building, playground, all grew new again. He stood at the foot of the steps and turned his back to the school, surveying the playground. It really hadn't changed all that much, he hadn't changed all that much.

Then, to his right, he saw the clump of lilacs, spindly reeds grown tall and leafless near the base. It was his special place—had been his special place. A circle of bushes eight or more feet tall, their leaf-freighted tops bowed inward to create a canopy over the cool and shaded spot he'd often gone to eat his lunch, or tell the summer stories that all children brought to Vineville in the fall.

Cool. And shaded. Beneath the overhanging bows the earth, nearly black and satin-like, felt smooth against his palms. Harold sat against the thickest clump of stalks and stared out through the mottled shadows at the school again. If he let his imagination play, he could almost hear the others—Billy Reimer and the Kipness girl, Dorcas Schmidt and all the rest—playing pom-pom-pullaway or prisoner's base in the hot sunlight while he lay in pleasant shadow and observed. He felt the coolness of the earth, smelled orange peel and tasted peanut butter, heard the teeter-totter creak its grating rhythms.

Harold's head came up. His eyes opened. He started to laugh, softly, then checked it, embarrassed to make the sound with no one there to listen. He slid a foot back and pushed himself up. Bits of dying grass drifted from his trousers. The frozen sunburst of a burr slung to his cuff.

252

He tasted the salt on his upper lip, tried to reconstruct. He remembered sitting down in the lilac clump. He didn't remember falling asleep.

His watch, and the disc of the sun, showed him he hadn't dropped off for long. He bent and pushed his way out of the lilacs. Though pleasant as a sentimental exercise, his return to Vineville now struck him as foolish. If he had hoped to find some clever answer to the problem of demolishing the place—or even an answer to the troubling question of why he was concerned at all—he hadn't. Moving with purpose over the shimmering playground, he was pleased that no one watched him, had been watching him return to his special place. These days there was no room for special places, and little understanding of the need for them. One schoolroom, one physical plant—one life—had to resemble the next. His included.

He hurried, conscious of the searing heat of the blacktop through the soles of his oxfords. A two-thirty meeting with the chairman of the junior high science departments. To discuss - what? The sun addled him; he shook his head.

Yes. Centralized purchasing of lab supplies. Put your mind back on it, Harold. There was no way on God's earth to perpetuate his whim, to preserve Vineville School nor any good reason why he should try.

He remembered dropping his coat on the concrete steps. The coat was gone.

Angry with himself—forgetting things already, Harold, sure sign of old age—he stalked back to the Chevy. Though the windows were down, the inside was an inferno. And empty. No coat.

Slowly, beginning to understand even then, he turned. He squinted through the filmy summer haze, to the school door between the plywood squares which seemed to stare back at him. Take a step or two, closer -

He saw the vertical strip of blackness, wafer-thin but unmistakable. The door no longer touched the doorframe.

Without even asking the question, he believed he knew who had opened it. There was fear in his knowledge, but of a strange, almost relaxing quality. He started walking up the drive again, his chest tightening across its entire width.

He seldom allowed himself to think of that particular

series of memories. Only when he'd had a beer or two, or when some reminiscent scent caught him off guard, did he invite those recollections back from where they lay hidden; they made smiling easier, at certain times. He did not exactly think of the memories now, either. But they lay inside him, bright as images on the videotape monitors all new high schools had to have - and his stomach hurt with excitement, anticipation.

Climb the stairs, not quickly, in fear, but with awful expectation. Awful, in the original meaning of it

His freckled hand barely touched the greenly corroded handle. The door swung in. He smelled hot dust and shuttered animal droppings; saw the metal-framed desks, four rows creating aisles which narrowed into distant darkness. He push'ed the door back. His throat felt thick. He moved from light to the inner shadows, expecting cruel heat. Perhaps the heat was there, and he was so cold he couldn't feel it.

Several plywood battens on the side windows hung agape, no longer a tight fit. Shafts of light penetrated, enough to show him his coat, resting across the top of a desk someone had dusted. The coat was carefully folded. Then in dappled shadow he saw Mrs. Baker, waiting.

He turned once. Out the door he saw the flare of sun on the Chevy's hood. And, distantly, the span of expressway, a diameter across the world, a disconnected span beginning nowhere, ending nowhere, yet endlessly busy

When he turned back, Mrs. Baker was still there.

She smiled at him. "Hello, Harold. Won't you sit down?"

He squeezed into a front desk, not caring about the years of accumulated dirt that smeared his trousers. "I I've never seen you here before."

"But I've seen you, when you came occasionally. I thought the time had come to speak to you."

Mrs. Baker rose from her chair. She wore the outfit he remembered: a skirt, sweater, plain shoes. A gold heart locket on a chain of tiny links, the heart lying there between her breasts, where he'd so often stared at it, with longing. And with shame.

Mrs. Baker's sweater looked warm. Her forehead did not. Cool and curved as he remembered, it rose to the sweep of her fair hair. He had never gotten used to her name. A girl . . . Woman? What was she? Twenty-four, that much had been certain; twenty-four when he last saw her. He had never gotten used to her being *Mrs.* Baker. And now she still wore the cheap silver band on her left hand.

Harold had seen Mr. Baker from across the street as he emerged from Silbey Brothers' Funeral Home, at the end of that week in July when it had rained without stopping. Mr. Baker hadn't looked old enough to be studying for a graduate degree in engineering at State. But then, Mrs. Baker had never looked old enough to be a teacher, though she was two years out of Normal, and driving to State every day that summer for advanced work. On a Tuesday morning their used Hudson blew a tire on a rain-slick curve—

Damn him for not getting her a good car! Harold thought.

Then he felt foolish, foolish as he felt, at times, among his memories. A rational corner of his mind kept reminding him: he hadn't looked old enough, back then, to care about a girl—a woman—a *Mrs.* Baker—twice his age. But then, there was no explaining how you were marked in the yesterdays.

"I never knew how you felt till afterward, Harold," Mrs. Baker said. "I've never had the chance to tell you . . . I didn't want to frighten you—I hope you're not afraid of me now, but . . . It touched me a lot. It really did. I've wanted to take your hand and make you feel how much."

Harold wiped the back of his hand across his mouth. He noticed the top of the desk, now partially hidden by Mrs. Baker. *Mrs.* It still sounded wrong to him. Her fingers had been resting on the desk when he groped his way in. No marks disturbed the dust.

"You've watched me before?"

"Yes, whenever you've come. It's nice to have someone come back. No one else does."

"How long have you been here?"

"Actually, ever since the accident. What you see of me can't leave. A person's always a part of where they lived and breathed, you know. Perhaps they're never seen —or not often—afterward. But if they did more than

255

just pass through a place, a part of them remains in it forever."

He lurched to his feet. "They're going to tear the school down. I'm the county school superintendent now "

"I know, Harold. I have ways of keeping up."

"Even I can't stop it."

"That's why I knew I had to speak to you. You mustn't let them just destroy this place. It meant too much, to many people. And of course I'm being selfish. Once Vineville's gone, I don't know what will become of . . . this part of me."

"But why here?" Dust motes lifting on the slanted sunlight sparkled in the air between them. Harold squinted, leaned toward her. "You had another life, with . . . with *him*. Why here?"

"Now I know what really mattered." Her smile was warm, and real. It was! He knew that as he'd never known a thing before. "He and I were different, Harold. It took some time for me to see that. Even after—"

"He's married again, did you know?"

"It doesn't matter anymore. What matters is the present. We have to talk."

"Yes, Mrs. Baker." He sat again, folding his hands on the scarred desktop. One nervous finger traced initials carved and blackened in the polished wood.

She turned away, moving gracefully to the blackboard at the front of the room. "Arithmetic, Harold. Shall we work at numbers now?" Her smile drew a shy nod of response. "Good. You always enjoyed arithmetic, didn't you? I could see it in your eyes, the eagerness to move along, impatience with the others not so quick as you. Try this." She wrote on the blackboard: $12 + 30 =$

"Forty-two."

"And this." Again she wrote, the chalk whispering across the board, her wrist and arm an ivory blur before him. "Add this, Harold." $24 + 0 =$

"Twenty-four," he whispered.

"Aren't those numbers better?" She turned toward him slowly, her chin lifted high. "I waited for you, did you know? For all these years, each time I saw you passing by, the times you stopped and hesitated at the gate, and even when you thought of me and didn't know it, I was here. Waiting."

Without willing it, he was on his feet. "I have to tell you something." His voice was harsh, hoarse, and rasping. "Wait! There's something you don't know. I saw you and . . . you and *him*. I was outside your house one night, when . . . I couldn't help it, really! Walking past, and the shades were up, and . . ."

"I know." Gently she laid a hand on his cheek. "I knew at the time. It was you I was thinking of, only you. Even then, but what could I say? A boy half my age . . ." Her eyes were black and bottomless, her hand the scent of anise, sherry, tangerine.

"No!" He jerked away and stumbled clumsily against his desk. "Not yet." He sucked desperately at the fetid air. "Let me say it all. Those letters you got, *I* was the one who sent them. Vile! Terrible! How could I—"

"Not terrible, Harold. Pure and lovely. You were only twelve, how else could you express what you felt? There's nothing to forgive, except your shyness, and the time you've made me wait." Again she reached to touch him.

Something flickered in the darkness to his left. He pulled away and peered into the haze-filled corners of the room. Nothing there. No one. As his eyes returned to hers it came again—a flash of light, a winking glitter. He ignored it. Her hands lay cool upon his cheeks and pulled him nearer, closer, toward her. The husky taste of copper filled his throat and made each breath a labor both of pain and promise. Through misted eyes he watched his own hands rise to rest upon her shoulders. Bare. Cream and honey to the touch, her sweater gone as easily as that. He ran a thumb along the straps which drew depressions in the softness of her flesh, and they were gone. Slowly his hands drifted down her back and traced the velvet hollows of her.

Then her voice was in his ear, each sibilant a rush of ocean or the summer wind across a plain of wheat. "Talk to me, Harold," she whispered. "Tell me you won't let them kill me. Not again. Not another time. This is me, here. This is you and I, here. Say you'll save me, save us, say that we can always meet like this."

Something rustled in the darkness at his back.

"Please?" Her lips caressed his ear, his shudders made him draw her closer till his arms ached from the strain of trying not to crush the warmth he held, finally, after

257

all this time, held in his own arms. "Please? They'll never know. No one comes here now but you. The road's abandoned, no one passes by. How would they know?"

"I can't. How could I explain?"

Then she was hands. The shirt slid from his trembling shoulders as he stood in anguish. To protect her—somehow. To keep this moment. There had to be a way. "But if they found out—"

"How could they, Harold? Blind and hurrying, all of them, all the time. That road out there, this building, these are us. Not them. Let them have their highways, all the furious treadmills that they travel like some mindless creatures, driven, blind."

Whispering. The rush of yellow winds across a swamp.

He flinched and turned to look. Her nails scored fire down his back and then his ribs, traced circles on his chest. The snicker of a buckle, and his belt released to free him from the bind of clothing dropped in whispers to the floor. "Is someone . . . ? Did I hear . . . ?"

Then she was tongues.

His hands explored, caressed, and kneaded while he trembled gravid with his need for her. He blinked against the hint of movement on all sides but couldn't wrench his gaze away from haloed shining hair that bobbed enticement on his chest. Her head tilted back, and she was all abandon, waiting now for him to act.

He choked back arguments, denials. "I'll try. You know I'll try."

Damp clouds surrounded him.

"I will," he said. "I will." And bent to cover lips that held a crimson welcome for him and his years of misted recollection.

Giggling voices. Breath at the nape of his neck.

She drew him lower. Settling, floating, drifting down. The floor a bed of clover now and musk that welcomed him. There was satin, tulle, and corduroy beneath his hands, while metronomes of light began their pulsing beat. He held his breath and felt the tension drawing bands across his chest.

"Har-uld's got a gir-rul, Har-uld's got a gir-rul, Har-uld's got a gir-rul."

He lunged in panic. His feet slipped on the dung-littered floor and he crashed awkwardly to his knees.

258

"That will be enough of that, boys and girls."

Mrs. Baker stood over him, tapping one toe impatiently. She posed in anger with her arms folded, and the sweater hung from her shoulders fluttering in the wet winds that rushed through the room.

"Well, Harold? Are you going to lie there all day? Take your seat, please. And the rest of you, stop that noise this instant!"

He stood up, wondering if he resembled an old-time burlesque comic, the way he reached—no sense hesitating and pulled up his trousers and buckled the belt. In the light-slants, Dorcas Schmidt's thousand dollar's worth of wire and bands winked again before she covered her mouth. She couldn't cover her laugh.

"Harold? I'm waiting—"

"Ooo, Har-uld, she's waiting, better kiss her," Billy Reimer giggled.

Harold forced his eyes away from the shadow-children, their faces moving now and again as if created of smoke. Yet he recognized each one, and each detail: Billy Reimer's perpetual ink-stain, a shapeless smeared tattoo on the inner side of his right index finger; the puckered vertical scar on the chin of the Kipness girl where she'd caught a hard-hit baseball one recess.

"Harold?"

He let the near-reality around him darken, drifting, faded, until his eyes bore down a tunnel into her eyes. Amused eyes, but not unkind amusement. The sharing of private, feverish matters, matters for two, no less, no more. Her eyes changed then; he saw a coppery inquisitiveness. He looked past her to the board.

12 + 30 =

And back. *I'm waiting*, the eyes said.

"Let me go outside a minute," he told her.

"We know where you're go-ing," Billy Reimer began, and was joined by chanters: "We know where you're going—"

He tried to speak without words. She understood, and nodded. "It will be time for the dismissal bell soon. Class, stop that silly singsong. Open your social studies book to the section we were studying yesterday. As you'll remember, we were talking about natural resources . . ."

He turned and stumbled up the dung-pelleted aisle,

his coat over his arm. He closed the door behind him and sat on the concrete steps, blasted by the day's open furnace. The pain in his left upper arm increased, his heartbeat seemed quicker, the thrilling flutter of a trapped sparrow. He breathed with difficulty.

He fished out a second pill—the maximum he was allowed in eight hours—and swallowed it, blinking away sweat from his eyelashes.

Across the distance, the blurred span of the superhighway began and ended in unknown places. He half-heard its repetitive hum. The thought of the annual budget, of crying pregnant girls, playground fights, coaches struggling for their livelihood—

One of them, Wodmer, a heap of debts and a record of 0-19 for his basketball team, had done it, finally, inside his thirty-six-payment station wagon, with a vacuum cleaner hose through the window. And only six hours after Harold had bought him a beer, trying to convince him that there were other positions; that, with his influence, he might be able to ask for reinstatement, though of course he had no hope of it. Two influential board members wanted a new coach, and that was that. So much motion. Waste motion. Like the endless heat-snake that sped along the distant superhighway . . .

He sat a long while, adding it up. He wasn't happy with the total, but at least the process of calculation enabled him to reach a decision.

How difficult would it be? He was surprised that it was no more difficult than reaching out to pick up a drink of cool water. He simply—decided.

At once the heat began to bother him less, his left upper arm stopped aching. His heart no longer clattered within his chest; he couldn't even feel it.

Was it all that easy?

Apparently.

He hunched back in what little shade the eaves provided. He closed his eyes, feeling both a little sad and certain that he'd done the right thing. It was best this way, as well as irrevocable.

Presently a jingling inside the school—her hand-bell—brought a scurry and the treble drone of voices. He stood. His body felt light, virtually weightless. He positioned himself beside the door, waiting for them to come out.

The door didn't open, but all at once, on the steps beside him, he glimpsed a bandaged kneecap, a merry eye, a winking upper brace, and freckles, the children insubstantial as autumn leafsmoke. Their voices grew indistinct as they ran off around the corner of the schoolhouse, on up the dusty road—homeward. He couldn't see them clearly in the day's shimmering blaze, and yet he could. He relished watching them run, carefree, unburdened.

Only when the sound of nearby crickets humming in the weeds had covered their fading voices, when the children were finally gone, did he turn to enter. He found it no longer necessary to operate the handle of the door. That amused him somehow.

"Look, I've been thinking about you—"

"I'm glad you have, Harold. Have you decided? Can you stop them from destroying this place?"

"There's no way. It's too late, even if I wanted to try. You see, something changed while I was thinking out there. That is, I changed. At least I think I did—I wanted to, decided to. One of the reasons I did was because I knew there's no way on God's earth to stop them from tearing down the school. What I'm saying to you is, we'll have to go from here. Leave before they kill this building, and us in it. That way, we can at least be together. I want us to be together . . ."

The drowning, beautiful eyes swallowed him in their wonder: "You don't want to go back?"

"The thing is, I can't—anymore."

He extended his hand for her to touch. It was a different touch than when he'd held her only moments earlier, unreal, yet much fuller of sensation—like and like caressing.

"Harold, kiss me."

"Can we ?"

"Harold, make love to me."

"Is it possible? I mean, the way we both are—?"

"We're the same now. If we can't make love . . ." The fire in her eyes bloomed like embers suddenly blown. She laughed. "If we can't, you certainly made a bad decision. Harold, I'm only teasing. If you couldn't stop Vineville coming down, why, yes. We'll take our chances one and one."

"I honestly don't feel bad about it," he said, walking past her, his eye on the board. "Not a single regret. At least so far."

"I'll try to keep you in that frame of mind."

With sudden insight, clear and sharp, he sensed another change—he now guiding her—and smiled. "I just added it all up, and it came to—to a hell of a lot of wasted time." Chalk in his fingers. "This way, I'll have something." He erased the equal sign following "12 + 30," added a plus, a zero, an equal sign, then two numerals. He stepped back, pleased, and proud, the equation now correct.

$$12 + 30 + 0 = 42$$

He turned, dropped the chalk into the darkness, aware in passing that he never heard it strike the floor as his arms reached for her.

They watched from a distance, a distance measureable in many ways, as two sedans pulled into the dusty drive later that night. Roof lights whipped red swirls across the weed tops.

Then the ambulance came, and a towtruck for Harold's Chevy. He wasn't able to get a close look at the shape beneath the stretcher sheet. Two young kids loaded the stretcher at the school steps, but because of the darkness Harold couldn't be certain whether they were loading something, or nothing. They certainly weren't loading him; that is, any of him that mattered.

When the last state police cruiser raked its front wheels noisily onto the country road and disappeared behind the silent ambulance, Harold felt a little regret. But not much. He turned his back on the diminishing cruiser; in the turning, his eyes drifted past the span of superhighway. At night it was distinct: a hard black swath through the night, marked with dotted patterns—red beads strung one direction, white the other.

Harold smiled and said Mrs. Baker's first name aloud. Aloud, to them. He drew her down in the privacy of the lilacs.

THE WARM
FAREWELL

by

Robert Bloch

Although ROBERT BLOCH has written hundreds of short stories in a long and distinguished career that spans four decades—beginning as a colleague of the late H. P. Lovecraft—he has only produced a moderate number in recent years, turning his hand chiefly to novels and scenarios. Which is a great loss, for at his best he's one of the consummate practitioners of the terror tale, his style incorporating cutting irony and character studies meshed with the experience of horror and the supernatural. This suspenseful tale might be called a social fright, operating admirably, as it does, on more than one level of terror simultaneously, and winding up in fine Blochian fashion.

It must have been around ten o'clock when the cars arrived.

Rena could see them coming down the side road as they turned off the highway from Freedom—there must have been more than a dozen of them. They crawled slowly in a weaving line, like a long black snake inching closer and closer along the gravel.

None of the cars had their headlights turned on, and all of them had little pieces of cardboard stuck over the license plates. They came very slowly and very quietly.

Mrs. Endicott didn't notice them because she was busy making a last-minute tour of the house. Since they'd sold the furnishings along with the place, there wasn't too much to pack, but she wanted to make sure.

Mr. Endicott didn't notice them either, at first. He was closing the car trunk and arranging the extra suitcases in the back seat.

But Rena saw them coming, and she tried to keep the panic out of her voice when she called, "Dad!"

He looked up and then he must have heard the sound of their motors chugging along in low, because he came inside fast.

"Looks like we're going to have visitors," he said, trying to smile.

Mrs. Endicott went over to the window.

"Don't pull the blinds," her husband told her. "They know we're here."

"Aren't you even going to lock the door?" she asked.

Mr. Endicott shrugged. "What's the use?" he answered. "Now don't worry. There won't be any trouble. They probably just want to make sure we're going."

Mrs. Endicott looked at Rena. "You better go in the bedroom," she said.

The girl bit her lip but did not move. "I'm not afraid," she told her mother. "Those White Hopes can't frighten me."

Mr. Endicott looked at her. "Your mother's right," he sighed. "You better go in the bedroom. No sense taking chances."

His wife sniffed. "I wish you'd thought of that yourself, in the first place. Then maybe we wouldn't be running away like this. We had a nice home here. The paper was doing well. But you had to go to work and write those editorials. You had to bring Scotty down — "

"Stop that," said Mr. Endicott. "No sense crying over spilt milk. I had to write those editorials. You know I did. Now be quiet, both of you, and let me handle this."

Father, mother, and daughter fell silent as the cars drove into the yard. They angle-parked in a wide circle, blocking both driveway exits. Now car doors slammed and the white figures emerged—the hooded, sheeted figures of thirty men. As if by signal they converged on the doorstep, forming a smaller circle.

For another moment there was no sound; then a buzz of voices rose from just outside the door. Presently the knocking began.

Mrs. Endicott put her hand on Rena's shoulder. She reached out to touch Mr. Endicott, but he shrugged free and went to the door.

Just as he was about to open it, Rena gasped.

Her father turned. "What is it?" he whispered.

"I just happened to think," she said. "I know why they've come. They want to know about Scotty."

"Oh, no!" Mrs. Endicott fluttered her hands. "Lock the door," she gasped. "Please lock the door!"

Mr. Endicott made a helpless gesture as the knocking sounded again. "Leave this to me," he warned quietly.

Then he opened the door wide.

The man standing in the doorway might have been six feet tall, at the very most. But in the long white robe

266

and the tall hood he was a giant. A ghost-giant, with hidden eyes and a voice that came forth in a croaking whisper.

"Greetings," he said.

Mr. Endicott didn't answer.

The ghost-giant snickered. "What's the matter, cat got your tongue? Or you just plain too scared to talk?" The figure moved forward. "Well, we ain't gonna make trouble. Not if you cooperate."

He turned and addressed the hooded man directly behind him. "Come on in," he said.

White sheets rustled.

"No, the rest of you wait there," the ghost-giant called. "Just the four of us, like I said. Guess that'll be enough to handle our business. If we need help, we'll holler." He snickered again, and an answering chuckle arose from the sheeted circle.

Four hooded figures entered the parlor. The ghost-giant closed the door.

"Well, now," he said. "Looks like you folks was all set to pull out. Is that right?"

Mr. Endicott nodded.

"Guess you packed in pretty much of a hurry, way it looks. Reckon you wasn't expecting visitors. Or did you have a notion you could hightail it before any visitors arrived?"

Mr. Endicott shrugged.

The hooded giant gazed at his three companions and chuckled again. "See what I mean, boys? This is your Yankee hospitality. Come to pay a friendly farewell call, and what happens? They offer you any dopes, or maybe even a little jolt of corn? Not likely. Don't even ask a feller if he'd like to set down. And after all the ways we traveled just to get here."

His chuckle mingled with the answering sounds from under the hoods of the others. Then he moved over to Mr. Endicott and rubbed his white-gloved hands together briskly.

"Gonna have to ask you to speak up," he said. "Guess you all don't realize you got distinguished visitors here."

Mr. Endicott glanced down at the feet of the sheeted

men. His eyes traveled over shoes and protruding trouser cuffs.

"I realize it," he said, quietly. "You'd never make much of an actor, Jess. And as for Race and Pud, here, they'll have to invest in a second pair of shoes if they want to sneak around in disguise."

"Ain't nobody sneaking around in disguise," the hooded giant rumbled, abandoning the whisper. "This here's the White Hopes, and don't forget it. No names among the Brothers."

"Brothers!" said Mr. Endicott.

"Now that's enough of that," the man identified as Jess said. "We've had all the sass we need out of you, Endicott. You and your stinking editorials. You been asking the good citizens of Freedom enough questions. Now it's our turn to do the talking. And all we want out of you is a few answers."

He walked over to the fourth hooded figure, whose shiny black patent-leather shoes and creased seersucker trousers offering a striking contrast to the sandals and work pants of the others.

"You want to take charge, Brother Hood?" he asked.

The sheeted head shook slowly.

"All right," said Jess. He turned to Endicott once again. "I told you about distinguished visitors," he went on. "This here's our Brother Hood. I guess you heard about him. Head of the whole organization in this territory. He come all the way from headquarters in Atlanta, just to help us say goodbye. Just got in tonight."

Mr. Endicott ran a hand across his bald spot. "Look here, Jess," he murmured. "We're all ready to go. Say what you have to say and get out."

"Now wait a minute. Wait—a—minute!" Jess walked up to the small man and gazed down at him through the slits in his hood. "I guess you ain't really learned your lesson after all."

"I've learned enough," Mr. Endicott answered wearily. "I've learned you can't hope to sell freedom here in Freedom. I've learned enough to get rid of the paper and the house and leave town. What more do you want of me?"

"Not much." Jess turned to the silent Brother Hood.

"See? Spunky little cuss, just like I told you. But we showed him a thing or two. Just like he said now. He's shut up shop for good. Had to dump the paper for a song. The bank squeezed him on the mortgage here and he was lucky to get half what he paid for the house and throw his furniture in on the deal. Reckon he'll think twice before he pulls any more smart-aleck stunts again."

"I know when I'm licked," Endicott said. "Does that satisfy you?"

Jess didn't answer him. He talked to Brother Hood. "And it was all done peaceable, too. No rough stuff. Everything clean and legal-like."

"What about those bricks through the window?" Mr. Endicott asked. "What about those notes, and the phone calls, and expelling my daughter here from school?"

"We was just protecting our own youngsters," said Jess. "We got decent girls in this town. We don't aim to have them spoiled and corrupted by any Northern nigra-lovers .."

Mrs. Endicott put her arm around Rena. "Shut up!" she cried. "Shut up and get out of here!"

"You really want us to go, Mizz Endicott?" Jess bowed, his hooded head bobbing grotesquely. "Well, seeing as how you feel like that, ma'am, we're on our way. Sorry we troubled you. But just one thing before we clear out."

"What's that?" Mr. Endicott answered for her.

"We come here for information," Jess said. "That's all we're after. Just information." He paused and moved closer. "Where's the nigra?" he rumbled. "Where's Scotty?"

"Mr. Scott has left town," Endicott answered. "I thought everyone knew that."

"You mean you told everyone that," Jess corrected him. "But the White Hopes know different. We got eyes that see in the dark." The hooded head shook. "Oh, I admit we was fooled at first. That was a pretty slick trick of yours—bringing down a nigra from up North, an educated nigra if you please, that looks and acts like a white man. I bet you laughed aplenty when you put him on the paper and started him writing those highfalutin stories about segregation and what-all. Oh, you fooled us good,

269

you did! Until he up and wrote that dirty lying piece for the magazines about the White Hopes."

"That was a mistake," Mr. Endicott said. "I didn't know he was going to write that article. I'd never have authorized it."

"I'll bet you wouldn't," Jess chuckled. "Like you say, it was a mistake. A real mistake. And you made another quartering him here at your own house, a lousy nigra living right here in a white man's home. Passing for white, and you helping him!"

"That was my business."

"That's our business, mister. That's the business of every decent, respectable white man in these parts. And when anyone forgets it, the White Hopes are here to remind them."

"Why can't you forget it?" Mr. Endicott asked, wearily. "It's all over and done with. Mr. Scott left town last weekend."

"Oh did he?" Jess glanced at the others. "Did he really? We happen to think different. If he left town, how'd he get out—walk? We been watching the buses, Endicott. We been watching the train. Ain't no nigra comes in or goes out without us knowing it, anytime. And we been watching sort of special for Scotty. On account of we didn't want him to leave without us saying goodbye. Right, boys?"

Race and Pud guffawed.

"He's not here, if that's what you're thinking," Mrs. Endicott said.

"We know that," Jess assured her. "But we got a pretty good idea you folks can tell us where he's hiding out."

"I don't know," Mr. Endicott said. "That's the truth, so help me. I don't know where he went. He came to me Saturday and said he was leaving—said he wanted to leave so there wouldn't be any trouble. And he made a point of not telling me where he was going."

"You've got to believe us," Mrs. Endicott said. "He told us nothing."

"But he didn't go," Jess said. "We would of seen him if he did. So he's got to be around these parts, someplace. And if he's around these parts, he's got to eat.

270

Somebody's looking after him. Somebody's feeding him."

"We have nothing to do with it," sighed Mr. Endicott.

"Who else could it be?" Jess asked. "There ain't a white man in the county that'd touch that nigra with a ten-foot pole. Ain't a darky that would dare lift a hand for him. They know how the White Hopes feel about a bad nigra like Scotty. The word's out we're gonna give him a farewell celebration."

"I tell you, we don't know anything!"

"And I tell you you're lying." The white-gloved hands fumbled under Jess's sheet and emerged holding a leather strap. "I didn't come here aiming for trouble. But the boys ain't taking no for an answer. Maybe we got to do some persuading."

Mrs. Endicott let out a strangled sound as Jess advanced on the little man. He said nothing, nor did he move. The gloved hand swung the leather strap. It swished through the heavy humid air of the room.

"Better grab hold of him, boys," said Jess. "This is liable to be kind of messy."

Brother Hood stepped forward. His voice was a soft whisper. "Wait a moment," he said. "Might I make a suggestion?"

"Sure. This is your party, really."

"You haven't asked the girl yet."

Mr. and Mrs. Endicott looked at Rena. And now Jess was looking at her too, looking at her through the eyeholes in the hood. The room was suddenly very silent.

Jess coiled the strap in his gloved hands, caressing its length. "Why that's right," he said, slowly. "Looks like we clean forgot about Rena, here."

He walked over to her and stood balanced on the balls of his feet, rocking from side to side .

Rena's eyes went wide.

"How old are you, honey?" Jess drawled. "Fifteen, sixteen, thereabouts? Funny, I never noticed before. You're right pretty. Too pretty to waste your spit on a nigra like that Scotty. You're a white girl, honey. Reckon maybe you need a white man to teach you what that means "

"Keep away from her!" Mrs. Endicott sobbed.

Jess swung the strap slowly. "I'd sure hate to spoil that

pretty face. Yessiree, I'd sure hate to have to do something like that." He raised the strap. "Suppose you help me out, honey. Suppose you tell me where Scotty's hiding. Before I count up to three, maybe. One, two——"

"Look at her," Brother Hood said, sharply. "She won't talk. Not that way."

Jess paused and turned. "You got any other ideas?" he asked.

"It's my party, like you said." Brother Hood approached Jess and bent his hooded head. He whispered something. Jess nodded, snickered, straightened up.

"Go ahead," he said. "Go right ahead."

Brother Hood nodded. Then he took two quick steps forward and gathered the girl in his sheeted arms. She screamed and struggled, engulfed in the billowing folds that enmeshed her. Brother Hood fought her, a great white bird flapping his wings over his prey.

Mr. Endicott came across the room. "Damn you, let her alone!" he shouted. "Let her——"

Jess drew the strap back and hit him across the mouth. Then he hit Mr. Endicott with his fist. The little man fell down and his glasses dropped to the floor.

Jess stood over him. "One more move out of you and you'll really get it," he grunted. "And that goes for your wife, too. You, Race——hang onto her."

Race was already grasping Mrs. Endicott's elbow, twisting her arm behind her. He didn't twist any harder than was necessary, but he did a job.

The hooded man named Pud flung open a door. "Right here's the bedroom, Brother Hood," he said. "Reckon that's what you're looking for."

Brother Hood nodded. He jerked the struggling girl through the doorway, dropping the strap and using both hands now. Pud started to follow behind, but Brother Hood snapped, "I don't need you in here. My party."

He started to laugh, and then the door banged shut, and there was silence.

Mrs. Endicott began to cry, noiselessly. Mr. Endicott crawled along the floor and picked up his glasses. They were unbroken, and when he put them on he could see Jess standing over him with the strap poised.

He could see Race, too, and now Race had a gun in his gloved hand.

So nobody moved.

Nobody moved when the gasps came, or the thud, or the scream. Nobody moved when the thumping sounds rose from behind the thick door.

Nothing moved in the room except the hands of the clock on the wall.

A full fifteen minutes passed before the door opened Brother Hood came out alone.

"Come on," he said. He was panting and his voice had submerged to a conspiratorial whisper.

"Did she—?"

"Come on," Brother Hood repeated, nodding. "Let's go."

"Where is he?" Jess asked.

"The old Jasper place, if you know where that is. Hiding out in the barn."

"I might have guessed," Jess said. "Way off on the side road down there. Been deserted for years."

"All set?" Brother Hood panted.

"Got everything right out in the car," Jess answered.

"Then let's go. You boys lead the way—I'll have to follow in my car."

Jess chuckled. "Man, you sound beat! Must have had quite a workout "

Brother Hood cut him short with a curt nod and moved over to the door. Jess and his two companions followed. Jess stood in the doorway for a moment after the others had made their exit.

"You all don't forget us now," he said. "Sorry we got to be running along so quick like, but we got this little surprise party all arranged." He paused. "Mebbe you better forget us after all," Jess murmured. "Yeah, that's the best idea. We never been here." He shifted the leather strap in his gloved hand. "Mind, now. We never been here, none of us."

The Endicotts didn't answer.

They didn't look at him, nor at each other, as the white-robed man went out. They didn't move as they heard the receding murmur of voices drifting down the driveway. They waited until the motors started, roared, and droned away in the night.

Mr. Endicott turned as the bedroom door opened and Rena came out. Her face was white, and she let the door slam behind her fast and hard.

"Gone?" she whispered.

Mr. Endicott nodded.

"Then we'd better go, too. Right now."

Mrs. Endicott stretched out her hands. "Rena—"

The girl shook her head, brushing the tangled hair from her eyes. "Don't say anything," she murmured. "Please don't say anything. Let's get out of here."

Mr. and Mrs. Endicott exchanged glances. He nodded and led his wife to the door.

Rena paused and bit her lip. "I forgot my purse," she said. "Start the car and I'll be right out."

She raced back into the bedroom as they left. By the time Mr. and Mrs. Endicott had climbed into the car she was back, snapping out the lights and closing the front door behind her.

"Don't use your lights," she told her father. "Just head for the highway. The faster the better."

Mrs. Endicott patted her arm. "Don't worry, honey. They're gone now, to the old Jasper place." She paused. "How did you   ?"

Rena didn't answer her directly. "Jasper's? That's good. It's a long way out. And they'll surround it, and go inside to search. They've got kerosene, of course, and they'll plan on burning him. They like to burn, you know."

The car mounted the rise to the highway just ahead, and they could see the panorama below. Suddenly Mr. Endicott turned and said, "Look!"

Turning, they gazed behind them, staring at the side road. The White Hopes were on the prowl now, and they'd lighted their torches, two to a car, thrusting them out of the front windows so that a line of fire blazed in the night. A long chain of bobbing flame stretched down the side road leading to the old Jasper place.

"You see?" Rena whispered. "I was right. They'll go there and hunt around the barn so that they can burn him." Her voice broke and she began to laugh.

Mrs. Endicott shook her. "Stop it!" she cried. "Stop it!

I don't care what he did to you in there—you shouldn't have told them. They'll burn Scotty alive. Why did you tell them where he was?"

"Yes," Mr. Endicott said. "And how did you know?"

Rena shrieked and gurgled. "I don't know," she said. "He must have made up the whole story when he came out."

"Who? Brother Hood?"

"That wasn't Brother Hood," Rena giggled. "That was Scotty. I still don't know where he's been hiding, but he'd sneaked back here to tell us goodbye. And when he looked through the bedroom window and saw Brother Hood drag me in there, he crawled in. I saw him, but Brother Hood didn't. He hit Brother Hood on the back of the head with a big rock."

Mrs. Endicott gasped. "Did he—kill him?"

"No. He was just unconscious. Then Scotty tied him up with bedsheets and gagged him good. And he put on Brother Hood's pants and shoes and gloves and robe and came out. He told me we'd have to get away fast. He's taking Brother Hood's car, and when the White Hopes get to the barn he'll sneak off in the confusion and make his getaway. By the time they find out there's nobody in the barn it'll be too late." She giggled again.

Mrs. Endicott touched her daughter's cheek. "Thank God," she said. "You're all right."

"I'm all right," Rena repeated. "Now let's hurry!"

Mr. Endicott shifted and the car moved out onto the highway. "All's well that ends well," he muttered. "I think Scotty will make it—he just whispered and nobody recognized his voice. Once he's gone and we're gone there won't be any trouble." He glanced at his daughter. "I—I know what an ordeal this has been for you. But you mustn't be bitter about it. You've got to remember they're not all like that. Plenty of decent folks in Freedom and all over. It's just the minority, the ones who haven't learned, and they're disappearing fast. The big danger isn't in what they do, but in how they feel. That bitterness—it's contagious. Makes you want to fight back, their way. And you mustn't. Only leads to more trouble."

"Fight fire with fire," Rena said. And giggled again.

"Look down there!" Mrs. Endicott cried.

"Never mind," Rena insisted. "Keep going!"

"No—stop! Look at the flames!"

The car halted. The trio gazed off in the darkness as a sheet of fire rose suddenly in the night.

"But that's not Jasper's place," Mr. Endicott gasped. "That's that's *our* house!"

"And Brother Hood is tied up in the bedroom," Mrs. Endicott said. "Rena, you said you were going back there for your purse. Did you—?"

Rena was silent. They were all silent, staring down at the fire. Now they could hear the roar of the flames and, above it, something that might or might not have been a single piercing scream.

Rena giggled again.

"Fight fire with fire," Mr. Endicott sighed. "They'll blame it on the White Hopes and nobody will ever know. But I hate it, it's wrong, we've got to go back."

Mrs. Endicott gripped his arm. "No," she said. "It's too late. Rena's right. We'd better get out of here, fast."

She didn't look at her daughter, even when she began to laugh louder and louder, and after a minute Mr. Endicott started the car again.

He shifted into high and the car sped forward, heading away from the flames, heading due north.

END GAME

by

Gahan Wilson

It is perhaps appropriate that a book of scary stories should close out with a funny fright, a sort of sigh of relief after a roller coaster ride of terror. And probably the person who, in the public mind, is most identified with the macabre and the funny is GAHAN WILSON, creator of hundreds of wonderfully oddball cartoons in Playboy, Fantasy & Science Fiction, *and other magazines. But Wilson is not simply a humorist of surfaces: his outré depictions are often gentle moralities and commentaries on social conditions and happenings in the modern world. Wilson is also the author of ingeniously conceived short stories, as can be seen in his forthcoming collection from Doubleday and in this bit of dark merriment.*

Balden's mouth worked, chewing sidewise like a parrot, or a turtle, or some other hard-beaked creature, and he moved his bishop to his queen's knight four with a sparse, economical shove of the hand. I leaned back in an ostentatiously casual fashion and lit my pipe. Balden's eyes remained fixed stonily on the board. I wafted forth a tiny plume of smoke and watched it drift slowly over Balden's head like a small cloud working its way past Abraham Lincoln's portrait on Mount Rushmore.

"Did I ever tell you about the circumstances surrounding Mannering's death?" I asked.

"No," said Balden shortly, his voice, as always, muffled and remote.

"I speak not of the circumstances before, nor those during. It is the circumstances that came after of which I speak."

I gazed at the ceiling, ignoring Balden's obvious disinterest, and continued.

"The instructions in Mannering's will concerning his post-mortem treatment were peculiar, to say the least. As his lawyer, however, it was my duty to see that they were properly carried out, no matter how bizarre they might seem."

"Your move," said Balden.

I lazily advanced a pawn and went on with my narration, seemingly all unaware of Balden's glaring indifference.

"He had always been a great traveler, as you doubtless know, and, thanks to the family money, was able to indulge his predilection to the full. Reports of his activities came in from the most exotic places. Amazonian explorations, dizzying mountain climbs in Tibet, deep African probes—he seemed always to be investigating some new corner of the Earth."

Balden's eyes glittered coldly as he moved a knight to one side, exposing a thrusting rook.

"He died in a fitting room at Abercrombie and Fitch while preparing for a polar journey. He was being measured for an insulated parka when he suddenly keeled over and died."

"A pity," said Balden, tapping meaningfully at the edge of the board.

"The strange conditions of his will were a direct outgrowth of his lifelong passion for travel." I moved my hand vaguely this way and that over my pieces. "I shall never forget the growing expressions of stunned incredulity on the faces of the beneficiaries as I read the terms out, one by one."

I absentmindedly interposed a bishop between Balden's rook and my threatened queen. He sighed.

"The body was to be dressed in a specified wool suit, placed in a natural-looking position, and coated with a clear, nonreflecting plastic. The general effect to be strived for was that of an elderly gentleman, comfortably seated, with his eyes alertly open. The slightest suggestion of the macabre was to be studiously avoided."

Emitting a rasping cackle, Balden captured my queen knight with a rook. I let him study my expression of benign serenity for a moment, and then picked up my tale.

"Thus prepared, the body was to be sent perpetually from one part of the world to another on an eternal global tour. Always first class, of course, and always accompanied by someone familiar with the area so that the corpse would not miss any local points of interest."

Balden had taken to clearing his throat rather noisily and I was forced to raise my voice.

"The family put the whole business into the hands of a carefully chosen undertaker and travel agent, who to this day remain in their employ. Both did their jobs well and, for a period of several months, everything went beautifully."

A slight but unmistakably convulsive movement on the part of Balden pulled me temporarily back to the business of the game. I moved my queen one square to unpin my bishop, doing it with the air of one who is only dimly aware of his surroundings, and continued my account.

"Then, in Hong Kong, the whole plan went dreadfully awry. In an ill-advised attempt to show Mannering's cadaver an interesting quarter of the city, his guide had installed the body in one rickshaw while he took another. They had barely reached their destination, an unbelievably crowded sector, when a street riot broke out. Horrified, Mannering's guide saw his client's vehicle vanish into the swarm. The desperate fellow struggled frantically to follow after, but he was hopelessly pinned by the howling multitude to the wall of a bean curd factory. There was nothing he could do to alter the ghastly course of events. Mannering was gone."

Some time since, Balden had made his next move. He brought the fact home to me now by repeatedly indicating the piece's change in position with jabs of his index finger. It was a bishop, and I captured it quietly and unobtrusively with one of my knights.

"A search was initiated instantly, of course. At first it was thought that the task would be a fairly easy one. We broadcast a description of Mannering and, considering his unique condition, had the firmest expectation it would quickly bring results. It did not."

"Check," said Balden. With some force.

"Nor did any of our other efforts meet with the slightest success. We tracked down every rumor and followed up each clue, but all to no avail."

Abstaining from giving it so much as a glance, I moved my king one square to the right.

"After two full years of fruitless search, the police of a dozen nations were ready to admit defeat. The small army of private investigators which we had hired fared no better. The corpse of Arthur Mannering was conceded lost."

"Check," said Balden, again.

"It was at this gloomy moment that I received a midnight telephone call from Mannering's nephew, Charles Addison Vaughn." I blocked Balden's attack with a move of my bishop. "He had a remarkable tale to tell. It seemed that he had wandered into a Forty-Second Street sideshow emporium, drawn by a poster advertising an attraction billed Oscar, the Roumanian Robot. Oscar, so the poster claimed, could do lightning calculations, play chess and checkers, recite poetry, and execute pastel portraits of surpassing charm."

"Check," said Balden, yet again.

"Imagine Vaughn's astonishment when the curtains of Oscar the Roumanian Robot's booth parted to reveal nothing less than the corpse of his uncle, clothed in mandarin attire, seated on a large wooden throne, a chessboard before it and a blackboard at its side. While Vaughn gazed on, appalled, the corpse did indeed do lightning calculations, play chess and checkers, recite several atrocious poems, and essay a number of rather muddy drawings. The jerky movements of the jaw, arms, and torso which accompanied all this were accomplished by means of an intricate system of wires and pulleys connected to an involved, cog-wheeled machine built into the body of the throne."

My next move, which I made with my eyes fixed on Balden's, simultaneously captured his attacking piece and placed his king in jeopardy.

"Check. I joined Vaughn and we both went at once to the Forty-Second Street place of entertainment, but we arrived too late. Oscar, the Roumanian Robot, had severed his connections with that establishment. The boards of his accustomed booth were bare."

For the first time, Balden seemed undecided as to his next move. His hand went here and there over the board, then retreated to scratch nervously at his thick beard.

"We traced the history of Oscar and found the trail led straight back to Hong Kong. His first appearance had been in an alley theater, an unsavory den provided over by an Arabian midget, Salaman Ruknuddin."

Balden pushed a piece several squares to the right,

then attempted to take the play back. I forestalled him with an upraised palm.

"No fair changing the move after you let go."

I captured the piece, smiling thinly.

"Ruknuddin closed his theater shortly thereafter, and he and Oscar began a meteoric rise in show business. First in the Far East, then in Australia, on to England and Europe, and finally to America. Everywhere they went the audiences flocked to see Oscar's marvelous performance. Then the fatal flaw in the robot was uncovered and, overnight, Oscar turned from a wonder into a laughing stock."

"Check," said Balden, a little shakily.

"Stonewosk, the Polish master, discovered that Oscar was a patsy for the Ethiopian end game." I took Balden's piece. "An absolute sucker for it. No matter how many times you pulled it on him, he'd tumble right into the trap. Shaken badly, his confidence gone, Oscar's other talents coarsened or disintegrated altogether.

Balden's next move was done with a spastic gesture which very nearly knocked several men from the board.

"Check," he said, in a voice so faint as to be hardly audible.

"Oscar's career, and Ruknuddin's, went into a speedy decline, and then into total eclipse. The last that was heard of them was their pathetic final stand at the Forty-Second Street dive. The Ethiopian end game had pursued them to the end."

My voice rose.

"It pursues them even now, Balden," I said, moving my king. "Checkmate!"

Suddenly the figure sitting opposite me began to twitch and shudder in a remarkable fashion. I stood, reached over the board and plucked off the false beard worn by my opponent to reveal the face of a tired-looking, certainly dead Arthur Mannering.

"The game is up, Ruknuddin!" I cried.

Abruptly the figure stopped its struggling and, as if to compensate, the chair on which it sat began a series of violent movements. After a moment or so a cog-bedecked panel in its side flew open and a tiny figure dashed out, spun, and streaked for the door. The curtains behind me were pulled apart and a group of anxious men rushed into the room.

"We must stop him!" shouted Charles Vaughn, and he was seconded by the others, but I held them back with a gesture.

"Let him go," I said, watching the desperate fugitive scuttle out of the apartment. "He is finished. He can do no more harm."

I saw that the mortician had already begun to restore Mannering to his former seemliness. I was glad to observe that there was no serious damage. The travel agent was also present and he stepped forward, a quantity of folders and timetables in his hand, to look at me expectantly. Mannering's journeyings were, of course, to continue. I suggested a quiet sea voyage for a restful start.

AFTERWORD

The tale of terror is one of the oldest forms of story-telling, inherent to every human culture. It has been with us from the very beginning, whether in stories told around campfires or represented in art, drama, and literature. Men who don't write books have always whispered over their night fires—or in broad daylight, for that matter—of brushes with scary things. And men who have put their experiences of awe and fright in written form have done so from earliest times, from the *Odyssey* of Homer forward to the date you see on your daily newspaper. Many of the great literary figures have created works of terror and the supernatural: Shakespeare, Goethe, Poe, Balzac, Dickens, the Brontë sisters, Tolstoy, Pushkin, Maupassant, Kipling, Mann, to name only some. The appeal of "things that go bump in the night" is very basic everywhere. And now this form is perhaps the last strong outpost of Romantic expression in the arts.

And yet, for all that, particularly in America, there is a kind of stubborn, supercilious refusal in many quarters to recognize this kind of story as a literary form worthy of attention by serious, intelligent readers. The reasons for this are doubtless many, but one is surely the tongue-in-cheek interest in bad horror movies and their overworked reliance upon familiar supernatural characters, Dracula and Frankenstein the two best known. All these stereotypes have their place, but how big a place is the question. Where the interest seems to be destructive is when the essential inspiration and attitude is irreverent or sadistic. Concerning the former, I am among those who believe that the magazine *Unknown* and magazines in its tradition failed because their predominate premise was too whimsical. *Unknown* did run a good many excellent stories, but also a good deal of "cute, clever, and amusing" material written by writers having a condescending, self-indulgent kind of fun at the readers' expense. People do occasionally like humor in their supernatural tales and, indeed, there is an element of ironic humor near the heart of the good story of terror; but it must be carefully controlled or the reader is unlikely to engage in the sober kind of pondering necessary for maximum enjoyment of the strange story. The mainstay appeal is the chill of probing the unknown, as the bestselling books in the genre testify. And the tale of the humorous macabre is usually most satisfying when written by those who have reverence and love for the *non*humorous supernatural and who themselves write it well— a W. W. Jacobs, a Robert Bloch, or a Gahan Wilson. One knows in reading their funny supernaturals that it is an affectionate and respectful use of humor and, probably deep down, a usage that is made with an occasional look over the proverbial shoulder. Many of those attracted to the light and whimsical tradition have, I would suggest, weak credentials in the respect and reverence department: their true loves are elsewhere—and it shows.

The intrusion of the sadistic into the supernatural terror story is more serious and perennial. Any genre that frequently has to do with fear and death must naturally approach territory that is ripe for sadistic treatment. But not only is there a difference in treatment between the sadistic story and the true supernatural story, there is an equally great difference in inspiration and appeal, as Fritz Leiber ably points out in the introduction to this book. Tales of the supernatural appeal on many levels, but none of them involve a focus on physical suffering and unpleasantness for its own sake.

Labels are always tricky. What does one call this

rather broad but same-spirited form? I tend to prefer the term "terror," but it seems to me only one of several satisfactory ones. Many are turning away from the word "horror," but I like all the terms: stories of horror, wonder, terror, fantasy, the inexplicable, the supernatural, as long as the inspiration is not that of the dilettante or the sadist. *FRIGHTS* is the title of this collection because it seemed to me to convey a welcome to a broad variety of eerie and suspenseful stories. Additionally, I aimed to collect stories which are a bit different, that struck me as more than *another* vampire story or *another* deal-with-the-devil story; the somewhat off-trail modern tale of suspense and horror was my goal. And—important, I think—all the stories in this book have never been published before. There are, I believe, some very vital and fine things being written today in this field, and there should be more places to showcase those new works. In a small way I hope this book enlarges that showcase.

—Kirby McCauley
New York City
January 11, 1976